MASON'S Fool

Cynthia J Stone

TREATY OAK PUBLISHERS

PUBLISHER'S NOTE

This is a work of fiction. None of the characters or events is based on actual people, living or dead, or their lives or circumstances. If you think you recognize someone or some place and want to make anything of it, you're dreaming and should trying writing your own book. Seriously, it's just a coincidence and purely unintentional.

Printed and published in the United States of America

TREATY OAK PUBLISHERS

ISBN-13: 978-1-943658-14-5

ISBN-10: 943658-14-5

DEDICATION

To the friends who, by doing it so well,
have taught me to reinvent myself.

TABLE OF CONTENTS

CHAPTER ONE: The Go-To Girl   1

CHAPTER TWO: The Fever   4

CHAPTER THREE: The Workout   11

CHAPTER FOUR: The Mouseburger   19

CHAPTER FIVE: The Producer   25

CHAPTER SIX: The Flying Saucers   30

CHAPTER SEVEN: The Celebrity   37

CHAPTER EIGHT: The Poet's Corner   41

CHAPTER NINE: The Honky Tonk   49

CHAPTER TEN: The Job   59

CHAPTER ELEVEN: The Last Resort   63

CHAPTER TWELVE: The Rocker   71

CHAPTER THIRTEEN: The Graduate   78

CHAPTER FOURTEEN: The Lowlights   88

CHAPTER FIFTEEN: The Frying Pan   96

CHAPTER SIXTEEN: The Fire   104

CHAPTER SEVENTEEN: The Highlights   112

CHAPTER EIGHTEEN: The Talking Horse   118

CHAPTER NINETEEN: The Ups and Downs   128

CHAPTER TWENTY: The Tour   133

CHAPTER TWENTY-ONE: The Detour   142

CHAPTER TWENTY-TWO: The Poet's House   148

CHAPTER TWENTY-THREE: The Other House 154

CHAPTER TWENTY-FOUR: The Des Res   163

CHAPTER TWENTY-FIVE: The Green House   169

CHAPTER TWENTY-SIX: The Wee Tot   177

CHAPTER TWENTY-SEVEN: The Librarian   181

TABLE OF CONTENTS

continued

CHAPTER TWENTY-EIGHT: The Big Baby   187

CHAPTER TWENTY-NINE: The Dictator   192

CHAPTER THIRTY: The Talking Pony   197

CHAPTER THIRTY-ONE: The Stalking Horse   204

CHAPTER THIRTY-TWO: The In-Laws   212

CHAPTER THIRTY-THREE: The Rule of Thumb   216

CHAPTER THIRTY-FOUR: The Awakening   222

CHAPTER THIRTY-FIVE: The Hot House   228

CHAPTER THIRTY-SIX: The Hot Seat   234

CHAPTER THIRTY-SEVEN: The Out-Laws   239

CHAPTER THIRTY-EIGHT: The Detective   245

CHAPTER THIRTY-NINE: The Suspects   250

CHAPTER FORTY: The Next-to-Last-Resort   257

CHAPTER FORTY-ONE: The Diddling Trickster   264

CHAPTER FORTY-TWO: The Marina   272

CHAPTER FORTY-THREE: The Gormless Pillock   277

CHAPTER FORTY-FOUR: The Sweet Boffin   285

CHAPTER FORTY-FIVE: The Row Boat   290

CHAPTER FORTY-SIX: The Escort Service   295

CHAPTER FORTY-SEVEN: The City of Lights   301

CHAPTER FORTY-EIGHT: The Cake Hole   308

CHAPTER FORTY-NINE: The Merry-Go-Round   314

CHAPTER FIFTY: The Home on the Range   322

MASON'S Fool

CHAPTER ONE
The Go-To Girl

In my family, I'm known as the Go-To Girl. Made a mess? I'll clean it up. In a tight spot? Call me, and I'll get you out. Whirling like a dervish? Calm down and just follow my example.

For good reasons, my family sees me as the reliable one, patient, unwavering, and faithful. The list goes on. Over the years, especially as an adult, I have never disappointed them. Or surprised them, either, come to think of it.

My schedule never lacks an opening and my gas tank is always full. I am the Finder of Lost Objects, the Battener of Hatches, the Taker-Up of the Slack. In a crisis, my MO is to take a deep breath, fix what needs it, and stay put until the storm passes.

Without complaint, I have always done—and been—what my parents and my husband and the rest of the good folks in Mason's Crossing expected of me. From straight-A student who kept her room spotless to devoted housewife, Sunday school teacher, Heritage Society member, library docent. Descended from a long-respected and honorable family. A modest and upright citizen. Not even a traffic ticket. Ever.

As careful guardian of her own universe, my

whole life was dull and predictable. Like following the same recipe over and over. And that's exactly the way I wanted it.

So why am I sitting in a Paris jail, handcuffed to a notorious British rock star, accused of kidnapping and dognapping, criminal trespass, undocumented entry, and maybe worse, without a clue how to fix this disaster? No reasonable explanation. No alibi. No luggage.

And I can't find my passport. That would almost solve the undocumented entry charge. Not my fault, not entirely, but we were in rather a hurry at the moment. They're going to ask me about the yacht before it exploded and sank off the coast of Normandy. I swear I didn't know what was... Oliver only said... well, never mind. The justification for the whole sordid mess will come out eventually.

Leaning across the desk, a mustached French police officer, a stern specimen of the Sûreté Nationale, has blackened my right thumb on an ink pad and is pressing it onto my rap sheet. He has already telephoned Interpol. My stomach churns.

Oliver sits next to me, waiting his turn. He has to. We're joined at the wrists. He's grinning, his one blue-black eye somehow twinkling. He's been arrested before, so the cheeky ass is accustomed to things like this happening. If I could, I'd smack him in the other eye, except it would add to the count on my rap sheet.

The international *paparazzi* is camped outside the door of the police station, clamoring to get more photos. While the police were bustling us inside, I thought I recognized the logo from *Life Magazine* above the brim of one man's hat. But, even ducking behind Oliver, it was hard to see anything beyond the glare of all the flash bulbs going off in my face.

Why did I let him talk me into taking Simon's prize-winning terrier and... oh, I can't even think straight about the rest of it now. I'll wait until the judge questions me and try to answer in order of what happened when and where. He'll have to believe my statement. Although I'm not sure I would.

It won't be too long before this unsavory misadventure hits the evening news in America in cataclysmic proportions. Maybe Walter Cronkite has never watched "The Tonight Show Starring Johnny Carson" or never heard of Oliver Knight and the Goodknight Lads. Fat chance.

Maybe my family won't recognize me with my newly bleached blonde hair. Dim hope. But even Uncle Walter can't save me.

Between moments of shock-induced quiet and laughter or sobs, I am hyperventilating. Much more of this, and I'll faint.

How on God's green earth did I get myself in this jam? So nice of you to ask. It started with a kiss.

Don't you dare laugh.

CHAPTER TWO

The Fever

Let me back up a few months. Three, to be precise.

One day my husband came home and informed me he'd joined a new health club on the outskirts of Austin. I encouraged him in his effort to lose a few pounds. After several weeks, Dwight looked a tiny bit more trim and muscular. Sexier, if that's possible for a balding, forty-one-year-old medical supply salesman who danced like a kangaroo and wore knee-high socks with his sandals.

Several nights a week, dinners at home were delayed while he got sweaty as he pumped iron, crunched his abs, and pounded the treadmill at the gym after work. Another new hobby kept me busy while I waited. Mother had taught me how to knit cables and I made him a sweater. Light blue, to match his eyes.

When Dwight showed up at the breakfast table one morning wearing a pink shirt under a plaid sport jacket instead of his usual dark gray suit, he said, "It's the early 80s. I have younger customers now. I have to look more hip." He had also combed his hair forward to cover his receding hairline.

For a moment, I considered spilling orange juice all over him. Just to save him from himself.

He took twice as many vitamins and wanted toast without jelly. "For a change," he said. "What are you doing today? Lunch with the girls, then a nap?"

I reminded him that 'housewife' as my career choice was his idea.

That night, he skipped dessert, his favorite cherry cobbler. Not my preference, but that didn't keep me from eating half of it in the kitchen while he watched sports on TV. After a while with no conversation, I went to bed feeling full but not satisfied.

Later that week, I exchanged the rep tie and matching hankie I had bought him, in anticipation of his upcoming birthday, for a pair of pleated khaki slacks instead. I decided against the tooled leather belt and the paisley polyester shirt. John Travolta, he was not. And Dwight never got fever on a Saturday night, from dancing or anything else.

At some point, it dawned on me maybe I should join the same gym. "We could work out together." Only in my mid-thirties, I could see that a middle-aged spread waited for me just around the corner. I blamed the cherry cobbler, which I had polished off all by myself at lunch the next day.

"No!" Dwight said. "You can't... I couldn't enjoy my workout with you watching."

"But I wouldn't be watching you. I'd be doing my own exercises. Or I could take a class."

"This is a guy thing. Just my buddies and me." He stood up. "And who would have dinner on the table when I get home?"

I sighed. Maybe I could just turn up the temperature until the boiling bathwater rendered my blossoming fat instead.

On Monday evening, Dwight told me his boss had announced a meeting for a new product line training and then a company golf game to be held on Saturday. It would last all day, followed by dinner at the country club in Austin. To my relief, wives weren't invited.

"Don't wait up," Dwight said that morning. "You know how Sherman likes to shoot the breeze with everyone, especially after he's knocked back a few scotches."

I'd been around his boss often enough to agree Dwight had a point. "Besides," I said. "I have to get up early the next morning to teach Sunday school."

"You'll have to go without me." Dwight pecked me on the cheek and dashed out the door, clubs banging together in the golf bag like castanets.

After morning chores and a light lunch, I ran errands in town, picking up Dwight's dry cleaning and his list of items from the hardware store. Nothing he could actually put to use. A chain saw and a power drill? Might as well give a monkey a stopwatch.

But I had spoiled him by taking care of everything around the house myself. If I left town, he probably couldn't find the light switches. Nevertheless, I paid for the power tools, knowing they wouldn't see sparks unless I used them.

A long trip to the grocery store helped me decide

on pot roast with all the fixings for Sunday lunch. Another of Dwight's favorites. I put the cold items in the styrofoam cooler I always kept iced down in my trunk, and headed to the library to return some books.

By four in the afternoon, I met Sally Avery at the Hot Crossed Buns Bakery on Mason Avenue. She and I had been Tri Delt sorority sisters and bridesmaids in each other's weddings. Mine was very simple, but hers was like a coronation. Her father had more money than mine, more than anybody's, actually.

We had just settled in our booth with our coffees and basket of pastries when I spied two of Dwight's male co-workers across the dining room. I stared at them until I caught their eyes and waved. Maybe they had skipped the golf game.

Sally and I resumed our chat. I was pleased to hear her marriage to Mike Avery made her happier than she'd been in her whole life. Her son Colton, from her first marriage, would be leaving for college in two years.

"But there are days I feel too old to chase a toddler," she said with a laugh.

"I envy you."

Dwight and I wanted children, but never had any. Somehow that was my fault, he had often reminded me.

I gave Sally a half smile. "Enjoy the gift."

As the co-workers stopped by our booth on the way out, I introduced them to Sally. "Returning to the club tonight?" I said. "It's a long drive back to Austin just for dinner with the guys."

One of them frowned. "What are you talking about?"

The other one shook his head. "I'm taking my wife to a movie later. Just the two of us. Some chick flick she's dying to see."

I set down my coffee cup. "Y'all weren't at the sales meeting today?"

"What meeting?"

While Sally squirmed, I blinked several times. "Maybe it was just a few of the guys. New product line and all?"

"The boss... uh, Sherman never mentioned anything about it," said the first one.

The other one jabbed him in the ribs. "We gotta run. Nice to see you."

They took off like there was a prize for who got out the door first.

While thoughts ricocheted in my head, I squinted at Sally. I took a deep breath and waited for the eye of the storm to bring its calm. "Seems like I need to ask Dwight some questions."

"I'm sorry," she said, squeezing my hand. "Maybe it's nothing."

All at once the last month became clearer to me.

"Until recently, Dwight hasn't been overly dedicated to his job, his diet, or his physique." Like me, he never changed his routine without a struggle. The working overtime might be a pretense while the working out signaled a new goal. It resulted in his coming home late almost every weeknight, but what did it add up to?

What got Dwight all fired up about nutrition and exercise? Who was he trying to impress?

Not his boss.

I shook my head at Sally. "Did you know Dwight takes pains to come in second in sales? Even third?"

"Why?"

"Because he believes the person who costs the company the most in commissions will be the first one fired in a slump."

Certainly not trying to impress his wife.

"Dwight never cared what I thought about anything," I said. "He'd let his tongue turn to dust before he paid me a compliment. And my spaghetti sauce is never as good as his mother's. It's her recipe, for pity's sake, and I follow it exactly!"

He never bothered to argue with me, but I could tell he tuned me out and did whatever he wanted anyway. After a while, I quit sharing my ideas with him.

I should just go home, hunker down, and wait for the storm to pass. It's what I always do.

Sally gave me a sad smile. "In almost thirteen years of marriage, did you ever tell him how you felt?"

For a moment, I sat motionless. Teetering on the edge. Hearing the rumble of approaching cannon. Shell-shocked already, I slid out of the booth, picked up my purse, and reached for my wallet. "I've got to go home."

With a wave of her hand, Sally took the check. "You paid last time."

"Paid? You bet I've paid." I raised my voice. "My whole life, I've paid for a ride in the back seat while I let that jerk drive any place he wanted. Never asking me where I'd like to go. Taking advantage of my good nature while he always put himself first. What a fool I am!"

I pounded my sternum with my fist. "I'm the one who knows how to use the darn power tools. Some lazy partner he's been, letting me do all the work around the house!"

Sally raised her eyebrows and glanced around the dining room. A quick scan over my shoulder told me people were staring.

I didn't care. "I'm through with letting him get away with that crap. He's never given a damn about me. Starting now, things are going to be different. I'm not heading home after all."

"Where will you—"

"To... to the..." Not to Austin or the country club. Too early to make a scene in public. Who would be there anyway?

I snatched a chocolate creme-stuffed eclair from the basket. "To the gym!"

CHAPTER THREE
The Workout

I circled the parking lot, passing the health club three times before I chose a parking place. It wasn't that crowded, not on a Saturday afternoon, and I had good reason to expect to find Dwight there. After all, I pulled into a space next to his Ford LTD, light blue like his eyes. Convertible, like his... oh, whatever.

For a moment, I sat in the front seat not moving. He wasn't where he said he'd be. So what? Maybe the meeting got out early. Maybe rain in Austin canceled the golf game. I peeked up at the cloudless sky. Maybe I was a fool.

Nothing in my boring life had prepared me for what might lie behind those glass double doors. A wave of fatigue washed over me and I rested my forehead on my hands as I gripped the steering wheel. Battened the hatches. Braced for the storm.

The storm didn't pass. It grew instead. From searching for signs I might have missed to wondering what I could have done differently, I berated myself for not speaking up sooner.

Perhaps that was my problem all along. Even as a child growing up, I did what others expected as opposed to what I really wanted to do. Trouble was, I wasn't sure what I wanted. No one had listened to me long enough for me to find out, not even my parents. Not even me.

When one of my poems was published in *The Journal of American Poetry*, Mother had cackled, "No one ever earned a dime from a rhyme." Behind her, my father grinned as he shook his head.

Now was as good a time as any to pose the question. Was I willing to make myself uncomfortable with the truth? No, make that *comfortable* with the truth. Connect the dots. Unbatten my own hatches and stick my head out. Take a chance on me for a change.

I opened the car door and headed toward the entrance. Turned sideways once, stopped in my tracks twice. Spun around again and marched through the double doors into the lobby.

The tanned, skinny young thing at the front desk looked up from her movie magazine and snapped her chewing gum as if she couldn't believe I had ever set foot in a gym. "Are you lost, ma'am?"

"Is Dwight Morehead here?"

"I'm not allowed to give out the names of our customers." She sat up straighter and poked her perky boobs at me. My eyes shot icy daggers at her until she blinked. "And you are?"

"His wife. Alice Morehead."

The gasp and the gaping mouth told me what I needed to know. "Where are they?" I headed toward the doorway to the main workout room.

"Wait!" she called out. "You can't go back there. You're not a member!"

I whirled around and jerked my thumb toward the exercise room. "Unless you want me to make a huge, ugly scene in front of all those panting, red-faced customers," I said through clenched teeth, "you'll take me on a little tour. Right now."

What compelled me to say that? I've never made a scene in my life, if you don't count the little one at the bakery a few minutes ago. What kind of maniac was I turning into?

She punched a button on her desk phone, but I was too quick for her. I grabbed the receiver and slammed it down. "Now!"

Maniac? I might come to like the new me. Determined and assertive. Scary.

Grimacing, she came out from behind the desk and pointed down the hallway past the locker room doors. I had two choices: sauna or pool-and-hot-tub. Dwight never liked to sweat that much. Door number two.

Several grandmotherly-looking types bunched together, bobbing up and down in the shallow end of the pool, while the rest of it was empty. No one lounged in the hot tub either, but I did spy two pairs of wet footprints leading from it to the door marked 'Laundry Room.'

Following the tracks, I stomped across the cement floor and flung the door open. Tonto would have been proud of me. Thank goodness I went steely numb within moments.

With his hands on her bare tummy, Dwight was kneeling butt-naked in front of a young blonde wearing nothing but a bikini bottom. His bright red Speedo lay on the floor next to him.

For a few seconds, I considered leaving the way I had come in, turning around and clicking the door closed behind me as quietly as possible. In silence I stood, waiting, until somewhere deep inside me, a different door closed. Slammed shut. I hitched myself up straighter.

She shrieked and grabbed a wet towel from the nearby bin to hide her glistening, king-sized breasts, while he twisted to look over his shoulder.

"Oh... my God!" he panted as he struggled to his feet. "Alice! What are you doing here?"

Not wanting to see her effect on him, my gaze wandered above his head while I tapped my foot. Once he wrapped himself around the waist in the towel he had snatched from her, our eyes met in mute challenge. With her arms crossed over her chest, she turned to face the wall.

After a moment, I wheeled around and headed back toward the exit. He trotted behind me, spewing explanations and denials, slathering blame on me like a mud bath, until he caught up to me, next to the pool.

"Alice," he pleaded. "I've been meaning to talk to you, but you never listen to me."

I stopped to glare at him.

"There's something important I have to tell you. Uh, ask you."

Icicles and a palpable hush.

"I didn't mean for you to find out like this. Everything came to a head very quickly."

After frowning, I raised an eyebrow and then glanced down at his towel, which had slipped below his rounded belly.

He sucked his stomach in and held it. "Okay, poor choice of words, but—" He heaved a big sigh. "I just learned... well, I've got to... I want to marry her... as soon as..."

His meaning almost made sense, but I couldn't seem to care. His rambling about how he needed to be happy and wanted a divorce, so I had to face the facts and let him go, should have been the signal that my world was crashing around me, but I didn't even need a deep breath.

Happy? His words became a droning buzz in the background, as all at once it occurred to me that the flip side of our marriage coin was also true. I couldn't remember the last time I felt joyful. Appreciated. Loved. When had we ever done anything—or gone anywhere—that was my choice? All these years, a really efficient housekeeper, who was also a good cook and laundress, could have met Dwight's needs. Most of them, anyway.

Could I accept the fact that Dwight found someone else, a younger, more shapely and attractive woman, and was leaving me for her? She'd find out he wasn't such a prize. Comfortable? Yes, I was getting there.

As he shuffled his feet by the edge of the pool, Dwight hiked the loosely-tucked towel up to his waist. "Don't you want to know why?" He ran a nervous hand through his thinning hair.

So far, his future bride had remained in the laundry room, but the grandmas at the other end of the pool had stopped bouncing and wandered a little closer, their eyes—and their ears—fixed on us. Words carried easily over the water.

I gazed at him and realized I was married to a grown man with the maturity of a seventeen-year-old boy. We never had children together, but I had spent the last thirteen years trying to raise this child. With no luck, evidently.

Shrugging, I shook my head and stared at the water in the pool. A future without him was starting to appeal to me.

Dwight cleared his throat. "Rhonda's *pregnant*." He waited for my reaction and seemed to appreciate my surprised expression, and then grinned. "I'm going to be a *daddy*."

Lunging forward, I tugged at the edge of the towel, while with my other hand, I shoved him into the pool. As I flung the towel toward the far wall, I spun around before I even heard the splash and made my way toward the exit.

As Dwight surfaced, cussing and calling my name, the grandmas whistled and applauded. One of them even hollered out a whoop-whoop. I was pretty sure none of them would offer to fetch his towel.

Back in my car, I sat for a moment and tried to sort through my emotions. Replayed the scene and the words. Why wasn't I angry with Dwight for betraying me?

Bit by bit, the anger surfaced, but it was directed at me. How had I permitted this treatment all these years? Why didn't I stand up for myself? Love myself better?

What ifs flitted around my brain like a bluejay chasing a grasshopper. Daddy had advised me to give up my dream of being a poet and be practical, while Mother said to get a MRS degree and find a hobby or volunteer until the children come along.

After graduation, Mother encouraged me to take Dwight's offer by hinting it was the only one I was likely to get. At the time, I couldn't argue her point. Before we stood together at the altar, Dwight had vowed no wife of his would work outside the home because taking care of him was a "full time job."

Marriage, home, community had all fallen into place without my really noticing who got left out. What had become of me? How did I disappear? I have always been perfectly capable of fixing the difficulties of others, but... until today, I didn't believe my life had any real misfortunes or serious losses.

Except one.

I bit my lip. As time marched on, I had come to accept my infertility.

Now Dwight would get what he wanted. Could I?

Raising my head, I stared out the front windshield. Enough is enough. I swallowed hard. As I fired up the engine, I determined to go home, sort through this mess, and find what I was looking for.

Me.

CHAPTER FOUR
The Mouseburger

A Mouseburger. That's what Helen Gurley Brown would call me.

I stood in line at the grocery store, thumbing through the latest edition of *Cosmopolitan*. 'Cosmo girls' are beautiful, fun, sexy, and smart. She hadn't started out that way, she wrote, describing herself as "plain and ordinary," a woman who had to "work relentlessly to make herself desirable and successful." But she certainly fulfilled her dream and became a 'Cosmo girl.' And more.

If this was a test, it was the first one I had ever failed. Ms. Brown labeled me perfectly: "A mouseburger is not prepossessing, not pretty, doesn't have a particularly high I.Q., a decent education, good family background, or other noticeable assets."

Before moving forward toward the cashier, I slid the magazine back into the rack.

What had I been doing all these years? Working at everything I did—okay, it was only volunteer and housework—so Dwight would at least see me as valuable.

Either he was blind. Or I was.

"Good morning, Mrs. Morehead." The cashier

gave me a sad smile. "How's everything these days?"

She knew about the divorce, final last week. Everyone in Mason's Crossing did.

Nodding, I said, "Fine."

"You getting along all right?" Her tone sounded almost weepy.

Wait! I am the Go-To Girl. Everything I have always done for my family I can also do for myself. Maybe I don't have to stay a Mouseburger. What a revelation!

I reached across my basket and pulled the magazine from its slot. Laying it on the top of the pile, I smiled broadly at the cashier and said in my bravest, cheeriest voice, "Never better."

On the way out, I ran into Sally on the front sidewalk as she struggled to settle her toddler into the child's seat of a grocery cart. Unruly red hair had sprouted on his head like monkey grass, and his blue eyes twinkled with mischief. The toddler kicked and wiggled non-stop.

As I approached them, I held up my keys in front of his face and jangled them. "What's with his adorable hair color?"

The toddler went slack as he grasped for them.

"Mike's father, Clyde, and my great-grandmother Patricia Mason. Aren't recessive genes fun?" Sally pulled his legs through the openings and plopped his bottom in the seat, and then said, "Thanks, Alice. You know just what to do."

We hugged each other, and her natural warmth

encircled me like a cloud.

"I hope that's true."

"What do you mean?"

"I have to figure a few things out, like what I'm going to do the rest of my life."

"Are you okay?"

"It's different without someone else at home, but frankly, it's better, less lonely even, without... Dwight." I sighed. "But I'm getting bored with volunteer work."

I told Sally about Dwight quitting his job and opening a frame store with his new wife. He possessed no skills with power tools or geometry and was color blind, but she loved to use rock concert posters in her decorating. I imagined Jimi Hendrix, his glorious Afro back-lit, hanging on their dining room wall.

"My income from his future employment, awarded to me in the divorce decree, will drop to below freezing. I think I need to find a job. A real job."

"Doing what?"

"My résumé is a little sketchy. My degree in Home Economics has been spent solving problems for everyone else's home life." I shrugged. "Not sure what I'm qualified to do. I don't even have a teaching certificate, but my father says I should be a substitute at the high school."

"Then you could work your way toward a certificate, right?" Sally dangled her car keys in front of her child's face. He exchanged mine for hers, and she handed them back to me, wet. "He's the superintendent and could hire you tomorrow. Why not?"

"I'd rather not depend on him. I need to be inde-
pendent for a change."

"But you love young people."

"Substitutes get tortured unmercifully, don't you
remember?"

As she nodded, Sally dug through her purse until
she found a business card. She handed it to me. "Call
this guy and say I referred you."

"Who is it?" I read the name on the card: Doug
Creighton, Producer. "What does he produce?"

"Remember my friend Angelique, the artist?"

"Who could forget her? She was like a second mother to you. How long has it been since she passed?"

"Feels like more than five years. Anyway, Doug
is Angelique's second ex-husband. He's a music producer in Austin, close personal friends with Willie
Nelson, but he's getting involved in something to do
with television. Seems very interesting."

"I don't know anything about music or TV, except
I watch a lot of it lately." Ugh, even re-runs.

"He told me there's some new channel about to
get launched, and Doug's always had a nose for the
lucrative ground floor, according to Angelique. She
once told me he's a genius."

Sally's smile was wistful. I guess some losses
never fade.

"Anyway, he needs a personal assistant, someone
who can keep his life on track while he expands his
business. Some big famous deal is headed his way,

and he says he's desperate for help. You don't have to know anything about his commercial operation, just how to manage whatever comes up in the other part of his demanding existence, so he says."

Sounded familiar, only this time I'd get paid for picking up dry cleaning and taking the dog to the groomer's. Or any similar last-minute emergency.

"Truly, Alice, you'd be perfect for it."

"Do you mind if I ask you something? Why did he and Angelique get divorced? Is he mean or something?"

"He's a pussycat, with a problem. He's terrific at business opportunities, but years ago Angelique revealed she had never met anyone so disorganized and unpredictable in his personal life. He never came home when he said he would, was always off somewhere working on the next recording contract or carousing with rock stars, letting everything else come unraveled."

I knew the type. Nothing I couldn't handle, but this one I could keep at arm's length.

"Thanks a bunch. I'll get in touch with him right away."

"Good, I'll let him know to expect your call. Then you'll have a fighting chance of getting through. He's a real character, but you'll like him."

Sally seemed like she glowed. Joy simply burst from her every pore. If I didn't admire her so much as a close friend, I would be jealous for the way her life had turned around.

I patted Sally's arm. "How's everything with you?"

"I'll let you in on a little secret." Sally nuzzled the top of her toddler's head. "My little boy is getting a sibling."

Tears stung my eyes at the corners. How perfect. "Congratulations!"

"We haven't told many people yet. My father is ecstatic, of course."

"I hear he's moving back to Mason's Crossing."

"He'll be here part of the year, and still keep the ranch going, too. He's turned out to be a pretty good grandfather. At least he works at it. We're trying to make up for lost time."

Now there was a magic trick if I ever heard one. But could you make up for lost time all by yourself? I was determined to find out.

Hugging her, I said, "I'm really delighted for you." I meant it. She deserved all her newly-found happiness.

"Call me if you need anything," she said as she aimed her cart toward the grocery store's automatic doors. "You know I'm always up late, waiting for Mike's shift to end." She told me he had taken a later shift so he could spend waking hours with their son.

"Thanks, that's nice to know."

"I mean it. Call me. Even midnight isn't too late."

Still wiggling, Nathan Farraday Avery waved at me as I, the almost ex-Mouseburger, headed toward my car.

CHAPTER FIVE

The Producer

After five phone calls back and forth over several days, I finally secured an appointment to meet Doug Creighton. While I cooled my heels for nearly two hours in his production office in Austin—what else did I have to do anyway?—his telephone rang so often, I considered answering it and taking messages. It would have been fun to schedule his golf game with Coach Royal and Willie for next Thursday.

The other messages made no sense with all their hip, technical jargon, and one sounded very important and downright mysterious. "The package has almost completed its assignment, will be released, ready for retrieval, Friday. Don't be late." I hoped it wasn't a drug deal.

The office door sprang open and Doug Creighton roared through it like a pickup truck with its tailgate down, trailing papers behind him. He dropped a load of videotapes on his desk and turned to face me. "Please tell me you're Alice, Sally's friend." He stuck out his hand.

I shook it and nodded, taking a moment to assess the man who scooted around his desk and checked the flashing light on his answering machine. Tall, good-looking, full head of black-and-silver hair, tailored but trendy dresser. I guessed his age at late forties or early fifties.

"I let myself in," I said in a timid voice. "I hope that's all right."

"Oh, crap, did I leave the door unlocked again?" He ran his hand over his forehead. "I must be losing it."

"Mr. Creighton, you've had fourteen messages since I've been here," I said, glancing at my watch.

"Please call me Doug," he said. "Any of them important?" He poured us both some coffee from a thermos. Mine tasted stale, but he didn't notice.

"Uh, well, Coach Royal and Willie—"

"Oh, yeah, golf. Is Larry joining us? We've got to go over the festival details."

I began to tingle all over, and it wasn't from the coffee. "Gatlin? He didn't mention him."

"Okay, I'll see if Kris'll be in town."

"Kristofferson?" My heart skipped a beat.

He nodded as he shuffled a stack of papers, muttering, "Got to get these contracts over to Carlos."

Doug deposited himself in the canvas chair behind his desk and gestured to another one across from him. Smiling, he said, "Sally tells me you can get toothpaste back in the tube." Against his tanned face, his teeth shone like-glow-in-the-dark Chiclets.

I laughed and picked up the stray pages from the floor before I sat down. "I don't know about that,"

I said, placing them on his desk, "but I'm good at keeping track of things, helping people stay on target, solving problems, handling details. My strong suits are patience, organiza—"

The phone rang and he grabbed the receiver like he wanted to choke the life out of it. "Yes... fourteen... maybe... Friday, far as I know right now... Plan B only if we have to... I'll keep you posted." He hung up.

"...organization, reliability, neatness, punct—"

Again the phone rang, but this time he ignored it. "My life is a constant storm, people and stuff blowing in and out all the time. I need someone who can keep calm and handle any situation. The live music scene in Austin is exploding, and I've got a finger on one of the major switches. My house needs to go on the market, one of my daughters should be starting college next fall if someone could figure out where to send the paperwork, and I have three ex-wives, two still living, both noisy and high maintenance, and a crazy brother-in-law who wants to mingle with the stars so he can pitch them their own tunes using his stupid lyrics. My mother and my sister nag me about it non-stop."

Doug flipped through his Rolodex and yanked a card from it. "There's a super-big opportunity headed this way—could be any day now—and I'm on the verge of cutting the deal of a lifetime, while I'm also trying to expand the studio space. I can't let all this other mess get in my way."

He jumped to his feet. "Sally says you're the Go-To Girl." He bent over his phone, checking the Rolodex card twice as he dialed.

"That's my nickname, just family use it, but only occasion—"

He spoke into the phone, more like barked into it. "Heard anything yet?... Thought we'd know by now... This better work, 'cuz I anteed up a lot of beans for this package."

My ears perked up and I waved my palm at him, then pointed to the answering machine. "You have a message about a package," I mouthed.

"Call you back." He hung up and sat down again, without noticing the card floating to the floor. "What'd it say?"

I repeated the message as best my memory allowed. "It's fifth in the sequence after two o'clock." I pointed to the floor until he picked up the card.

"Friday, hmmmm? Two days from now." He ran his hands through his hair, then stared at me for several moments.

Without flinching, I tried to look calm and pleasant. Normal. Capable. I tossed back the rest of the coffee, now cold, like it was straight bourbon.

"No telling what you'll be called on to do, and the answer always has to be 'yes'," he said as he lit a stale cigar for at least the second time.

I nodded, I hope not vigorously enough to seem over-eager.

"I assume no problem, then, and you won't need

much supervision, right?"

The salary, plus expenses, he offered me was forty percent higher than any teacher's paycheck. I couldn't wait to call my father and tell him 'no thanks' as kindly as possible. Truly, I'd rather be stripped naked and paraded through the school cafeteria at high noon than depend on my parents for the rest of my pitiful life.

"Can you start tomorrow?"

In a flash of brazen spunk, I picked up the stack of contracts. "How about now?"

Doug sighed in relief as he handed me a business card with his lawyer's address on it, and gave me instructions to hand-deliver only to him. No one else must see what the contracts contain or even know they exist.

His phone rang as I exited his office, and all the way down the hallway I could hear him yelling, "No! Stop! You're killing me!" at the caller, who must have been his brother-in-law.

Once in the elevator, I studied my reflection in a mirrored panel. Still plain and ordinary, but a slow grin spread across my face.

The Mouseburger had learned to roar. Or at least to speak up.

CHAPTER SIX

The Flying Saucers

Doug Creighton's attorney kept me waiting half as long as he did. Next time I would call first to be sure he wasn't in court.

While I sat on the Corinthian leather sofa in the lobby of his downtown office, I glanced through the contracts. With no legal training, I didn't expect to understand much, but it kept me busy and made me appear smart, at least to the receptionist.

And I was curious. What was Doug's big secret for his attorney's eyes only? Maybe this was the huge deal Sally had mentioned. Perhaps connected to Doug's "package" on the answering machine.

The first several contracts were related to the construction on the new recording studio. Dwight and I had remodeled our home several years ago, so the basic terminology seemed familiar, even if the details of acoustics and voltage far exceeded anything I had dealt with before. Nothing in our house ever needed to be soundproofed, and the square footage didn't require an intercom, much less a loudspeaker.

Maybe we could have saved our marriage if we had built a stage and learned to sing together. Maybe I was a fool.

The contract on the bottom of the pile was thicker than the others, so I saved it for last. It began with the usual language about identifying the parties involved, listing "Douglas Creighton, Producer" in the first line.

When I read the name of the second party, an electric shock jolted me from head to toe, and settled in my pounding heart. After several moments of thrilling excitement, I blinked to be sure I hadn't imagined it, then spelled out the name, letter by letter. O-L-I-V-E-R G-O-O-D-K-N-I-G-H-T.

Oliver Goodnight was a British rock star of the stratospheric order, an adrenaline-inducing cross between Paul McCartney and Mick Jagger. The quintessential musical bad boy adored by millions, including me, he had brought his tour to a screeching halt last year. He went into seclusion after the tragic death-by-overdose of one his "Lads," his bass guitarist, in Paris last year.

Now Doug would be bringing Oliver Goodknight—minus the Goodknight Lads—to Austin!

Closing my eyes, I thanked my lucky stars. Maybe I would get to hear him perform live. Or even meet him...

Wait, there's got to be more! I turned back to reading the contract.

... for a special recording session, filmed for a new television channel called MTV.

Sally was right to believe what Angelique had claimed. Doug was indeed a genius. How did he do it, see into the future, that is?

Maybe Doug would ask me to deliver Oliver's messages or order his catered meals. Then I'd have to ask him which foods he preferred, did he like Tex-Mex or barbecue? Golf with Willie and the guys? No problem, I'll set it up. Would he mind if we had a photo taken together so I could show my girlfriends? Of course not. Here, stand next to me, he'd say, so I can put my arm around your shoulder.

The receptionist interrupted my daydreams to let me know Mr. Trevino would be returning from court in about twenty minutes, if I could wait. With a smile, I nodded and resumed my fantasy.

When we met, Oliver's deep blue eyes would stare into my hazel ones and we would connect on a deeper level, sharing a rapport, a chemistry, an affinity he had never felt with any other woman. Nor I, with any other man.

He would cock his head sideways, smile down at me, and take my hand to lead me off the stage. "I have something really special for you," he would say, as he licked his full lips.

Without a backward glance, I would follow him to his dressing room and gaze at him as he stripped off his shirt. His smooth muscles would gleam in the lights from his dressing table, and I would scarcely be able to suppress an urge to stroke his bare flesh.

Before I could even unzip my skirt, he would turn toward me, hand me his shirt, and say in a lustful tone, "No starch."

Reality—or my own foolishness—will be the death

of me yet, I swear.

Deflated, I shook the papers of the contract as if to stack them in order, and started anew on page one. By page eight, I was exhausted by the specs for the stage, lighting, and sound equipment.

Page nine brought something entirely strange and different to the agreement. Oliver Goodknight demanded no green flying saucers in his dressing room. Any other color was fine, but green was absolutely not allowed.

Uh-oh!

Did Doug know Oliver was still on drugs, and had hallucinated, evidently many times before now? I had read rumors of his going through rehab, but here was manifest proof it didn't take. How would I break the awful news to Doug?

"Ma'am?" said the receptionist. "Mr. Trevino will see you now."

She led me down the hallway to a spacious corner office with a view of the Capitol. Mr. Charles Trevino, already seated behind his desk, stood for introductions. He looked vaguely familiar.

"Call me Carlos," he said. "Would you like something to drink?"

With a nod of my head, I handed him the contracts and paused, wondering how to warn him about the imaginary flying saucers. He gestured me to a chair.

"This won't take but a few minutes," he said as he breezed through the ones on the top of the pile.

"These are all pretty standard. I should know. I wrote all but one of them."

I waited for his secretary to set a tray with two tall glasses of ice water on the edge of his desk. A perfect round lemon slice garnished each one.

"The last one isn't," I said in a timid voice after she closed the door behind her. I took a swig of my water and waited.

Raising his eyebrows, he peered up at me over the rim of his reading glasses. "What do you mean?"

"Take a look at page nine." My voice was low, as if I sat in a confessional booth, baring my soul. "Oliver Goodknight is afraid of flying saucers." I gulped half the glass of water while he read.

Carlos snorted as he shuffled the pages. "With these guys, you never know."

While I polished off my drink, he spent a few minutes reading, then chuckled and nodded. "This is funny."

"Is he—"

"Not crazy."

"Still on drugs?"

"He has a purpose in putting this in the back of the contract." Carlos took off his glasses. "Oliver's foot got broken a few years ago when an electrician or a carpenter failed to secure a heavy prop. Since then, he's put detailed specs into every contract. Perhaps he's a little paranoid now, but the only way for him to be sure everyone reads the whole contract is to include the part about flying saucers near the last page."

"So if he sees green ones, he knows they probably haven't read the specs."

"Right." He shrugged. "Actually that's a very smart move."

"But how do you get flying saucers into his dressing room in the first place?" I figured that job would become mine.

Carlos guffawed. "Flying saucers are like candies, with sherbet in the middle. Brits love them."

"Ooohhhh," I exhaled, relieved my secret make-believe lover wasn't a candidate for a straight jacket in the rubber room of an insane asylum. I set my now-empty glass on the tray.

"Be sure Doug knows about this." Carlos handed me the other contracts, but kept the one for Oliver. "Tell him I'll go over it with a fine-toothed comb and clue him in on what's what. We musicians are a strange breed, that's for certain."

Now I remembered where I had seen him before. On stage at the summer music festival at Zilker Park, followed by a taping of *Austin City Limits* on the UT sound stage. Dwight's former boss was a regular donor to KLRU, Austin's PBS station, and we had received free tickets from time to time.

"You play drums for Los Fuertes, don't you?"

He grinned, revealing perfect white teeth, just like Doug's. "Music is my first love, but law comes in a close second. Besides, it pays the bills."

I stood up and stuck out my hand. "It's been a

pleasure meeting you. I'll let Doug know what you said."

He escorted me to the door. "Tell your boss to keep me posted when he gets the package. I'm sure you understand what I mean."

What package? Code word for what?

As I rode down the elevator, I wondered where in the world I would find sherbet-filled flying saucers.

CHAPTER SEVEN
The Celebrity

By the time I returned to Doug's office with the contracts, it was after five o'clock and the door was locked. Rats, I should have asked him for a key. I couldn't slip the documents under the door, since I didn't know when or if the nighttime cleaning crew would show up.

A juggler like Doug was bound to have a back-up plan, so why not a back-up key? I reached up over the door frame, and sure enough, my fingertips touched something skinny and metallic.

The key opened the door on the first try. Without letting the stinky air from old cigars deter me, I hurried in to answer the phone on Doug's desk, vowing to open a window.

"Creighton Productions," I wheezed.

"Is Doug there?"

The baritone voice sounded vaguely familiar.

"He's stepped out. May I take a message?" I shuffled through the papers on his desk for a pen and a notepad. Finding none, I pulled a discarded envelope from the trash can.

"Tell him I'll be coming in next Wednesday and can make the golf game after all."

As voice recognition took hold of my brain, I sucked in the muscles around my tummy, especially tightening the ones connected to my bladder. "He's looking forward to playing with you, Mr.—"

"Just Kris."

How idiotic I sounded! Dead silence. Then I gulped.

"Are Willie and Coach gonna join us?" the mesmerizing voice continued. "What about Larry? Or is he still on tour?"

"Only Coach Royal and... Mr. Nelson, so far," I squeaked. "I don't believe Mr. Gatlin can make it."

"Well, maybe another time. See you Thursday."

"Yessir."

He hung up, but I couldn't let go of the receiver. I stared at it as if I expected it to explain to me what just happened. I actually had a one-on-one chat with Kris Kristofferson. Granted, my side of it was inane, but it was my first encounter with a celebrity. Would he really see me on Thursday?

The phone company's off-the-hook signal buzzed like an alarm, and I shook myself out of my trance and replaced the receiver. After locking the front door, I spent the next half hour tidying up the office, replaying the conversation, practicing what I would say next time. No star-struck, speechless awkwardness for me. My behavior would be smooth, efficient, businesslike. No one would realize I hadn't been interacting with famous people all my life.

Doug would depend on me to help get them

settled or wherever they needed to go, find out what else they required, other than no green flying saucers. I would provide seamless assistance without missing a beat. I hummed "Always on My Mind" while I transferred stacks of papers from the floor to the credenza, careful not to mix them up, and deposited pens and pencils into a holder. Scattered paperclips went back in their box, coffee-stained styrofoam cups and cigar butts in the trash. Later I'd rinse out the coffee pot, now cold, on my way to the ladies' room.

As I began to imagine my new career reaching successful heights, the phone rang again. A feeling of intense calm came over me as I put the receiver to my ear. "Creighton Productions," I said in my most relaxed and competent tone, swinging the extra-long corkscrew cord like a jumprope.

"It's Oliver," whispered a voice in a heavy British accent. In fact, it sounded more on the cockney side than the Queen's English. But what did I know?

My heart didn't even skip a beat. My lungs inhaled and exhaled as usual.

As much as I might tighten my stomach muscles again, however, my bladder had a mind of its own. It dropped the full load of Doug's coffee and the gallon of water I had consumed at the lawyer's office, down my legs, into my shoes, and onto the floor.

"'Allo?" the voice said louder. "I say, is anybody there?"

My lips moved but no sound came out. All I could do was stare at the floor and watch the puddle spread.

And wait to regain my senses.

Meanwhile, someone in the hallway right outside the office jangled a keychain and then inserted a key into the door handle.

CHAPTER EIGHT

The Poet's Corner

The door handle jiggled again. At that instant, I would have given anything for a disguise, or even a towel. I would have put it over my head and pretended to be a three-year-old who believed in magic.

My eyes swept the room. Not a single useful thing.

"One moment, please," I said into the phone. Gee, whose calm efficient voice was that?

I set down the receiver, grabbed the quarter-full coffee pot, and sloshed its contents over the swelling puddle of pee. Then whirled around in time to stand behind Doug's desk as the door swung open.

A middle-aged man with a protruding belly stood in the doorway, surprise registered on his face. "Who're you?" he said in a demanding voice, as he took a step forward.

"Doug's new assistant." I stood my ground, a new skill I just developed, forced by necessity. "And you are?"

"Lynwood Walker." He grinned in a rather greasy way. "But folks call me Woody."

I didn't return his smile, but tried to look pleasant. "Do you have an appointment with Mr. Creight-on?" I shuffled through a pile on Doug's desk, know-ing it was pointless to search for a calendar.

"Not 'xactly. I spoke to him a little bit ago." As he strolled toward the desk, his eyes flitted around the room like a sightseer while he focused on framed photos of Doug with countless big-name music stars and other celebrities. "So this is Dougie's office? My, my!" He pointed to one in the middle. "That really Elvis?" He looked closer and nodded.

From the corner of my eye, I kept careful watch on the puddle. It had taken on a life of its own, spreading like gossip. When he came within a foot of it, I spoke. "Please watch your step. I just spilled some coffee."

He glanced down and sidestepped the puddle without looking disgusted. So far, not so bad. When he reached the desk, he extended his hand. "Nice to meet you, Miss, uh... what d'ya say your name was?"

I relaxed, but only enough to be courteous. "Alice, Alice Morehead. What can I do for you, Mr. Walker?" One at a time, I slipped my heels out of my soggy shoes, hidden behind the desk, and hoped I didn't appear to be dancing. Maybe he couldn't hear the slight sucking sound, like my insoles were gasping for air.

"Doug said I could drop by with some song lyrics. I'm a tad early." He laid a three-ring binder on the edge of the desk next to the phone, opened it, and popped apart the rings. Wearing a proud smile, he removed three sheets. "I been workin' on 'em for a while, and now they're almost perfect."

He held them out for me. "All they need's a little polishin' before Doug shares them with Willie and Kris next week."

My eyes widened. "You must be his brother-in-law." I accepted the pages and set them on the top of the desk.

"Doug tol' you about me, did he?" His grin turned tentative. "He pro'bly swore I had no talent, but I know I really got somethin' here. All's I need is a chance."

'Doesn't everyone?' I wanted to say. Instead I nodded and pointed to the door. "Mr. Walker, if you haven't been in here before, how did you get a key?"

Now his face turned reddish-pink, a hangdog attitude beating back the bravado, and he stared down at the puddle. I prayed it had eaten through the veneer and been absorbed into the floorboards. "My mother-in-law gave me hers this afternoon. I didn't think Doug would let me in if I knocked."

Woody sounded embarrassed, and I didn't have the heart to add to his discomfort. "Mr. Walker, I'm going to offer you a deal." I picked up the ring binder and replaced the three pages. "I just happen to be an award-winning published poet"—so what if it was one poem and one award, fifteen years ago— "and I'll be glad to take a look at your work and give you some feedback. No promises, however. Just my opinion. Clear?"

He beamed as he held up his palms and shook his head, eyes closed like he was at a prayer meeting. "Just to have a professional read 'em and—"

"Now that I have them, you mustn't bother Doug with these any longer. Never again. Understood?"

He nodded, a bit too eagerly for me to believe him.

I stretched out my hand and cupped it. "And in exchange, you must surrender the key to this office."

"But it's not mine, it belongs to my—"

Raising one eyebrow while staring at him, I tapped my palm. "Doug will get it back to its rightful owner." I made a mental note to get the office lock changed.

Woody sighed and dropped the key into my grasp. "How soon can you take a look at my lyrics?"

"As soon as Doug lets me know the rest of my responsibilities and I get my schedule organized." I dropped the key into my purse. "I'll get in touch with you. Not the other way around, remember? No calling Doug, no showing up here unannounced."

"Okay, that's fair." He turned to leave. "You've sure given me hope, Miss Alice," he said as he waltzed out the door and closed it behind him.

Relieved, but wondering what I had gotten myself into, I twisted sideways to look over my shoulder at the back of my skirt. No wet mark. A miracle.

After a beeline to the ladies' room for enough paper towels to fill a suitcase, I stuffed some in my shoes and then used the rest to wipe the floor dry until it left no trace of moisture. As I stood up at last, a distant voice made a sound like crinkled paper, and it came from the edge of Doug's desk.

Oh my goodness! I had left Oliver Goodknight holding the phone this whole time. I snatched the receiver and slammed it to my ear. "So sorry, Mr. Good—"

"May I speak to Miss Emily Fooking Dickinson?" His tone was crisp and frosty. Or maybe it was just his accent.

"What, uh... yes, I'm... how may I assist you?"

"I must speak with Doug immediately."

"Sorry, Mr. Goodknight, he's not here."

"Oh, good Christ!" His words snapped out, like he could fire bullets through his teeth. "At what hour do you expect him?"

My mind sorted through all of Doug's comments before we had gone our separate ways earlier that afternoon, but I had no clue where he was or when he'd be back, if at all, this evening. I added appointment book to my mental list of office supplies. "I'm not sure. He wasn't in when I returned from his attorney's off—"

"Will it be soon?" Now he sounded like a worried child, wondering when his daddy would get home. "I need him to do something for me without delay."

What was it Doug had told me? My answer had always better be yes, even before anyone asked the question.

"He didn't leave me a way to reach him, so I'll be glad to take care of it instead. Just tell me what you need."

"Transportation from—"

Rifling through Doug's Rolodex, I said, "I'll send a limo to the airport. What time do you arrive?"

"Bollocks! No limo, not the airport."

Why was he whispering?

"Doug will be surprised, pleasantly, of course. He didn't expect you until later in the week." Where had my boss gone tonight? Why didn't I ask him before he left? Mental note: keep better track of this wandering parakeet.

"What about you, Miss Poetess? Why cannot Miss Dickinson come fetch me up?"

Oliver Goodknight wanted to ride next to me, in my car. Just the two of us. He'd jump in and I'd give him a little peck on the cheek. "Welcome home, darling. How was your tour?" I'd whisk him away to our stately mansion overlooking our private lake, but before we got halfway home, I'd have to pull over so I could return his kisses without wrecking the car. My sweet little Jetta, a previously-owned 5-speed I had learned to drive last month.

Stop, no way would a British rockstar of his magnitude want to ride in something so... humdrum. What a fool I am!

"Mr. Goodknight, I'd be happy to arrange a rental car for you. How about a... Lincoln Town Car, or a Cadillac Seville?"

"My driving license was revoked." His tone was surly.

"Of course. Where are you?"

"Wait! How do I know I can trust you?"

I pondered for a moment, then tried not to laugh out loud. "Mr. Goodknight, I know all about the green flying saucers."

"Right-o, then. Come rescue me."

"Where?" A swank hotel, no doubt, but why did he need to be rescued?

"Some beastly petrol station on a corner in— Beg pardon, where am I?" Fumbling sounds came through the line as he shuffled the phone away from his mouth.

A distant voice yelled back at him.

More shuffling. "I'm in Fredericksburg."

"Virginia?" Must be some private rehab clinic outside D.C.

"No, Texas. Just west of Austin or somewhere out here in the bleeding desert."

"I thought you were not due out of, um... out 'til Friday. How did you get released early?"

A pause. "I escaped."

Thankfully my bladder was already empty.

There was simply no talking him into returning to the rehab center. By his refusing to hear of it, I learned some new phrases, cusswords actually, in British slang. Little did I know they would come in handy very soon.

Oliver recited the cross streets of the small town in the Hill Country, and I told him I'd be there in about an hour-and-a-half and could he find somewhere comfortable to wait inside the gas station until then? He didn't have to know I would stop at the mall and buy myself new pairs of jeans and shoes, plus panties, on my way out of Austin. With my new salary, I could afford it.

"But make haste, would you? I'm bored out of my skull, have been for weeks on end. There's nothing to do in this tiny backwater of civilization. No live music anywhere. What the bloody hell do people find to do here on Pluto? There must be something—"

"Wait right there for me!"

Doug would be pleased to learn I said 'yes' to his most important client without bothering him with any pesky details. His plan for the new TV show could proceed without a hitch, and he would achieve yet another major success.

Oliver Goodknight riding in my car. Just the two of us! Like captives who had escaped together and were headed back to paradise.

Not until I passed Johnson City did I ask myself what I would do with him when we got back to Austin.

CHAPTER NINE

The Honky Tonk

No one, especially not Oliver Goodnight, loitered in or anywhere near the phone booth at the gas station by the time I arrived in Fredericksburg. Already bored, maybe he had gotten hungry, too.

Trying not to panic, I glanced around. No lights left on inside any of the buildings. Three blocks ahead a traffic signal blinked, but no cars waited at the intersection. A sleepy little hamlet even smaller than Mason's Crossing, Fredericksburg rolled up its sidewalks before 8 PM.

Anywhere he might have gone, Oliver would've had to walk, unless he hitched a ride. My watch indicated I had last spoken with him an hour and forty-five minutes ago. A knot formed in the pit of my empty stomach.

Slowing my Jetta to a crawl, I peered from side to side as I progressed up Main Street. It wasn't like I expected to find him snoozing in a doorway, but he had already caused a major spike on my predictability meter.

On the corner utility pole hung a poster with 'Rodeo' for a headline. Calf roping, bronc busting, bull riding—nothing here to interest a Brit... unless you count the country western bands listed in small print at the bottom. Live music would attract him like a bear to a beehive.

I followed the directions a few miles up the highway towards Kerrville and pulled over to park on the edge of a grassy field outside a bright, noisy arena, with rows of white canopies and tents on either side. At one end, a ferris wheel lit the sky like a rocket flying in circles.

Finding Oliver shouldn't be hard among the jeans and cowboy hats, I thought. It wasn't like I could show everyone his photo, however, not without bringing unwanted publicity. Maybe I should just ask people if they'd met anyone with an English accent.

Caution played the better part of valor. Instead, I asked the local highway patrolman to point out the music tent to me and I trudged across the hay-strewn field through wafting barbecue smoke. My mouth watered. In my hurry to buy a fresh wardrobe at the mall, I had forgotten to eat anything.

Out of character for me, I had come this far without a plan, but now was the time to formulate a strategy. Find Oliver, feed us both if he's still hungry, get him in the car, drive back to Austin. What could be simpler? Perhaps by that time, Doug would magically appear and whisk Oliver off my hands, after he thanked me profusely for rescuing his most valuable 'package.'

After several moments inside the tent, my pupils

adjusted to the dim light. The lead singer of a quartet on stage belted out a song about broken-hearted lovers. Or maybe a stray dog trying to find a dead squirrel he had hidden for a snack. I couldn't listen to the lyrics without thinking about Dwight, so I tuned both out of my mind.

I scanned the crowd for any male head without a cowboy hat and finally located one in the shadows leaning against the wall across the room, but I had to stand on my tiptoes to see the face. Hard to get a good look, so I nudged my way through the herd around the edge of the dance floor, dodging boot scooters and others keeping time to the twang of the guitars and the beat of the drums.

When I got close enough, I confirmed the man's identity as one British rock star, newly escaped from rehab, MIA from the live music scene for the last year. He looked like he missed performing in some terrible, heart-wrenching way, like a starved child who peered through a café window.

No one else had recognized him yet, and I couldn't tell if he was relieved or disappointed. I kept weaving through the audience until I stood in front of him. Were his eyes really that blue? Like Wedgewood china... oh, stop acting like a fool and focus! Celebrity or not, I wasn't about to let him liberate the contents of my bladder a second time, so I tightened my stomach muscles and concentrated on getting his attention.

Despite my resolve, I melted anyway. "Mr. Goodknight?" I gushed.

Oliver looked down at me like he was in a trance. "Eugenia?"

The man to my right turned and stared at him. "Goodnight? Hey, you ain't related to Charlie Goodnight, are ya?"

"Who's that?" Oliver said, in a tone absent of any real curiosity.

"Y'all don't know?" He slurred his words. "Chizzum Trail?"

"Never heard of it." Oliver returned his gaze to the stage.

"Mr. Goodknight, I'm Alice. We spoke on the phone about two hours ago. Doug's been expecting you. We should go."

He made no movement, even when I placed my hand on his arm. What did I imagine would happen? Electricity?

"Which Goodnight're you? Cuzzin?" said the man next to us, in a voice that grew louder by the second. "How 'bout another beer for me and my buddy here?" He called to the waitress passing with a full tray near us. "Two... no, make that three, longnecks, ma'am."

"You're very kind," I said to him with a shake of my head, "but we must be going now." I tugged on Oliver's arm.

The band finished the song and the crowd applauded. The lead singer thanked everyone and then said, "Folks, we have a very special guest with us tonight, all the way from England..."

My head whirled around like it needed an exorcist. The lead singer pointed in our direction and the spotlight followed his gesture.

"...None other than our favorite limey lad, Oliver Goodknight!"

The crowd erupted into screams and whistles, which soon became the thud of boots stomping on the plywood floor. "Oli-VER, Oli-VER," they chanted.

What could one song hurt? I turned back to Oliver and would have shrugged a go-ahead, except for the look of unmitigated terror in his eyes. He gripped my forearms hard enough to cut off circulation to my hands and stood as if paralyzed.

"I... I can't go up there," he said in a voice as full of fear and pleading as I'd ever heard anyone's.

"You don't have to," I said. "Just wave to the audience and we'll leave."

"But I *want* to—"

The crowd that had pressed close around us now parted like the Red Sea, providing a clear path to the stage. With a huge grin, the lead singer waved Oliver forward, as if urging him to accept an award.

"Help me!" Oliver said, as his Caribbean Ocean-colored eyes drilled a hole into mine. He took a step forward, as if he were pulled by an invisible wire.

"C'mon up here, y'all!" called the lead singer. The stomping and whistling resumed.

I shook my arms free from Oliver's grip and, placing my hands on each side of his head, said, "What song is inside you, waiting to come out?"

After what seemed like a full minute, he said, "I feel... 'Crazy'."

"We don't have time and this isn't the place for you to be crazy."

Oliver swallowed hard and looked like he was about to cry.

"Oh, wait, you mean the song, 'Crazy'?" Patsy Cline's and Willie Nelson's were the only versions I'd ever listened to.

He nodded.

"Good choice." I pulled him behind me toward the stage. "Get everyone to settle down," I told the lead singer as we climbed the wooden steps. "And then take it slow. Give him room to breathe."

Facing Oliver, I said, "The only thing you should think about is how that song should be sung. Right now, it's just you, the tune, and the lyrics. Nobody else. Put what you've lived into it. And you can, because you know why Willie wrote that song."

He gasped and said, "Don't leave me!"

"I'll be right here." I backed away and sat on the edge of the stage where he could see me.

And waited.

He didn't adjust the microphone or nod to the band members for the opening chord. His expensive Saville Row leather loafers might as well have been nailed to the floor, as he stared over the heads of the couples who had stopped dancing and crowded around the stage. Everyone grew silent, either from awe or disbelief, it didn't matter.

I cleared my throat and his distant gaze shifted down to me. His lips formed a perfect 'O,' but no sound came out.

Tilting my head from side to side as if I heard the music, I closed my eyes and mouthed "Crazy," while rocking back and forth. "Repeat after me," I said in a low voice.

I opened my eyes. He frowned and nodded, but didn't sing a note. Couldn't sing a note.

The band members were getting antsy, and the lead singer approached Oliver from behind. I arose and held up my palm to stop him. Then I stood beside Oliver, blinded by the spotlight. Just as well, since stage fright is one of my leading characteristics.

"Crazy," I crooned in my timid, off-key voice which I prayed no one but Oliver could hear, while I signaled the band behind my back. "I'm crazy for—"

The guitarist strummed out the musical phrase.

"Feeling so lonely," Oliver chimed in.

The band and Oliver started the song over from the beginning, and he smiled. We never took our eyes off each other as I backed away.

Well, after such a rough start, he did manage to sing it. Not just sing it, but tell a story with each shading of his rich tenor voice.

The crowd might have anticipated some rocked up version of an old country favorite, with all his usual strutting and jumping around the stage, but what they got instead ripped their hearts out.

And mine. But somehow it wasn't over Dwight,

not this time around.

When he finished, at least ten seconds passed before the applause erupted, enough to blow the sides out of the tent. Hooting and hollering started up again, as if Oliver had just roped and tied the million-dollar, Grand Champion Steer in record time.

With a slight hiccough, I glanced at the audience. More than a few women wiped runny mascara from their cheeks, while several cowboys blew their noses into their bandanas. Dancers had frozen mid-scoot and leaned against each other looking wistful.

Yep, Doug would be delighted to learn Oliver Goodknight, newly clean and sober, still had that unmistakable magic. Even with a different genre.

When the crowd yelled "Encore!" Oliver's eyes leached into mine. He all but begged me to let him stay to sing another song.

But the sound of distant sirens caught my attention. Had the rehab hospital discovered his absence and called the police?

We couldn't wait to find out. With no small degree of regret, I shook my head.

He ignored my signal and turned to conspire with the lead singer regarding their next number, I assumed. While Oliver shook hands with the other band members, I leaped forward to the middle of the stage and asked the lead singer about any back exit. "May Oliver borrow your hat, too?"

"I'd be honored," he said through a gap-toothed grin as he handed me the black felt Manny

Gammage special. "He can keep it."

As the sirens came closer, I plunked the cowboy hat down on Oliver's head, told him to tuck in his long blond hair, and yanked him toward the back of the stage. I knew I had to use language he would understand. "The coppers are here. Move your fooking arse right now!" I said through clenched teeth. "And follow me!"

The sirens stopped, for all I could tell, right in front of the tent. We slipped through the rear flap just as a loud commotion commenced at the entrance. I grabbed Oliver's hand and took off running down the back row of tents. By the time we rounded the corner of the last one, we both slowed to a trot as we scuttled between pickup trucks and trailers.

When we reached the outer row of vehicles where my Jetta was parked, we resumed casual walking as if we had just finished a corn dog and a cold one. "How 'bout that barrel racin'?" I said when we strolled past a uniformed officer.

With a grunt, Oliver pulled the brim of his new hat lower and ducked his head.

Once I unlocked the car door, Oliver fell into the back seat and closed his deep blue eyes. He said not a word while I pulled onto the highway toward Fredericksburg.

As we slipped away into the velvet darkness of the Texas Hill Country, I wondered what Doug would think. Had I broken any rules? How could I tell?

One thing I did know. Doug would find a way to

hitch his highly creative wagon to this spark-fling-ing, orbit-busting megastar the moment he and Oliver Goodknight met, and I would get to go along for the wildest ride of my life.

What I didn't know was whether Oliver was recovered enough for the upcoming trip.

CHAPTER TEN

The Job

I thought Oliver would sleep all the way back to Austin, but he woke up hungry when we reached Dripping Springs. No more than a village, it offered nothing in the way of a café or even fast food. After another twenty minutes on the road, I pulled into the Night Hawk on South Congress, the only restaurant I could think of that was open late.

We didn't talk much, and I couldn't come up with idle chat anyway. I didn't know enough about Doug's business yet, didn't want to ask about rehab, and thought Oliver would find me mundane to the Nth degree. I tried not to stare at him and felt thankful other customers were seated too far away to recognize him.

He took his hat off and set it on the window ledge. A perfect gentleman.

"You'll want to turn that over," I said, pointing to the hat.

"What?" He frowned. "Why should that matter?"

"See how the brim is curved from front to back?" I picked up the hat and ran the back of my hand under it. "It fits the owner's head just right because he's pulled it into shape. If you set it down on the crown instead, it will keep its customized arch. That's one way you recognize a real cowboy, by how he treats his hat." I flipped it over and handed it back to him.

"Is that some kind of bleeding Texas folklore, meant to make us foreigners feel out of place?" His face looked serious. "Are you implying I'll never be an authentic cowboy?"

Mine turned hot and red. "Of course not," I squeaked. "I just thought you'd—"

"Furthermore, where I'm from, the word 'crown' refers to something and someone utterly different." He gave me an impish grin as he returned the hat to the ledge, upside down this time. "You are quite helpful indeed, Alice. Tell me about your employer. How do you enjoy working for Mr. Creighton?"

Fear of performing to the point of paralysis, moods that change in a flash, mischievous teasing taken to a new level, what next? But in the midst of all those shenanigans, how did he remember my name?

"He's a genius, of course, and so well-connected. We're still finding our way around each other. But I've already taken on lots of responsibility for him. It's my task to uncomplicate his life and keep him from getting overloaded."

"At which you obviously do a cracking job." His expression turned quizzical. "Hmmm," was all he said.

A waitress appeared at his elbow. Once he figured out that fries were the same as chips, Oliver ordered a hamburger plate. "I cannot resist any food called the 'Down South.' After all, that's where I am, right?"

"Well, sort of."

At first he tried cutting his burger into bite-sized

pieces and eating them with his fork. I watched in uneasy silence without dipping my spoon into my steaming bowl of chili. He might have believed I'm helpful, but I couldn't relax. I guess I must have gaped at him.

"Now what?" He raised his eyebrows until all I could see were two shimmering puddles of blue. "Am I eating it wrong?"

"Actually, a hamburger is meant to be held in your hand, like a sandwich. It's finger food."

"Well, fancy that, I thought it might be some sort of Beef Wellington, Texas-style."

When I laughed out loud, he said, "There, now the ice is shattered."

"I'm sorry, I didn't mean to seem distant. It's just that"—I couldn't tell him about wetting my pants at the first sound of his voice—"I haven't been on the job for very long and—"

"On the job?" He guffawed. "Do you realize what 'on the job' signifies in back in England?"

I shook my head.

"Having sex!" His eyes twinkled like blue diamonds. "Either you're still a virgin, or you haven't bonked anyone in a long time? Which is it?"

Forget the blue diamonds. I was speechless.

"Ooh, bugger, I'm a naughty boy, aren't I?" He picked up what remained of his hamburger and gnawed on the edge.

"Quite!" I sighed. Maybe he was flirting with me, just for fun, but I was afraid to enjoy it too much.

"But you're also sensitive and... kind."

Now it was his turn to stare at me. After a few moments, he said in a soft voice, "No one has ever told me that before."

"When you sang, back there in Fredericksburg, I got tears in my eyes."

"Really? Why?"

"You conveyed how it feels to lose someone you love. That tender side of you came through in your voice as you sang. Despite the fact we were in a tent in some rancher's field, people really related to you in that intimate setting. I know I did."

"Well, I... couldn't have done it without you. Getting on stage again absolutely terrified me straight past my knickers, but you, you were a solid anchor for me. If you hadn't put your hands on my face..."

I twitched. Where did I get the nerve to do that? Who was I turning into?

"...otherwise, I don't know what would have happened." Oliver took a deep breath and tilted his head sideways. "Have you also lost a person you love?"

"Not yet."

Twisted visions of Dwight danced across my mind, and I shuddered, then signaled the waitress for the check. She brought it and told me they were about to close.

Next I had to get Oliver tucked in somewhere for the night. Even this late, I was still on the job. The Texas definition, not the English one.

CHAPTER ELEVEN

The Last Resort

Oliver refused to go to a hotel. In fact, he stamped his foot on the sidewalk like a spoiled child. After considering what kind of trouble he could get into, both from room service and the lobby bar, I agreed.

Creighton Production's office telephone didn't answer when I dialed from the restaurant's pay phone, twice. I couldn't begin to find Doug anywhere else, so I assumed he had disappeared for the foreseeable future with his music cronies to a private club in the back alleys of downtown or East Austin.

We stood under the Night Hawk's porte cochere as I reviewed our options. Oliver expressed a desire to go bar-hopping along Congress Avenue and its environs, but I wasn't about to let him head off on a bender.

"Bender!" He grinned. "What could a Texas totty like you possibly know about benders?"

"My mother's brother has gone on a few. After he got home from Vietnam."

Oliver grew quiet. Had I said something inappropriate? Brought up painful memories?

"But he's okay now," I gushed. "He's been—"

"Clean and sober? Aren't those the proper words?" He grimaced. "For how long?"

"Three years."

"How did it happen, his survival, I mean?"

"He made it because he realized his family cared about him, despite his mistakes and his past. My uncle learned to accept and love himself in a new way. It was a struggle, but he managed... manages fresh, every day."

Oliver was thoughtful for a moment, then the grin he shot me was as bright as a neon Lone Star Beer sign. "I would wager my grandfather's squiffy bollocks that you played quite a large part of that process."

"Huh?"

He looped his arm through mine as we headed toward my Jetta, and his body radiated warmth. "Why can't I simply stay with you? Hmmm?"

I stopped dead in my tracks. Surely he didn't mean... no, I can't even let my foolish imagination go there, despite my fantasy in the lawyer's office earlier that afternoon. Where would I put him at my tiny duplex? On my second-hand sofa? We'd have to share a bathroom the same size as the trunk of my car. Absolutely not.

A megastar like Oliver required a comfortable wing of a large estate, with hospitable people—or better yet, hospital people—to keep an eye on him until I found Doug, and then tomorrow I could get him settled where he was supposed to be. My parents were out of the question as they had already been asleep for several hours, plus they didn't even know I had taken this new job.

That left my uncle's spare bedroom, but I wasn't sure if two unsupervised people in recovery, one of whom had yet to demonstrate it, would be good for each other. What would my uncle's sponsor say? What would Doug say?

For now, Oliver needed to be with someone whose authority he wouldn't question, who would take seriously his requisite for sobriety, and who wouldn't put temptation in his path. Didn't sound like that was possible outside of rehab.

All of a sudden, fatigue hit me and I couldn't wait to crawl into my own bed. Alone, of course. I couldn't stifle a yawn, and then the solution dawned on me. I glanced at my watch; 11:15 gave me forty-five minutes 'til midnight.

I grabbed Oliver's hand and dragged him back to the restaurant, flung open the entry doors, and marched straight to the pay phone. After fishing in my purse for quarter, I shoved it in the slot and dialed Sally's number.

She accepted my apology and agreed right away to host our guest, all the while consenting to wait for further explanation upon our arrival. What a dear friend!

Yakking all the way up the highway to Mason's Crossing, Oliver used British slang with meanings I couldn't always grasp. Once, I had to pull to the side of the road so he could 'take the mickey'—which he told me after he got back in the car had nothing to do with 'taking a piss'—and we reached Sally's house a few minutes before midnight. Communication was proving to be a challenge, but I was determined to keep up with him.

Sally didn't bat an eye when she met Oliver Goodknight. Shucks, her father had probably introduced her to the Queen already. She was delighted, of course, to offer him use of the guest cottage on the back of her spacious property. He had no luggage—left behind at the rehab hospital during his escape— so she put together a small bag of Mike's extra things.

Oliver wanted to stay up late and chat—not 'chat us up,' he assured us—as was his custom. Whatever that meant.

"Sally, you've been waiting up a while," I said. "Aren't you tired?" We stood just off the kitchen near the back door, and my body begged for recess.

"I rest or nap after Nathan goes to bed for the night, so I'm more alert when Mike gets home. We visit while he unwinds."

"Who's Nathan?" Oliver said.

"Our eighteen-month-old son." Sally smiled like an angel.

"Oh, lovely," Oliver cooed. "Will I get to meet the wee little chap at breakfast?"

"If you're up at 6:30 when Chica arrives. She feeds him while Mike and I sleep in."

"Perhaps later," he murmured, "as I'll be sleeping in as well."

At that moment, the side door opened and Mike, dressed in full sheriff's uniform, entered the kitchen. We turned and would have greeted him except for Oliver's reaction.

Oliver threw his hands straight up in the air and called out, "I'm clean. You will find nothing on me." From the side of his mouth, he growled at me, "No need to call the coppers."

"I didn't," I hissed back.

Mike looked puzzled. "Wasn't gonna search you, but maybe I'll reconsider"—his eyes twinkled—"now you've given me probable cause."

Oliver pointed at me. "Ask her. We have been together all evening. I have had absolutely no opportunity to—"

"Just who are you anyway?"

"Mike, this is Oliver Goodknight," Sally said.

Mike's eyebrows shot up.

"Yes, *the* Oliver Goodknight." Sally nodded and waved her husband closer to kiss him on the cheek.

"It's a long story," I chimed in. "Sally was kind enough to agree to let him stay here just for tonight, until I can get all his arrangements sorted out."

Hands still in the air, from the waist up, Oliver twisted toward me with a questioning look in his eyes.

"And this is my husband," Sally said.

I gestured at Oliver to bring his arms down.

After he did, he and Mike shook hands, then Mike backed up to stand next to Sally. All things considered, meeting Mike in uniform should be something Oliver found an encouraging, if not a restraining, influence.

"Mr. Goodknight, now would be an appropriate opportunity for you to get settled in the guest cottage and let Sally and Mike have their time together." I laid my hand on his arm.

"What time will you knock me up?"

My eyebrows shot up. "Huh?"

"Tomorrow morning?"

"Oh, I'll be back around ten, and we'll find out what Doug has in mind. I'm sure everything will fall into place smoothly, and you won't have a worry in the world."

Hah! What a good liar I'd become.

We left Sally and Mike to enjoy the rest of their evening alone, and Oliver and I trudged past her greenhouse toward the guest cottage. Inside, the space was much larger than my half of the rented duplex and decorated with Sally's usual exquisite style.

"I'm not sleepy," Oliver announced as he set the bag of borrowed items on the breakfast table. "Is there a telly here?"

I pointed to the one in the corner of the living room.

"I don't suppose you get the BBC in Texas? I would like to find out what is going on back in merry old England. Do they miss me?"

"I'm sure they do. Everyone does."

"I'm rather certain the tax man does, but you are very kind to say so."

The moment turned awkward, as he seemed as if he wanted me to hug him good-bye, or just hug him. I cleared my throat and waited.

"Do you... must you leave?" he stammered.

"Yes, I have to be at the office early and get instructions from Doug. Then I'll come back here and fetch you." I picked up my purse. "Try to get a good night's sleep."

We both smiled at the unintended pun.

"But I can't fall asleep, not by myself. That was the whole problem in that bleeding pokey in Fredericksburg. I didn't want to be alone." His expression turned sheepish. "The most difficult person for me to be with is... me."

A few more minutes wouldn't hurt, just until he was comfortable. I told him so, and we settled ourselves at either end of the long sofa after turning on the TV. Within five minutes, he laid his head on the armrest, stretched his legs toward me, and fell asleep, dead to the world, even to merry old England.

Taking my time standing up, I swept the room with my eyes for a cozy blanket or afghan to throw over him, tiptoed to the next room, and found one at the end of the bed. He didn't stir an inch when I tucked it around him.

Confronting your demons is hard work. Maybe

he was more exhausted than I was. Maybe I was a fool for leaving him alone.

Before I dragged myself home, I petitioned whatever angels there might be to watch over him. I was pretty sure I would have no solution or explanation—and therefore no job—should he escape again.

CHAPTER TWELVE

The Rocker

When I woke up, the clock read 9 AM. Damn, I had forgotten to set my alarm. Oh well, I could get ready in a flash. Besides, who knew where Doug was this early, and it wasn't likely Oliver had left Sally's yet. How would he get anywhere?

Oh, wait. He had escaped before, just yesterday.

I flung back the covers and trudged to the bathroom. A fold in the pillowcase had left a large crease on my cheek, so I took a hot, if speedy, shower. After phoning the office and getting no answer, I departed without make-up or coffee. Only one would have made any difference to me at that moment. Maybe Sally would have some leftover brew. Surely she and Mike would be up by now.

Still anxious, I arrived at her home at 9:45 and rang the doorbell. After a few minutes, Chica answered by herself, no toddler in tow.

"Good morning, Missy Alice," she smiled as she waved me into the entry hall.

"Is anyone awake yet?"

"Oh, sí. Miss Sally, she has breakfast now, but Señor Mike he still sleep."

"What about—"

"In here, Alice," Sally called from the kitchen.

After nodding at Chica, I followed the sound of Sally's voice. Once in the kitchen, I inhaled deeply and prayed for relief in the form of liquid caffeine.

"Coffee?" Sally said.

"You're a life-saver on all fronts," I said with a grin. "How's our lad from across The Pond?"

"When I returned from taking the dog to the vet, Chica told me Oliver had gotten up early—"

I gasped. "Oh no! Where did he go?"

"You can relax. He played with Nathan for a while, then they both settled down again after a pig-out breakfast. Right now, they're taking their mid-morning naps."

"Thank goodness. I'm a little skittish about him, not just because of who he is, but also since I don't have any instructions from my new boss. In fact, I can't find Doug."

"When did you start working for Doug?"

In three minutes, I gave Sally the highlights of the last eighteen hours, including the brother-in-law, but omitting the part about my accident, the flying saucers, and the mysterious package. I glossed over Oliver's stint in rehab, but mentioned the performance-that-almost-wasn't in the tent at the rodeo and our mad dash to get away. The whole story sounded beyond crazy to me, and I hadn't even been employed a whole day yet.

"I hope he sees me as a problem-solver. Someone

he can count on to come to his aid during his troubles. Performing is so important to him, but he's got some issues, and in some odd way, he depends on my help."

"He values your contribution already, I'm sure."

"I'm so grateful you introduced me to Doug. It will be a very fun job. Not without its challenges, of course, but I like to be kept on my toes." I sipped my coffee. "Uh, is Mr. Goodknight in the guesthouse? I better round him up so we can go find out what Doug expects."

Sally set down her coffee cup. "Come with me. I want to show you something."

I followed her across the kitchen to the back staircase. When we reached the upstairs landing, she put a forefinger to her lips and tiptoed to Nathan's room. Once she cracked the door open, I peeked over her shoulder.

Still wearing Mike's sweatpants and T-shirt, Oliver was sound asleep in the rocking chair. Cuddled up to him, head on his shoulder, legs sprawled around his torso, was Nathan, still in his jammies, also conked out. A pop-up storybook had fallen to the floor, but Nathan's stuffed animal, a little gray donkey I had given him for his first birthday, shared Oliver's lap with him. Oliver had one arm around the donkey, and the other around Nathan's shoulder, his palm cradling the back of the child's head.

Under our breaths, Sally and I sighed "Awww" at the same time, hard to say which of us with more fervent emotion. Different reasons, of course. She expected their second child, while I...

We tiptoed back across the landing and returned to the kitchen, where she served me leftover pancakes and sausage. When I finished eating, I asked to borrow her telephone.

"Guess I better see if I can find my boss. Other than his office, I've no idea where to look."

"Angelique told me what he's like, remember? Good luck."

After three rings, Doug answered. Right away, he complimented me on the tidy look of his office and asked how soon I'd be coming in. We hadn't set regular hours yet, he reminded me.

"Well, Doug, I've got a surprise for you."

When I told him Oliver Goodknight was asleep upstairs, I couldn't tell if he shrieked at the news or because he sputtered hot coffee on himself. I already knew where to get the paper towels he needed.

"Alice, you're a miracle-worker. This is the package we've all been worried about."

Ah, yes, I figured as much. "I didn't know what else to do with him, so Sally was kind enough to—"

"Don't worry. Just bring him over here to the office as soon as you can."

"Should I let him sleep?"

"Let him do anything he wants. Just get him here in one piece."

I would have to get accustomed to Doug's broad brushstrokes. 'Anything he wants' could get us all in a truckload of trouble. I hung up the phone and rested my chin in my palm.

"Now what?" Sally said as she refilled my coffee.

"I hate to impose on your hospitality, but it might be better to leave Nathan asleep on Oliver's lap for now. Maybe they'll wake up soon."

Sally looked beyond me and grinned. "Mornin', darling."

Mike wandered into the kitchen, yawning and scratching his ribs with both hands, wearing almost identical clothes to those I had observed on Oliver. He slowed down when he stood next to Sally and reached for the coffee pot.

They seemed perfectly suited to each other, especially in degree of attractiveness. In height and physique, along with intelligence and good-natured charm, they matched. Sally had a more intense personality and quick reaction time, yet it was balanced by Mike's analytical, easy-going temperament.

She had drawn a winner in her second marriage. Would I ever be so lucky? Where would I even get in the running for a next time around?

He nodded at me. "Did you stay here, too?"

My face grew hot. "Of course not. I went straight home."

He winked at me. "As long as you got a good night's sleep."

I would have protested further, but we all turned at the crackling sound issuing from the intercom. Then toddler chatter and laughter interspersed with what must have been a few British cusswords came through loud and clear.

"We better get up there!" I said, as Sally and I rushed toward the stairs.

When we reached Nathan's room, we found fresh disposable diapers scattered on the floor. Nathan, attended by Oliver, who had his back to us, lay on the changing table, cooing.

"Bleeding hell! How does one untangle these nappies?" He tossed another unused diaper over his shoulder.

Sally and I leaned against the door frame and giggled.

Oliver turned around and, in an exasperated voice, said as he stepped toward us, "Oh, thank God you've arrived. We've a disaster on our hands. Well, not literally on our hands, but—"

A stream of liquid hit him in the upper back, and his eyes widened as he froze where he stood. Un-initiated in the habits of small boys, Oliver had left Nathan uncovered from the waist down.

Oliver didn't move until Nathan finished three seconds later, but his expression begged to know if what he felt was what he thought it might be. Our gazes locked, and I, with a twitch of my nose, nodded in slow motion. Slack-jawed, he closed his eyes as if in earnest supplication.

Nathan began to whimper, and Oliver whirled around to face him. He snatched another fresh di-aper from the supply and applied it to the child's crotch, plastic side out. "There now," he cooed, "let's not throw a wobbly."

"Ooh, I'm so sorry." Sally stepped forward. "Here, let me."

Nathan's fussing stopped that very second, and he chattered, "Oh-oh!"

Oliver's expression turned smug. "My newest fan! Hear that? He can already say my name."

Was there no end to his charisma? Was anyone immune to his powers of attraction?

Keeping a finger on the only thing between him and another spray, Oliver bowed and said, "My good woman, you are the epitome of salvation from the ravages of man's natural urges."

Once he straightened up, he peeled off his T-shirt. I couldn't take my eyes off his broad shoulders, taut stomach muscles, and hairy chest, not until he handed me the soggy shirt and sauntered out of the room.

Values my contribution? I was such a big fool for believing it

CHAPTER THIRTEEN
The Graduate

After thanking Sally and Mike profusely, Oliver and I headed toward the office of Creighton Productions. We managed to get through the front door of the building without adoring fans spotting him. I couldn't tell if he were disappointed or not.

"Austin is pretty laid back," I told him in the elevator. "But you'll like it here. Lots of local talent, famous and not-so-famous, plus big-name performers like you. Well, not quite as radiant a star as you, but…"

He gave me a weak smile, which faded within seconds, then stared straight ahead.

What was going through his mind? Was he worried about his next live performance? Missing his friends, especially the bass guitarist who had died of a drug overdose?

Silently, I vowed to help him over every rough spot, not just because that was my job description and I needed a paycheck, but because I recognized that was my nature. This position wasn't just people-and-paper shuffling, at which I had excelled my whole life. I could throw my heart into soothing his fears and understanding his sorrows.

Right then, I decided to give form and shape to Doug's broad brushstroke. Mr. Goodknight could count on me for more than just handing off his stinky T-shirt. After all, I had already comprehended the reason for the flying saucers.

When we entered the office, Doug rose with athletic energy from behind his desk and extended his hand, drawing Oliver to a seat at the round conference table. Round table? I almost laughed out loud, but instead backed away while the two of them chattered about mutual friends in the music business. Oliver nodded at the mention of certain names— people I'd never heard of—and seemed to relax.

Without being asked, I poured coffee into a cup and handed it to Oliver. "Cream or sugar?"

"Tea." He handed it back without looking at me.

"Of course."

Nowhere could I root out tea, not in the piles of sugar packets Doug had already strewn on the credenza or in the drawer below the coffee pot. Could I find Earl Grey at the corner 7-Eleven?

When I murmured I'd be right back, Doug and Oliver didn't even notice. After searching the convenience store, I discovered all tea on the shelf had been produced and packaged by Lipton. Would it suit a fussy Brit? If not, he could drink bottled water. I added a six-pack of it to my purchases.

At the cash register, I asked for a receipt and wished I had raided petty cash before I left. Very soon, Doug and I would have to address the issue of my reimbursement. Payday was almost two weeks away.

By the time I returned to the office, another person had joined them, a teenaged girl who resembled Doug. With thick dark hair like his, she must be his daughter. The girl stared bug-eyed at Oliver, even when Doug introduced me.

If Doug hadn't acknowledged my presence, I would have believed I had become invisible. I had already learned not to expect gratitude from anyone, not even my family.

"Chelsea brought her college applications," Doug said to me, as he stood up and approached me. "See if you can make some progress with 'em while I take Oliver over to see Carlos."

The girl followed him. "No, Daddy, I want to go with you." Her trance was broken, and she glanced at me in a dismissive manner.

"You stay here with Ms. Morehead and get those forms filled out." He handed me a file folder. "She can help you with the essay questions, too. Your mother and I agree on at least one thing: you have to get into a good college."

Like a reluctant steam engine, Chelsea huffed back to the round conference table and collapsed in a chair next to Oliver.

"C'mon, Oliver." Doug jerked his head in the direction of the front door. "Let's get on over to my lawyer's office. Carlos is dying to meet you. He's a musician, too, you know."

Now Doug sounded like his brother-in-law. Oh,

dear, when would I find time to read Woody's poems?

The door closed behind them. I set the box of tea and the six-pack of bottled water on the credenza, then approached the table.

"Let's see what you've got," I said to the back of Chelsea's head before I took the seat Oliver had just vacated.

"I'm not doing it their way," she announced. "They can't make me, and neither can you."

Oh goody. Teenagers.

Then I remembered what I was like at her age, a one-eighty from this fire-breathing dragon puppy. I always did it someone else's way.

"What is their way?" I set the folder on the table.

"Mother wants me to go to some stupid private girl's college in Massachusetts"—she wrinkled her nose as she stared at the tabletop—"and Daddy says I should stay here and attend UT."

"But?"

"They're both full of shit."

"Where do you want to go?"

Chelsea raised her head as if I had stuck her with a pin. "No one has ever asked me that."

"Do you know the answer?"

She craned her head toward me and narrowed her eyes, ready for battle. "Mid-Coast Community College. But my parents say they won't pay for it."

"Why that one?" No wonder her parents were concerned. Its reputation centered around football and low SAT scores. My high school classmates who had attended MCCC later returned home to blue collar jobs.

"I might could get a scholarship. That's where Dominick is going."

"Your... boyfriend?"

Her feisty demeanor drooped until all I detected was sadness. "We can't stand the thought of being apart. We're going to get married when he graduates after only two years."

"Have you told your parents this?" Of course she had, that's why her mother insisted on sending her out-of-state.

She nodded, while the feisty side resurfaced. "Don't say I'm too young to know my own mind."

"Oh, I think you do know your own mind. As of right now."

"But what?"

"Do you believe people can grow and change?"

"I don't know."

"Well, I do. In fact, I'm working on change in my life because I want things to be different. Better. I want to be happier. But I have to fight for it, and the person I have to fight with most is me. I can't stay stuck where I am and be happy, even if it's familiar."

"Bully for you." Her tone was flat. "What does that have to do with Dominick and me?"

I opened the folder and pulled out her transcript. "You're an A student, in the top five percentile."

"So?"

"You can go anywhere. I wish I'd had that opportunity when I was a senior."

"What's your point?"

Good question. If I had made other choices, maybe I'd be happily married today. Maybe still with no children, but minus a deceitful, womanizing pig of an ex-husband as well. I would be someone else now.

"You know, Chelsea, it's one thing when the door gets slammed shut in your face. You don't get what you want. Sometimes you don't even understand why. It's something else entirely when you slam it in your own face."

"Did that happen to you?"

I detected a little compassion in her voice. "I thought I knew what I wanted, but it turned out I ignored some opportunities. Afterwards, when I could have made some better choices, it was too late. Nobody's fault but mine that I got stuck. I'd hate to see the same thing happen to you."

"But what am I going to do? Dominick and I want to be together after high school. He's got no other options."

I rifled through the applications in the folder. "Let's see if there aren't some possibilities, shall we?"

After shuffling and setting aside several on the top, I came to the one from Texas A&M. "What about this one?"

She glanced at it. "My older step-brother will have a fit. His blood runs burnt orange."

"It's a good school, and it's located close to Mid-Coast, but not too close to your parents. You and Dominick could see each other on weekends."

"So I don't have to do it their way, do I?" For the first time, she smiled at me and looked relieved.

I shared that relief. One less thing for Doug to fret about. My job security was increasing.

For the next hour we filled out the application together and I coached her on vocabulary for an essay about blended families. Although I had no direct experience with them, maybe one day I would.

Hah! First I'd have to get married again, which meant finding someone special to fall in love with, a man with children from his first marriage, if he even wanted to remarry, and ...

Doug and Oliver burst through the office door, arguing and wagging their fingers at each other. I caught short phrases, but couldn't grasp the full context. Chelsea kept her seat, still copying her notes into paragraphs, but I arose from my chair right away and stepped toward them.

"What's going on?" I said in a soft voice, hoping to pour balm on the roiling waters. "Is there a problem?"

Doug said, "Oliver won't go back to rehab!" at almost the same time as Oliver said, "Not written in my contract!"

I felt like I was watching an angry tennis match, each one hitting the ball harder on the next return.

"He doesn't realize the terms of our verbal agreement," Doug whined. "It's only for two more days. Alice, tell him he has to finish."

"I can't sleep in that place. Alice, explain it to

him."

The verbal fisticuffs resumed, and the problem became more clear to me, as well as a possible solution. I was glad Chelsea was present to witness our exchange.

"Please stop," I said in a firmer tone this time. "This squabbling is getting you nowhere."

They each turned their faces to me as if I could hand down a ruling from the bench. "I think I see both sides. Doug has to be able to guarantee certain participants in his new project that you"—I trained my gaze on Oliver—"are clean and sober and will remain so during its completion. Otherwise, there will be a major predicament of a financial nature to overcome. Am I correct?"

Doug nodded and looked smug.

"On the other hand"—I turned my scrutiny toward Doug—"it's to your definite benefit that Mr. Goodknight is in top form, which a proper night's rest will help provide. If he can't, then you have a predicament of a different nature, don't you?"

Oliver sniffed and raised his nose in the air.

"So the goal is to have Mr. Goodknight graduate from the treatment while letting him find quarters where he will feel at home and be comfortable. Can each of you guarantee the other person that commitment?"

They both stood silent, matched in stubbornness.

I folded my arms across my chest. "Well, what's it going to be?"

After another moment, they nodded and shook hands.

"Now, Mr. Goodknight—"

"Please call me Oliver."

"So, Oliver, where would you like to reside during your stay in Austin?"

"At Sally and Mike's, if they'll have me. I've grown rather fond of Nathan, and he... reminds me of someone I miss very much. Besides, I left my cowboy hat there."

I remembered reading somewhere, perhaps a cheesy fan magazine at the hair salon, that a while back he'd had a child with a British actress. A boy? Didn't matter. He had missed out on fatherhood due to his touring schedule, as well as the custody problems which the drugs and alcohol had created. Rehab couldn't fix that.

"All right, I'll call and ask them."

"What about finishing rehab?" Doug said.

"I'll phone the clinic in Fredericksburg and ask if they can send the doctor here for the last several sessions. Will that do?"

Both men bobbed their heads with growing enthusiasm, and then Oliver added, "Tell him to bring my clothes and other items, would you be a sport?"

I then realized he wore the same outfit as last night, something I neglected to notice when we left Sally's that morning.

"One more thing," Doug said. "Alice, I think you should stay at Sally's, too. She's got plenty of room, and you'll have to drive Oliver around anyway."

"What?"

Oliver's eyes lit up like a short circuit. "I quite agree!"

I liked it better when they argued.

Oh, well, maybe it would only be for a short time. I could pretend I was back in the sorority house.

What could possibly go wrong?

CHAPTER FOURTEEN
The Lowlights

Hard to believe, but Sally and Mike agreed. Maybe not such a stretch, as Mike was a well-known amateur musician with an Elvis routine. Dwight and I had danced often at the Pioneer Festival in Mason's Crossing when his band played.

After a week or so, Oliver and I settled into a routine at their home, he in the guest quarters on the back of their property and I in the guest bedroom at the main house. Half the time, Sally and I found him napping with Nathan in his room, whenever he was home after lunch and before rehearsal. And it only took Sally two weeks to locate a source for flying saucers and have some shipped to her house. Someone who owed her father a favor, of course.

The doctor from the clinic in Fredericksburg came for several more visits and accepted the proposal to let Oliver "graduate" from rehab. Plus he'd stay on call as needed, if any situation turned overwhelming.

I vowed not to let that happen. Besides, Oliver hardly went anywhere except when I drove him. Doug rented me a bigger car, a Buick newer and nicer than my Jetta. After the first week, I insisted on a gasoline credit card, too. He saw my point.

If I stopped to think about it, I liked the person I saw myself becoming. Less submissive, more confident, willing to venture into unknown territory. My behavior was still appropriately self-effacing and, despite Helen Gurley Brown's advice to the contrary, my appearance mousy, but I didn't regard it as a problem. Not yet.

My parents didn't know how to react, so they spent the little time we had together warning me about drugs, musicians, bosses, millionaires, British playboys, and sleazy tabloid photos. My mother reminded me that "nothing good ever happens after midnight." My father said I could still apply to be a substitute teacher any time I needed to.

I never outright rejected their suggestions, not to their faces anyway. But I thought they were stuck in some old-fashioned time-warp where I was the docile, obedient daughter. Why couldn't they see the new me?

Oliver seemed to be making progress performing a new genre, but one hitch still loomed, which I hadn't mentioned to Doug thus far. How would our lad behave in front of an audience? Even a small one in a closed setting such as the stage on *Austin City Limits*. Truly, it was about the same size as the tent at the rodeo.

Oliver didn't bring it up, and I didn't see the need to approach him on the subject. If something went wrong during his performance, the director could always call "Cut!" and Oliver could start over. The audience would be charmed, I bet, to hear his British cussing.

On the day of the taping, my plan was to deliver him backstage at the appropriate time, not too early, so he wouldn't get anxious, then take a seat in the back row of the studio. I had heard that's where Coach Royal liked to sit, so I could enjoy a close-up glimpse of a national sports hero. Doug would be too wired up to sit, since this was Oliver's Texas debut, far as he knew.

Oliver didn't talk much on the way to the KLRU studio, and when we arrived, a person in headphones whisked him away for hair and make-up overhaul, not that he needed any improvement. I stayed out of the way of the technicians and stage prop handlers, and in a short while found myself standing next to the woman who was blow-drying Oliver's thick blond hair.

She looked up and smiled at me. "Hi, I'm Binky Gonzalez."

Returning her warm smile, I said, "Alice." I strolled around the chair behind Oliver. "Looks great. Oliver, I think you'll like it."

Binky handed him a mirror and let him inspect her work.

"Needs a slight trim soon, just for shaping it," she said. "Here's my card. Come in anytime for a private session. My salon is right off Lamar and 29th, west of campus."

Oliver took her card and handed it to me. "Set up a standing appointment for Thursday afternoons."

"You come see me, too," she offered, as she reached up and fluffed the limp hair on the right side of my head. "A few highlights would be just the thing. It'd give your hair more body, too."

Was she channeling Helen Gurley Brown? Her voice sounded almost apologetic, as if someone should take the blame for my appearance. I stared at the mirror, and a plain, frumpy woman in her mid-thirties, slightly overweight, returned my gaze. Not much to look at, but maybe with a little help...

Following another twenty minutes of primping at the hands of the make-up artist, Oliver was ready to go on stage, his chiseled cheekbones emphasized with just the right amount of contour cream. I knew because after he got out of the chair, I peeked at her supplies while I searched for her business card.

Doug waited offstage behind the main curtain, where he could see every move Oliver made and still have a view of the audience. He paced in a narrow circuit, and grabbed my arm when I came to stand next to him. "How's he doing?"

"He should be fine. Everyth—"

"If anything goes wrong, I'm screwed. MTV will never..." He put his other hand over his eyes and squeezed his fingers together, until I thought he would pull out his eyebrows. "This is only the first part of the launch"—he stopped pacing—"and it has to be a killer."

Doug didn't release my arm, so I abandoned my plan to sit near Coach Royal. My boss appeared to forego breathing as Oliver stepped onto the stage to riotous applause. The crowd turned delirious when Oliver waved to them and grinned, strutting to the front of the stage and bending down to shake hands with the lucky souls in the first couple of rows.

After what seemed like more than several minutes, the frenzy subsided enough for Oliver to approach the microphone and thank everyone for coming. At the sound of his accent, the uproar resumed. I guess they liked being called, "Barmy!" or being warned, "Don't bite your arms off!"

I glanced at Doug, who acted like he had forgotten I was there, even though he still gripped my arm. His eyes were wide and full of expectation, like a kid about to open a long-awaited birthday gift.

First the director cued the camera operators, one of whom rolled in for a close-up, then the back-up musicians. I held my breath and waited.

And waited.

Oliver stood as if in a trance. It was the rodeo all over again.

Doug's mouth gaped open. Like a pale robot, he turned his face toward me and then back to witness a disaster in slow motion. "Alice," he hissed. "Do something!"

I edged onto the stage behind the camera and moved toward the center until I caught Oliver's eye. Smiling and nodding, I rolled my hand and forearm in a circular motion, urging him to get started.

Not one note.

The director cued the camera operators to take five. The audience buzzed, but with a feverish curiosity this time, as if confirming rumors. Doug approached the director, and they put their heads together.

Before they could take a step toward Oliver, I came up behind them. "What's his first number?"

With a puzzled frown, the director said, "Why do you ask?"

"I know something that might help."

"It's 'Blue Eyes Crying in the Rain'."

Perfect.

"Doug," the director whined, "what have you gotten me into, for crying out loud? I warned you this guy couldn't reinvent him—"

"Cameras aren't rolling, are they?" I said.

The director shook his head, which was all the prompt I needed. "With luck, this should only take a few minutes. Watch me, and when I get out of the way, start the cameras, okay?"

Doug stared at me as if I had adopted Oliver's British accent and pronounced myself the Queen's Commander of the Royal Guard Musicians.

Acting as low-key as I could manage, I inched toward Oliver and spoke to him in a hushed voice. "This is your song now," I said. "Those blue eyes are yours. And you know why they're crying, don't you, Oliver?"

Oliver gazed at me and nodded.

Ignoring the blinding spotlight, I jerked my head toward the audience. "Tell them about the rain." I moved to stand next to him. "They want to hear your story. They're crying with you."

Behind my back, I gestured to the musicians and prayed they would interpret my signal to begin. The first notes glided toward us again, and facing away from the microphone, I warbled, "In the twilight glow..."

Just like at the rodeo, Oliver picked it up from there and I scooted away as gently and quietly as possible. The director cued the camera operators, and the rest of the two-hour performance went without a hitch. During his singing, the audience behaved as if they were hypnotized zombies, then exploded into raving, cheering maniacs when he finished. Even Doug was wowed by Oliver's singing talent, and I imagined my boss had already seen and heard the best.

I felt like an Olympic champion, or maybe some drab version of Superwoman. Doug and the director thanked me several times, and Doug hinted that I would need to explain in more detail later what had transpired between Oliver and me. He told me I was worth every dime of my salary.

How could I account for my magical effect on a Colossus such as Oliver Goodknight? Did I intuit his fear and put my finger on the source, allowing him to overcome his panic? Was it my innate kindness or my history of problem solving?

Outside the studio, I leaned against the wall and waited for Oliver to emerge from the backstage door. A few stragglers from the audience lingered at the end of the driveway, their laughter floating up to the starlit sky. I sighed, feeling a deeper exhilaration and gaiety than I had known in months.

Until I spotted Dwight's former boss, and behind him, my ex-husband. Next to Dwight stood his new wife, bulging abdomen—Dwight's long-awaited baby—leading the way.

Then the stars came crashing down and shattered all my joy

CHAPTER FIFTEEN

The Frying Pan

Recently Sally told me Angelique had given her some guidance a few years ago, especially when she needed answers most. Sally then grew to understand her father better and learned to accept him for the person he was. Angelique was the one who helped Sally get over her anger at Nate Wallace.

Was no one in my life who could help me understand myself? There I stood, in the alley outside the studio, believing I was a champion, and yet the sight of Dwight and his pregnant wife made me feel like an angry, jealous failure.

Not that I wanted Dwight back. Rhonda could have him, for as long as she could put up with him. After all, he was a liar and a cheat, and she was a co-respondent to his infidelity. They each deserved whatever the other miscreant brought to their nauseating party.

As I watched Oliver emerge from the backstage door, I struggled not to peek at Rhonda's puffy belly. How would it feel to have another life growing inside you? I'd never find out. And that made me cringe.

I would simply have to find another way to

define myself besides motherhood. Or being someone's wife.

Maybe acting as caretaker to the rich and
famous—not to mention crazy—would be my new
identity. Maybe I was a fool.

When I got home, I dug out Binky Gonzalez's card
and left a message on her answering machine. Time
for the Mouseburger to take some positive action.

She called me back the next day and we set up an
appointment for the end of the week. "Allow several
hours," she warned me. I couldn't wait and spent
the week preparing myself for the thunderbolt I had
launched.

When my parents saw my new hairstyle and
streaked color—yep, a dazzling blonde mixed in with
my frumpy brown—they offered to pay for coun-
seling. I declined with as much politeness as I could
manage.

Doug complimented me right away, calling it
"snazzy." Oliver seemed not to notice, even when I
took him to his weekly appointment with Binky.

"How do you like it?" she said, as she tweaked the
ends. "We should try more blonde next time."

"Um, okay, I'll think about that."

All blonde? Do I start the changes at the top and
work my way down? Begin on the outside and work
my way inside? Perhaps both.

Meanwhile, keeping track of Oliver kept me too
busy to think about what slice of life might have
passed me by. We spent a few hours of every day
trekking, anti-clockwise according to Oliver, the

hike-and-bike trail around Town Lake. He donned sunglasses and wore his thick blond hair tucked inside a knitted cap. If any runners recognized him, they didn't interrupt their jogging to ask for an autograph.

"What an inane name for this body of water, which isn't even a real lake," he complained. "You're lucky those blinkered, unimaginative souls didn't christen your city, 'You Are Here'."

"Maybe one day they'll name it after someone famous as well as worthy." My voice sounded meek and apologetic.

"Who are the local luminaries?"

I thought for a moment. Who indeed? A musician such as Willie Nelson? Not that he lacked respectability, but maybe he was a little too radical when it came to personal recreation choices even for the liberal City Council. No, it should be someone who appreciates Austin for its treasure trove of natural beauty. A dignified celebrity nobody could criticize for anything.

"Well, there's Lady Bird Johnson," I said.

"Is she an ornithologist?"

I couldn't tell if he were teasing me or not. "Were you raised in a cave? She's our very own First Lady, married to President Lyndon Johnson."

"Oh, that. What else is she famous for?"

Oliver seemed to enjoy hearing about her beautification projects and marveled that she had stayed the wife of a polarizing public figure for such a long time. He told me his own father was recently divorced from his fourth wife, and then grew silent for the remainder of our quick-paced march.

Some days, he started on the path around the lake in abject silence, as if he'd received bad news or his dog had died. My goal was to get him cheerful by the end of our walk.

Other days, he chattered like a grackle and my job was simply to listen. The doctor had warned us about possible mood swings as evidence of a 'trigger' to relapse, but I didn't think there was anything to report.

In certain ways, I believe Oliver was simply spoiled, even though he once excused his mercurial behavior by saying, "Today I'm a stroppy old bull who's got the hump."

I had to ask him what he meant. Thank goodness, it had nothing to do with sex.

"Then," he winked at me, "I would have said 'having a hump'."

I'm pretty sure I blushed.

By the end of the second week, my clothes hung loose on me, especially my pants. Since I liked the new skinnier me, I donated the baggy stuff to the Settlement Club for their garage sale, and went to the mall for a brand new work trousseau. Out with the frumpy old, in with the sleeker new had become a pattern.

On Friday, Doug told me Oliver needed a special wardrobe for the video they would be shooting in a few weeks for a new channel called MTV. My instructions were to provide our lad with guidance for authenticity, but to let Oliver make his own choices. I called a local western wear store and made arrangements for after-hours shopping, explaining it was for a friend of Willie's, at the end of the week.

Oliver already owned the cowboy hat, courtesy of the musician from the rodeo outside Fredericksburg. Our retail adventure hurtled downhill from there.

"No, real cowboys don't wear pink shirts," I told him, "not even the button-down variety. How 'bout all black, like Johnny Cash?"

He frowned at me.

"I didn't make the rules," I sighed, with a glance at the accommodating, enchanted store clerk. We had been at this for three hours after their 6 PM closing, and Oliver had tried on every pair of jeans in Callahan's General Store. And all the shirts. Vests. Belts. Belt buckles. I'd have another birthday before we got over to the boot department. Next time I would leave one of us at home.

"No, I don't think we'll find a leather vest in the style of a Nehru jacket." I tried to channel the popular country-and-western singers. What would Glen Campbell or Kenny Rogers wear?

The problem was that Oliver didn't want to copy anyone else. He wanted his own signature look, with his personal flair. If he were here, Doug would suggest developing a line of men's western wear under Oliver's logo.

I turned to the clerk. "What do you have that's traditional, and yet unique?"

"Well now, I might could suggest—"

"Spurs!" Oliver called from across the aisle near the boot department. "I need a set of spurs, don't you think?"

Oh, right. He'd probably wear them when he sat on the floor and crossed his legs to meditate.

"We have some jewelry made of spurs," the clerk offered. "In real silver."

"Anything for a guy?" I said.

Oliver reacted like he had struck gold. Or rather pound sterling. While I sat and rested my aching feet, he selected a large silver belt buckle, cuff links, a key chain, a pinkie ring, a bolo tie, a hat band, and some ankle bracelets which fit over a pair of boots, without the wheel, or rowel, on the back.

"I want something to jangle when I walk," he said with a child-like smirk. He spun around to model his complete outfit, including the "Chisholm" style boots made of calf and gator leather. They cost more than six months' rent on my apartment.

Oliver grinned at me in anticipation. "How do I look?"

Like the Duke of Cowchips. But I didn't say that. "Eye-catching ensemble," I squeaked.

His face fell. I should have guarded my facial expression and shown more enthusiasm.

"What's wrong with it?" He furrowed his eyebrows.

"You've made some nice selections, excellent ones." I stood up. "I guess I'm used to a little more... uh, subtlety in my ranch hands. I've never seen a cowboy dress with so much... attention to detail."

"You're saying I should return all this to their proper bins?"

The clerk put her hand over her mouth, but her gasp escaped anyway. Gobsmacked, Oliver would have said. Right away, I felt sorry for both of them. All that time and hard work.

"Not exactly. It's just that—"

Oliver glared a hole through me. Without looking at her or even blinking, he said to the clerk through clenched teeth, "I intend to purchase all this, plus that mound of togs over there. Here's my charge card." He almost tossed it over his shoulder to her.

At last, clarity reigned in my head. The only influence I had over Oliver was on stage, when he couldn't croak out a note. Everywhere else, I was reduced to his driver and baggage handler. I schlepped the nine bags out to the car and put them in the trunk.

We hardly spoke on the way home. He didn't seem furious, despite my having made him look foolish in front of the clerk. His mind showed signs of being absent, and I guess he wished he were back in Merry Olde England, instead of stuck here with me.

What would Doug say? I had failed to turn Oliver into a regular Texas cowboy, insulted his taste in apparel, and possibly delayed the filming of the spot for MTV.

The heat was sizzling, and I had to figure out a way to turn off the fire. Or I'd get fired.

CHAPTER SIXTEEN
The Fire

Doug had hired a Los Angeles director-script-writer named Bertie Hudgens to come up with a scenario built around the song Oliver would sing in the new video for MTV. Meanwhile, Doug contacted a modeling agency in New York for a supermodel to pose along side Oliver as he crooned his latest love song.

At Sally's house, I listened to Oliver rant and pontificate during his breaks from composing. It was like he was trying to learn a new language. But, for whatever creative sparks flared, we both were grateful, because the process kept him focused and his mood evened out.

My next assignment was to pick up Hildegarde Kandler, a young model who had appeared in the pages of *Vogue* magazine. Right away, I could pinpoint her country of origin: Germany, when she said, "Ver iss zee limo? I am not riding in zhat cahr."

Maybe I should have picked her up in my Jetta. As it turned out, the trunk of my Buick barely held her seven suitcases, all matching leather, designer-monogrammed. She tucked her long limbs into the back seat and spoke not a word until I pulled up to the entrance of the Driskill Hotel on 6th Street in Austin.

As I checked her in and tipped the bellboy a generous amount, I hoped they gave her one of their haunted rooms. With her pale skin, dark eye makeup, and windblown white-blonde hair, any ghost would have met its match, especially when she fixed her frosty gaze on it.

On the day shooting began, I had little to do except trail around behind Oliver and be sure he didn't freak out when it was time to sing. I had learned to bring a supply of British tea and locate hot water, along with coffee for Doug and anyone else who required some.

Following the first afternoon of rehearsal, the sound and lighting guy, Leo, and I became friendly. Aptly named, he was a shaggy-haired hippie holdover from the sixties who had spent too much time in the sun, judging from his leathery wrinkled face. He smelled like sweet tobacco, but I didn't mind. I brought him fresh coffee often, which gave me a chance to retreat into his booth and watch the proceedings go with hitch after hitch.

Hildegarde and Oliver were never satisfied at the same time because either the lighting or the sound or something else wasn't quite right. They both demanded the identical camera angle for every shot. She insisted he not touch her hair when they kissed at the end. He looked like he'd rather lock lips with a rattlesnake. I couldn't blame him. Her petulant mouth protruded like boiled sausages.

Leo and I agreed it was like watching two spoiled brats squabble over who got to sit in the Queen Mommy's lap. He reckoned the Queen Mommy only had one knee, if you believed their arrogant reasoning.

Doug kept his demeanor in control, exhibiting patience and calm in the face of über-irrational, superstar oneupmanship. Hildegarde and Oliver had to act as if they were reunited in love, he told them, and show some passion. Iciness reigned instead, although they tried to appear obsessed with each other. In my book, they didn't even manage to look mutually attentive or attracted, only preoccupied.

In the control booth, I sat on a wooden stool next to Leo as he traded instructions with his technicians on the set. His microphone was hooked up to their headsets, and every now and then he would flip another switch to address Bertie over a loud speaker so everyone would know where the spotlight or a hidden mike had been moved. Bertie would yell "CUT!" and then re-block the scene for Oliver and Hildegarde, and they'd start over.

We hadn't even gotten to the singing part yet, and I could tell Doug was growing more anxious by the minute. If we got down to splitting hairs, this wasn't technically a performance because Oliver wouldn't be standing in front of an audience. But he was a loose cannon when it came time to execute, and I was on the alert.

"I'll be right back," Leo whispered as he stood up. "Gotta take a coffee leak." He stepped around his chair and gestured for me to sit in it. "You're in charge while I'm gone."

In silence, I rolled my eyes at him as I plopped down. He winked at me and stepped out of the booth.

Imitating his posture, I leaned forward and propped my elbows on the edge of Leo's desk to watch yet another take of the scene of counterfeit lust. Oliver was supposed to wait in agony until she appeared, then take her wrist and spin her into his arms before he kissed her. They went through the motions several times, minus the smooch. I reckoned Hildegarde didn't want to smear the two pounds of pale glossy lipstick she wore.

When Oliver finally did kiss her, it didn't seem genuine and honest enough to me. Too much moving up and down and not enough connection. "You call that kissing?" I said under my breath. "More like he's eating an ice cream cone."

Oliver's arms went limp and his head fell back in what must have been either irritation or defeat, face toward the ceiling. As Hildegarde stomped two steps way from him, Doug and Bertie both whirled around to glare at the sound booth. My mouth dropped open.

"Leo!" Bertie shouted. "What's going on in there?"

I jumped up and swatted the controls. "Oh, no!" I squeaked. "The microphone is—"

Within seconds, the entire set went dark. I pawed at the buttons again and half the lights came back on.

"Alice, what's happening?" said Leo, as he came

up behind me.

"Oh, Leo, I accidentally—"

"Never mind," he grinned as he clicked something on the console. "I'll get things squared away for those two prima donnas."

While I sat horrified at what I had done, Leo fixed the sound and the lighting, and then Doug and Bertie told everyone to take ten. Hildegarde huffed off to check her makeup, and Oliver strolled away from the set in the opposite direction.

After a few moments, I decided I had to apologize for my egregious faux pas to anyone who would listen. I started with Doug and Bertie. Once my eyes turned teary, they were slightly more forgiving.

"You have to fix it with Oliver," Doug said in a stern voice. "I don't know how he'll handle this."

I agreed and went in search of him. After ten minutes of pursuit, I couldn't find him anywhere. I returned to the set and, needing some useful busyness to keep me occupied, picked up empty coffee cups. When I turned around from depositing them into the trash can, I all but crashed into Oliver. My face caught fire and I stuttered like the half-witted fool I was. How could I rectify this situation, soothe Oliver's offended ego, and rescue my job?

Before I could say anything intelligible, he grabbed my wrist and dragged me to center stage, right in the middle of the spotlight. He spun me around into his arms and wrapped me against him. The next thing I knew, he leaned down and planted his soft full lips on mine.

Oliver Goodknight was kissing me!

Certain I would die within seconds of a lightning strike, I decided on the spot to make the most of it. Eyes closed, I tilted my head sideways and pushed my lips against his, matching the pressure. He moaned or hummed, I couldn't tell which, but didn't break contact as he had with Hildegarde. Instead he worked his lips enough to get me to open mine just a wee bit. My heart pounded like a kettle drum in heat.

Doug would fire me, no matter what else I did, and I would end up serving defrosted synthetic slop to disrespectful oversexed teenagers in the high school cafeteria. Might as well go for broke.

I threw my arms around Oliver's neck and parted my lips a little bit wider. He tightened his grip, and I felt his tongue explore the edge of my mouth.

Come on, lightning, go ahead and hit me! You're no match for this guy's electricity! I feel it all the way to my heels.

Now was my chance for immortality. I raised my right thigh sideways and wrapped my calf around the back of Oliver's leg, then arched my back and leaned deeper into him, from my pelvis up. At the same time, I thrust my tongue into his mouth. We must have scorched each other, because he groaned again, no mistaking it this time, and I felt him get hard in his crotch.

Oh, my sainted granny, what have I done?

Before I could stop him, Oliver pulled my shirt-tail out of the back of my pants and plunged his hand up toward my ribs, digging his fingers into my flesh beneath my bra strap. Just as he was about to reach in front for my breast, the director yelled, "CUT!"

Everything we owned or touched froze, locked together in an inexplicable clinch. I didn't dare open my eyes, but somehow I had to get out of there and away from everyone.

As I unlaced my arms from around his neck, my right leg dropped like an overweight sack of wet laundry. I pulled my head back to peek at Oliver, although I couldn't bring myself to look much above or below his collar bone. His mouth gaped while he struggled to control his panting breath. I had to put my hands against his chest and bear down to get him to release me.

Without hesitation, I turned to run off the set and would have made it to the exit, but Doug raised his hand as I raced past where he and Bertie stood, heads together. "Hold on a sec, Alice," he said in a mysterious tone.

I halted and turned around. Lurking in the shadows just beyond them stood Hildegarde, glaring at me with her spooky eyes. What had I done to deserve her ill will?

Bertie gestured for Oliver to join their pow-wow, and he ambled toward them. I couldn't overhear anything they said, but every now and then, one of the three glanced toward me. Oliver was the only one who smiled, even if it seemed to be an unfriendly expression, so I figured he would be pleased to see me go.

While I waited for Doug to fire me, I tucked in my shirt—I could at least look professional on my way out—and straightened my hair. Too bad I wouldn't be able to afford Binky's services on my substitute teacher's wages. I would go back to being a Mouseburger after all. My parents would be thrilled. I stared at my feet.

When Bertie called out, "Okay, everyone, let's get her into makeup and then take it again from the top," I raised my head to find Oliver beaming at me like a Cheshire cat. Dadgum him!

Wait... Get who into makeup?

This whole mess started with a kiss, didn't I tell you already? If I weren't such a fool, I would have kept running out the door.

CHAPTER SEVENTEEN

The Highlights

By the time the make-up artist finished with me, I didn't recognize myself. Probably a good thing, as I still didn't know what I was supposed to do.

Had Bertie changed the storyline of the video? Without question, I was no substitute for Hildegarde, but how could someone like me interact with Oliver and be plausible?

I stared in the mirror and inspected the results of the toner and blush. More contour across my cheeks and color around my eyes. Unlike my new blondish locks, which I had come to accept and even enjoy, this new face would take some getting used to. Still maybe I could pick up a few pointers and improve my overall appearance in everyday life, but not so much that my parents would try to have me committed.

"Alice, we've got the revised segment all worked out," Bertie said over my shoulder as I stood up from the make-up chair. "Doug and I decided you're going to be the shy girl in the background. You're the one Oliver really loves, and so you get his attention away from Hildegarde at the last second."

Did they think I had a death wish? Hildegarde would never agree to be defeated by an underachiever like me. She hadn't ever been a Mouseburger and wouldn't be caught standing in line next to one, even at the Pearly Gates.

And how would I face Oliver after that display of lascivious taste-testing? I must have gone certifiable for those moments when I flung caution to the four winds. Maybe my parents were on the right track about my mental stability.

All of a sudden it hit me. With the blonde hair make-over and new cosmetics, I was not the same old Alice they raised, the naïve girl who had married and tolerated Dwight out of desperation, the one who complied with everyone else's demands and sacrificed herself for their needs. I'd become the new Alice, adventurous, intrepid, and successful beyond measure.

Stand aside, Hildeghost, and take notes.

With Bertie's encouragement, Oliver insisted on multiple retakes until my arms had all the energy of day-old helium balloons and my lips felt like someone had danced a cha-cha on them. Did I mind? Heck no, I was living my dream. In two hours, I got more kisses from Oliver than from Dwight in the last two years, and our lad kissed me with greater gusto.

Wouldn't my parents be surprised—no, shocked and astounded—to watch MTV and see me on screen with a world-famous rock star? So would my friends and my ex-husband. The new Alice would be introduced to the whole universe. Maybe Mick Jagger and Paul McCartney would form a line.

Not what I had expected when I applied for the job with Creighton Productions, but where was it written that a Mouseburger couldn't be reinvented? Helen Gurley Brown had managed it. I vowed Doug would get triple his money's worth.

The only other difference in the rehearsals was how Hildegarde reacted. Once on the set, she upped the ante on passion and Oliver seemed to make the most of it. Both Doug and Bertie were pleased.

By Thursday, I decided to take Binky's advice and let her turn me into a full-out, unmitigated blonde. Maybe my parents would offer to send me to a spa for a week's recuperation instead of an asylum. While Doug gushed compliments, Oliver exhibited his usual obliviousness.

On Friday, Oliver dragged himself to the breakfast table in the glummest mood I'd ever seen, even for him. During our morning trek around Town Lake, he asked me if I had any children.

I gulped. The new Alice hadn't quite left the old one behind. "No," I said in a sad voice, "I wanted children, but somehow... we never did."

"Your husband didn't want any?"

I shrugged and let him take that for an answer. What good would it do to explain that it had been all my fault. Wasn't the new Mrs. Morehead's distended abdomen proof enough?

"I thought I didn't either, before George was born. But now..."

"Your son with May Farnsworth?" I had read in *People Magazine* about the young British actress and decided I didn't need to pay the price of a movie ticket to see more than one of her gritty portrayals of a drug-addled prostitute finding redemption through sultry sex with a defrocked priest or of an uptight innocent schoolteacher ripe for a fiery awakening of a similar nature. A scorching, green-eyed redhead, her nickname in the press was May-Day. Perhaps she suffered from type-casting. Or not.

He nodded and removed his sunglasses to wipe his eyes. "May and I never were married."

"Not such a big deal these days, is it?" I tried to sound comforting.

"It is if you want your son to inherit the estate and title of Earl of Stockmore." He sat down on a bench and squinted as he stared across the lake at a team of rowers in a canoe.

I had forgotten Oliver was the second son of a member of British peerage. "Why don't you marry her?" I sat beside him. "I thought you two were a hot item."

Eyebrows raised, he turned to gape at me, as if I had suggested jumping naked off the Town Lake Bridge. "That beastly prat! She cares not one crusty dragon for anyone except herself. Stop listening to Chinese Whispers."

Huh? I would never fully understand Oliver. "Um, how old is your son now?"

"Georgie is around eighteen months, I think,

about the same age as Nathan. I was rather pissed at the time."

No wonder Oliver relished staying at Sally and Mike's. I began to see him through eyes more tender and benevolent. "I don't blame you for being angry."

He frowned at me. "Not angry. I was plastered."

"On a bender?"

With a nod, Oliver said, "I'm not very fatherly... didn't have such a good example, but I do love my son and want to care for him properly. If Georgie were a direct heir, he could become Earl some day."

"But what about your older brother? Doesn't he have any children? Mine does, three of them."

Oliver smirked. "Simon? Such a sad bastard my half-brother is, a result of my father's first unfortunate marriage, and too boring to appeal to any woman, much less convince her to have his child. Sits around all day reading poetry. Like Doug's brother-in-law."

"He can't be all that bad."

"You have no idea. His previous girlfriend lasted less than two months, according to Miss Entwhistle." Oliver shrugged. "Simon would likely have daughters anyway."

I bristled. "What is wrong with having daughters?"

"Only sons can inherit." His head waggled up and down. "I know, I know, it's an archaic system."

"So you don't want to marry Georgie's mother, but why can't you adopt him? Would she grant you custody?"

Oliver snatched off his knitted cap with the UT Longhorn logo and ran his fingers through his crumpled blond hair. "If I paid her enough quid."

"That shouldn't be a problem."

"We could get it sorted, except for one thing."

His voice flooded with emotion that threatened to swamp him. Waiting for him to continue, I tried to look sympathetic.

"She insists I settle down in England near her parents and live a normal family existence, including wife and home and hearth. May doesn't care whom I marry, but there's to be no more world tours, only special concerts on occasion." Oliver stood and pulled his cap down over his ears. "She's either off her trolley or wants my pickled bollocks in a jar on her pantry shelf. Either way, her goal is to make my life a bloody hell."

Now I understood him. Who knew a woman could have such bargaining power? As I arose and reached up to tuck his hair inside his cap, I wondered what possible solution I could find. After all, that was my job.

CHAPTER EIGHTEEN
The Talking Horse

Rehearsals continued through the afternoon. Bertie was pleased at our progress, and therefore Doug was more relaxed.

Beyond the palpable pleasure of kissing Oliver, which happened about every thirty minutes or so, I paused between takes to wonder what my family's reaction would be, once they saw the final video on MTV. What would they think of their daughter, former Mouseburger extraordinare?

I didn't fill them in on all the details, but I did mention that my job description now included an appearance on a program soon to be released on a new music channel. Sally was the only one who expressed genuine excitement when I told her. My parents worried whether my real name would appear in the credits.

Hildegarde upped her game, too, and Bertie took extra pains to compliment her after every take. Why would a woman who looked like that require such honeyed words? Maybe insecurity plunges all the way to the core. Don't I know it? My parents had always told me beauty is only skin deep, as if they needed to apologize for my looks.

Oliver's days of depression became more frequent, and I struggled to find a way to help him. Listening only worked if he felt like talking. When we spent our morning walks in silence, I had to be content with the possibility that being there was enough.

The day I set up an interview with a realtor to get Doug's mid-century modern Westlake house ready for the market, Oliver wanted to come along. Why not? He said he was interested in seeing how other Americans lived. He thought, rightly so, Sally's home wasn't quite average.

The realtor handled the shock of seeing Doug's cluttered house better than she reacted to meeting Oliver Goodknight. I thought we'd never get out the front door. Oliver was patient and promised her tickets to his next concert. Which left him off the hook until he could get his act together by himself. No way was I going on tour with him.

But that appointment left me with extra work of a dubious nature. How would I know which stuff to get rid of? I had organized Doug's office and things were flowing much more smoothly there, but his house was different, of course.

"Would you live in a des res such as this?" Oliver asked me. When I frowned, he continued, "Desirable residence."

I glanced around at the straight lines, angles, and floor-to-ceiling plain windows. "Nice view of the wilderness out here, but not exactly my style. I'm more of a old manor traditionalist. And a gardener."

Oliver smiled. "Excellent."

The excellence of it was lost on me. I wouldn't ever be able to afford this level of domesticity, never mind the style. No point in dwelling on it either, since I had to deal with the hodgepodge of contents very soon.

"Do whatever you think best," Doug told me later. "I'm not there much, ever since I began seeing DeeAnne. She'll want to pick out something for us anyway."

Was he getting married again? What would his children say about wife number four? One more, and he'd catch up to Oliver's father.

The next time I encountered Chelsea when she dropped by the office to visit me, a recent frequent habit, she had changed her mind about Texas A&M. "I guess it's the East Coast after all."

"What happened?"

"Dominick and I broke up. I caught him with someone else. That cheap slut, Maggie Vargas." She burst into tears and flung her arms around my neck, crying against my shoulder. "She's not even a cheerleader."

I felt a slight stab to my heart. After a moment, I stood up straighter and put my arms around her. When her wailing subsided, I stepped back and decided to share my scant wisdom.

"I know this hurts, and I can't lie and say it doesn't." I put my hand under her chin and lifted her face to look directly at me. "But I want you to remember, his bad behavior says more about him than it does about you. And what it says is, if he lies and cheats, he's not good enough for you."

"How do you know? You never met Dominick."

But I knew his doppelgänger, Dwight Morehead.

"Chelsea, do you trust me?"

She nodded.

"So then, trust me when I tell you that you will recover from this wound, if you choose to. You'll feel terrible for a while, and then one day you'll want to get up and start living again. You'll realize you've been given a gift."

"What gift?"

"The gift of learning how special you are, as an individual, not as part of a couple. See yourself as exceptional on your own and deserving of the best, even if Dominick didn't see you that way. And you can't let what he did drag you down."

"Is that how you did it?"

"Did what?"

"After your divorce… Daddy told me you divorced your husband, but you're over it."

Glad someone thought so. Some days, I wasn't so confident. And as Rhonda's due date approached, I felt myself becoming even less convinced.

"I work on it every single day. And I get stronger every day, too." Okay, maybe that last part was a stretch.

"I wish my mother was like you." She burst into tears again and I hugged her tighter, unsure I had ever received a nicer compliment.

Eventually, she quit sobbing enough for us to work on her other applications to universities along the East Coast. I would have killed for that opportunity when I was her age. In hindsight, of course. But my parents wouldn't have agreed, and not just because they couldn't afford the tuition. Their plan for me was what I did. Always.

While Chelsea scribbled on applications, I looked back at myself at her age. Too young to know or trust myself, too willing to let others run my life. I didn't need to gaze in the mirror to discover those days— and that submissive attitude—were behind me. If I made mistakes from now on, I'd simply chalk it up to experience and move ahead. If? More like when.

We were almost finished with the next-to-last application when Oliver showed up at the office. An hour ago, I had dropped him at Binky's salon for his standing appointment.

"You're out early. Did she give you a lift?"

Oliver's expression turned quizzical. "No, I used the stairs."

"I mean, how did you get here? I would've come to fetch you in fifteen minutes."

"One of her customers gave me a ride, a trifle scatty, that's all." He leaned down, clasped my wrist, and raised my palm to rub his cheek. "After my facial, a glorious escape."

"What does scatty mean?" said Chelsea.

Arching my eyebrows, I grimaced at Oliver.

"You Yanks might say, um... scatterbrained."

"Oliver, you know the rules. No rides with strangers, scatty or otherwise, no going out on your own."

He gave me half a grin. "My dear Alice, you certainly are more than your job's worth."

"At the moment, and for the rest of the afternoon and every evening until we finish filming, you are my job. We are joined at the..." I would have said lips because it rhymed, but it sounded ridiculous.

"Ah, yes, thank God for that. Well, since you're the talking horse, according to Bertie, we'll simply get on with it."

Talking horse? Would I ever understand his British slang?

Back at the studio, I had a chance to visit with Leo over coffee in the booth. He seemed never to get enough of the "liquid jolt," as he called it. We laughed as I told him about my difficulties in understanding Oliver's jargon.

"For example, I have no idea by what he meant by 'talking horse.' He said that's what Bertie called me. But Bertie isn't British."

Leo's smile disappeared as he set his mug on the edge of the console. "Just let that one go." His voice sounded strange and he wouldn't look at me, as he pretended to check some knobs and dials.

I rested my hand on his forearm. "What's going on, Leo?"

"Maybe you better ask Bertie what he meant." After a moment, Leo sighed and turned to face me. "I don't want to be the one to tell you this, but..."

"But what?"

Enjoying the first time I had made anyone squirm, I watched as he hesitated again and fidgeted in his chair. "Tell me anyway. I can handle it."

"Oliver misunderstood what Bertie said."

"So I'm not a talking horse? What am I?" I giggled. "Some other farm animal, a talking sheep perhaps?" Wait. That sounded like the old Alice.

"Not 'talking.' You're a *stalking* horse." He shrugged. "Bertie's idea."

Squinting, I caught my breath and held it, as I struggled to make sense of what he said.

"Oliver doesn't appreciate the nuance," Leo said, "or the hunting terminology. They didn't explain it to anyone because Doug figured it would spoil the chemistry on the set."

"Then how did you find out?"

He glanced at the knobs on the console. "Nothing happens out there I don't know all about."

"What does a stalking horse have to do with an MTV video? I don't get it either."

"You're just there so the German iceberg will thaw out. Hildegarde was too worried about smearing her makeup to display any passion, so Bertie suggested using you to create a little competition, a challenge. It all came about after Oliver kissed you and they observed how much—"

I held up my palm and tried to ignore the unease in my gut. "I've been making a fool of myself, believing my enthusiastic participation was based on something totally real and necessary and... and honorable."

Looking solemn, Leo stared into my eyes. "You looked real to me, if that's any consolation."

"So my illustrious career acting in music videos is already over." I shook my head in disgust. "That Bertie is something else, isn't he? Using people as if they had no feelings."

"He's total Hollywood. Naturally, he's an asshole."

"What am I going to do now?" I sank into the chair next to him. "Act like I don't know?"

"Can you do it?"

I pursed my lips and considered my next move. After a moment, I stood up and nodded at Leo. "Lightning is going to strike again. Just you watch. And be ready to record!"

He grinned. "Atta girl!"

The door to the control booth flew open and Doug raced inside, panting. "Alice, we need your help, right this minute!"

With a wink at Leo, I flung my hair over my shoulder. "Ready when you are. Just let me check my lipstick."

"No, no!" Doug all but shouted. "It's Oliver!"

"Isn't it always?" I smirked. "What about him?"

"He's gone!"

"I reminded him earlier today not to accept any rides with..."

Doug eyes widened 'til I thought they'd fall out of their sockets. He gripped my arm with one hand and waved a sheet of paper with the other. "You don't understand. He's on his way back to England to rescue someone named George."

"What do you want me to do?"

"You have to stop him."

"George is his son, and he's been very concerned about the boy's future." I shook my head. "I doubt anyone can stop him."

"Then you have to go with him and help him get everything settled as soon as possible, and then bring him back. You're the only one he trusts."

"How do you know?"

Doug thrust the paper at me. "He wrote it down. Oliver needs your help. Go get your passport."

I scanned the page in disbelief. "I... I can't go to England!"

"You have to. It's in his contract."

"What? How did that happen?"

"During the time he committed to the video, Oliver was to be assigned a personal assistant who would help him with any situation or need that might arise." Doug poked my shoulder. "That's you!"

"But surely my service was limited to Texas. Or at least to the U.S."

"No location was specified or restricted. Of course, we never dreamed he would decide to go home for a personal emergency. You just stay with him and get him back here as soon as you can."

"But what about your house? And Chelsea? And the new production studio? And your golf games with Willie and Kris and Coach Royal?"

Doug waved his arms like he was erasing a chalkboard. "They can wait. Shouldn't take more than a few days, right?"

With Oliver, who knew? I rolled my eyes with as much drama as I could muster. "I'll do my best."

"I knew we could count on you, Alice." Doug grinned, looking relieved. "Bertie and I are confident you won't let anything happen to him."

I glared at him and his goofy grin faded. "We'll certainly talk about that Hollywood ass... hole later."

From the corner of my eye, I caught Leo's wry expression as he nodded.

After a pause, Doug said in a meek, pleading voice, "You'll have him back by early next week, won't you? In one piece... and sober?"

For that miracle, I figured Oliver and I would have to be joined at more than our lips.

CHAPTER NINETEEN

The Ups and Downs

Oliver and I were the last to board because he said it would be the best way to avoid getting caught up in a fan frenzy. I had just hoisted my blue canvas carry-on bag to the overhead bin when the flight attendant for first class appeared at my elbow with two glasses of champagne on a tray.

Within seconds, Oliver, now recognizable since he had removed his UT Longhorn cap and sunglasses, opened his tray table and sat up straight, beaming at her from his window seat.

She returned his smile and set down the first crystal flute. From her seductive expression, she might as well have included her room key and left a trail of fish-and-chips for him to follow.

Now I had a choice. I could leave Oliver to his own devices, or I could execute my responsibilities. I snapped shut the door to the overhead compartment and scowled. "What's this?"

Oliver winced like I had poked him with a fork. "Ummm, I—"

"Please take that away," I said in an authoritative voice to the flight attendant. The new Alice had taken charge.

She stopped with the second glass in her hand, mid-delivery, and raised her eyebrows. She regarded me with disdain and a hint of suspicion, as if I were Oliver Twist asking for more gruel. "But he—"

"Juice, coffee, water, tea, only if it's served hot, or a soft drink. That's it." Before sitting down, I waited for her to collect both glasses. Darn, I bet it was the good stuff, too.

"Thank you," I said to her back as she retreated up the aisle.

Oliver's voice took on a wheedling tone. "Now Alice, we're not under the old rules any longer and Doug isn't here." He took my hand in his and stroked the back of it with his fingertips. "We can let our hair down a wee bit, can't we?"

"Of course, we can." I grimaced at him and snatched my hand away, ignoring the electricity that shot up my arm. "Then you'd be in violation of your contract and I'd be out of a job. Is that what you want?"

He sighed and sank back in his seat, staring out the window at the baggage handlers. I settled in and fastened my seatbelt, all the while wishing I had brought something distracting to read. I pulled the in-flight magazine from the seatback pocket and thumbed through it.

After a moment, he turned to me. "Alice, there's something I have to... I want to tell you."

I put down the magazine and tried to make my expression neutral. After all, if he was about to confess, I didn't want to seem judgmental or critical. As I waited, the plane backed up from the gate.

He looked me straight in the eye. "I have no problem with alcohol." Both his tone and his gaze were earnest.

"But you were in rehab... and your band member died of an overdose." I thought of my uncle and all his desperate, crazy denials before he agreed to enter treatment. "What about the drug usage?"

"I'm not an addict."

Thoughtful for a moment, I glanced up at the same flight attendant as she went through the motions to instruct passengers on the proper use of a seatbelt. Dwight had tried disclaimers like this one on me before, and I resisted rolling my eyes at Oliver. I kept my voice even, so it wouldn't sound like an accusation. "Then what were you doing in Fredericksburg at the rehab clinic?"

"Hiding."

"From whom? Federal agents?"

My parents' warnings echoed in my brain. *See, Alice, you're in trouble already. We cautioned you about heroin-soaked rock stars, didn't we?*

"Uh, not exactly. You see, Bennie was the one with the habit. And when he got caught..."

I had some vague recollection of reading headlines at the grocery check-out about Benjamin Lockeheart's drug troubles.

"... I tried to bail him out."

I shook my head. Never works, does it? I'd been

through that already with my misguided mother and her brother.

"How?"

"I offered to pay his dealers in full."

"Didn't that solve the problem? Surely, you could afford it."

"It wasn't the money. You see, it turned into what you call a sting operation."

My eyes bugged out. "You wore a wire to help the narcs catch drug dealers?"

"Yes, but they were actually after the smugglers." He made it sound like a choice between paper or plastic.

My eyes relaxed. "Oh, well, then there's nothing to worry about, is there?" My tone vacillated from sarcastic to hopeful. "Please tell me everyone got arrested and sent to prison."

He paused while the engine roared and the plane took off. Still atilt as we gained altitude, he continued. "Not quite."

I squinted at him. "Then what haven't you told me?"

Squirming in his seat, Oliver bowed his head. "They... those bastards have threatened..." He bit his lip.

"Who? Your family?"

He nodded and looked up at me, teary-eyed.

"You don't mean your son? They've threatened George?"

"That's why I had to leave Austin immediately. I

have to rescue my boy."

"Did you call the... who is it? Scotland Yard? What about your bodyguards?"

"No, the smugglers said that would only make it worse. And my bodyguards were in on the drug sales. Ben told me before he..."

By now, I wanted the flight attendant to return with the champagne, not that I felt like celebrating, but surely something bubbly would supply some much-needed fortitude. At least that's what my uncle had told me before he got sober.

"Alice, I don't know what to do. You're the only one I trust. You have to help me."

Of course, I do. After all, I am not the Mouseburger any longer. I am the Go-To Girl. The new Alice, who is fearless, efficient, and cost-effective because I go the extra mile to do my job.

While Oliver slept like he was over-medicated, I had something to distract me—and keep me awake—all the way across The Pond until we landed at Heathrow. Nothing like this was in my contract.

CHAPTER TWENTY
The Tour

Traveling with a rock star had its perks at first. A seat in first class on British Airways, a custom Bentley limo at Heathrow, although Oliver wondered where his vintage Jaguar XKE was stored.

How did he have time to drive himself anywhere? And he could forget driving anyway, as he had told me his license had been suspended.

Oliver's disguise, the same UT cap and sunglasses he wore around Town Lake, protected him from any screaming fans. The drab and efficient woman (shades of my past life) who met us at the gate, Penelope Entwhistle, assured us Oliver's half-brother, Simon, would have sent her, had he been at home to receive Oliver's message, to escort us to the country residence—a "des res" as Oliver termed it—of the Earl of Stockmore, Ramsden Grove, from Heathrow a two-hour drive southeast of London.

We arrived after midnight, exhausted and hungry, but too tired to eat. After Miss Entwhistle left us at the front door, Oliver led me through the grand entry hall. I wish I'd felt more energetic to notice the exquisite furnishings, but figured I'd see everything

in the morning, if my body recovered enough to recognize daylight. Elegant ancestors watched from the
frames on the walls as we plodded up a wide staircase, I lugging my own suitcase, and turned left when
Oliver pointed to the first door beyond the railing.

"In there," he said. "You should be comfortable in
the birdcage."

More English slang. "What about in the morning?" I had presence of mind to ask.

"We can sleep late, and then I'll come knock you
up."

"But what time—"

He had already disappeared into the shadows.
With a resigned murmur, I opened the door to my
appointed bedroom. After a little fumbling, my fingers found the light switch. The room was not volu-
minous, but the magnificent canopied bed appeared
soft and inviting. Indeed, when I wriggled into my
old cotton nightie and slid under the covers, I sank
down into the feathery mattress until I could barely
see over the top of the pillows and bed linens.

If I hadn't been so dog-tired, I would have been
more enchanted by the decor of the room. Another
thing to enjoy with the morning light. Before long,
I couldn't keep my eyes open, so I gave in to fatigue
and drifted away to the land of smooth sailing and
easy living. No one in my dreams came to me with
a single problem or errand, not even a message. A
quite contented Alice relaxed on the beach, lolling
under a palm tree and listening to the waves crash

on the crystal-white sand. So serene.

A crowd of tourists disturbed my view of the ocean as they clustered between me and the horizon. The noise of their chatter grew much louder. And closer.

I opened one eye, but couldn't move a muscle. Gravity seemed to have sucked me deeper into the non-resistant mattress, and I didn't want it to let go.

"This room is known as the Birdcage Chamber," said a voice in crisp, formal tones.

With both eyes drowsy, I stared at the wall next to the bed. Little gold birdcages hung on branches of lovely pink cherry blossoms. Inside each cage sat a colorful bird on a swing. Why didn't they chirp? Where had the ocean and the palm tree gone?

"In a style known as Chinoiserie, from the early 17th century when trade with China became popular," the voice continued. "Please step this way to admire the frieze around the fireplace, then turn and have a look at the carved mahogany headboard."

Gravity shifted gears and I bolted upright, both eyes popped wide open.

The tour guide and I screamed in unison, while the crowd of tourists took a step backward. I clutched the bed linens and drew them up toward my neck.

"Who are you?" the tour guide demanded in a loud voice. "How did you get in here?"

Words failed me and all I could do was bounce my stunned gaze from her angry face to those of the bemused tourists, who must have numbered in the twenties.

"What's all the ruckus about?" A shirtless Oliver sat up in bed next to me, undetected until now, and rubbed his sleepy eyes.

I squealed again, while as a unit, the tourists and the tour guide all caught their breaths is one gigantic inhale, strong enough to ruffle the canopy and the curtains. Otherwise, I was paralyzed from shock.

Oliver yawned, stretched his bare arms above his head, and smirked at me. Then he leaned over to give me a peck on the cheek. "Good morning, sweetheart," he murmured.

Cameras flashed and the tour guide spread her arms from side to side as if to protect her offspring from a firing squad. A buzz of recognition warbled through the crowd, its volume escalating by the second. Oliver preened and twisted among the linens and posed for more photos.

Ignoring the cold air, I jumped out of the bed, whirled around, and yelled at Oliver, "What are you doing here?"

Amid high-pitched squealing, more flashbulbs went off. I grabbed a pillow and held it in front of me like a shield.

"I'll report you to management this instant!" The dowager tour guide didn't know or care who Oliver was, as she herded her charges out of the room with a vehement harrumph. A frosty silence ensued, at least on my part.

I glared at Oliver. "What do you mean by sneaking into my bed in the middle of the night? Are you crazy?"

He looked like I had just slapped him, and I could have bitten my tongue off.

"Sorry," we both muttered at the same time.

"I know you're not crazy, and it was unkind of me to ask—"

"No, you're absolutely right." He sighed and turned weepy. "This whole bloody mess has got me a little unsettled, and... well, you know how I hate to be alone, especially at night."

"Yes, I remember." I kept my tone sympathetic but without any real warmth. "But you can't just—"

"Alice," he whimpered, "you're the only one I trust. I know you'll be there for me, and for Georgie, through thick and thin."

He held out his arms for me to come around the bed and give him a hug. I fell for the bait. After all, I had just spent the last few weeks learning to kiss him for the cameras. What harm could a comforting hug do?

I moved around the end of the bed and came to stand next to Oliver, my back to the door. That way, I figured, if any more tourists wandered through, I could dive under the bed with no risk of showing up later in someone's vacation photo album.

Oliver pulled me close and laid his head on my shoulder, enfolding me in his arms. All at once, it dawned on me that I was dressed in only my thin cotton nightie and I had no idea what, if anything, Oliver had on under the covers.

The sudden awareness must have hit him seconds later, because he turned his face to nuzzle my neck and slid his hand forward, up my ribcage and under my arm.

My back stiffened by reflex, or maybe anxiety about another tour group. Or because I was out of practice. I held my breath, while his other hand reached down for the hem of my nightie, his fingers grazing my thigh as he clawed at the fabric.

"Alice, Alice," he cooed in a beguiling tone that wrapped me up in a cocoon of quivering desire. When he lifted me off the floor and tugged me to the edge of the mattress, all my wisdom and self-control vanished like the palm tree in my dreams. Now was another dream come true, a different one, the one where I was bewitching and irresistible. This was the Alice I wanted to be.

"We've been practicing for weeks," he whispered in a husky, passion-laced voice. "Now let's make it real."

Balancing on my extended arm, I propped myself across his lap, gazed up into his deep blue eyes, and melted. He could have his way with me, anything he wanted. Tour groups or not.

In that moment, I was his and he was mine. No one in Texas, especially my parents, would ever find out, unless I wanted them to.

While he covered my face with slow kisses, I pondered what kind of maneuvering it would take to get me under the covers next to him. I couldn't exactly interrupt him by detaching and rolling off the bed to start over. How could we throw off his bed linens without breaking the passion?

The best choice seemed to be to let nature take its course and not make any sudden moves. I wanted to be tucked away in the sheets, however, before we reached the point of no return, and not let daylight on my bare flesh spoil the mood.

From that concern, logic took hold of my mind. I had no illusion that sex with Oliver would be the start of something wonderful that would continue beyond his contract with Doug, and *Austin City Limits*, and MTV. In fact, it might ruin our somewhat unusual friendship.

Sitting up, I took his face in my hands, palms against his cheeks, a move that had gotten his attention several times in the recent past. "Oliver?"

"Yes," he panted.

"Are you sure you want to do this?"

"Oh, yes!" He closed his eyes and tried to kiss me on the lips.

I backed up. "You know it will change our relationship in the future, maybe not for the better."

His eyes popped open and scanned my face. "But we can have a fantastic time right now."

Why did I expect a man in the throes of passion to stop and think? He had no blood circulating through his brain.

Hesitating, I sighed. What he said wasn't incorrect, but somehow it seemed...

"Alice, don't tease me," he pleaded. "You know I care for you—"

"I wouldn't tease you, Oliver. I'm not that kind of girl."

"What kind of girl are you?" came a deep voice from across the room.

Oliver and I both jumped, and he shot a puzzled look over my shoulder while I twisted sideways and attempted to duck under a corner of the bedspread. Instead I slid head-first off the edge of the bed and landed on the floor with a loud thud.

After a moment, I staggered to my feet and prayed to become invisible. The pillow I clutched in front of me proved useless.

"Simon!" Oliver's face broke into a broad grin. "We thought you were abroad."

Standing in the doorway, Simon scowled, shifting his glare from Oliver to me and back. "Obviously, I am not." His half-brother took a step inside the room. "What are you doing here? You're supposed to be—"

"I know." Oliver slumped forward and scooped up another pillow to lean against his bare chest. "But things have gotten complicated."

One eyebrow lifted, Simon regarded me like a blight on the perfect English rose garden. "I see."

"No," said Oliver with a shake of his head, "you don't understand. She's here to help. This is..." He turned to stare at me, renewed fear in his eyes and his mind a palpable blank.

"Alice," I said, squirming behind my pillow. I felt like such a fool.

"Well, pay her and then send her off. We need to talk." Without another word, Simon whirled on his heel and left the room.

At least he didn't have a camera.

CHAPTER TWENTY-ONE
The Detour

When Oliver slid out of bed, I had my back to him. I didn't dare turn around to see what he might—or might not—be wearing.

After the door closed behind him, I scurried to my suitcase, yanked it open, and pulled out the first outfit on top, a pullover beige sweater and dark gray slacks. Modest, sensible, ordinary. Exactly the way I hope Oliver's half-brother would learn to see me. Not as a hooker.

Once groomed and dressed, I returned to the scene of the crime and fluffed the pillows and the mattress, pulled up the sheets and the bedspread, fluffed the pillows again, and stood back to inspect my work. Even my mother would not have been able to detect the presence of two bodies in that bed, since its mattress and a sinkhole were constructed of identical materials.

A sound escaped from my lungs, up into my throat, but I couldn't tell if it were a sigh or a moan. Despite either one, I'd have to leave the room and somehow find Oliver and his brother, and clear the air. My stomach growled. When had I last eaten? Right after we landed at Heathrow the night before today, except is it really morning for me? How many hours ago was that? My watch and my body, craving dinner and not breakfast, were still on Central Texas time.

I opened the door and peeked out into the hallway in both directions, then took a step toward the carved mahogany railing. Below me, a wide staircase led somewhere. Is that the one I trudged up in semi-darkness last night? Where would I find myself if I descended?

Doug's warning rang in my head. Now was no time to hesitate, so I headed for the stairs and went down, retracing the way I had come. I didn't remember the two 90-degree angles halfway down, and had a choice of left or right. Either way, I predicted I would end up in the grand foyer leading to the front door. I backtracked once and tried to remember to turn the opposite way when I returned to my room.

Before I reached the bottom, my ears picked up angry male voices coming from behind double doors left ajar. One I recognized as Oliver's, and the other one, deeper and more melodious if that were possible, had to be Simon's. At the door, I hesitated. What person in her right mind would insert herself into the middle of a spat between siblings? But my job consisted of All Things Oliver, and if he needed my assistance—

"You've got it all wrong about Alice," Oliver said.

I knocked. In moments, the door flew open and Oliver, barefooted and dressed in pajama bottoms and a sweatshirt, grinned at me as he clasped my arm and shuffled me into the—I gawked at the overstuffed bookcases which seemed to reach to the sky—library. I'm sure my mouth must have dropped open, until I tore my gaze away from the thousand-plus books and found Simon leaning against the carved marble mantle, arms crossed and glaring at me. Oliver's half-brother wore a beige cardigan over his white shirt, and steely gray slacks. His thick wavy hair was close-cropped and medium brown, not blond like Simon's. If I hadn't dyed mine, we almost could have been twins.

"Simon, this is Alice Morehead, my personal Girl Friday."

Simon shot him a faint sneer, then gave me the once-over. "Not your usual uneducated slapper this time? Quite original." He reached into his pocket and pulled out a money clip, then peeled off several bills and laid them on the nearby table between us. "I trust fifty pounds is enough? Then you'll be on your way. Miss Entwhistle will show you out."

Oliver guffawed like a teenager hearing his first risqué joke. "Bloomin' hell, Simon, put your quid away. She's not a cheap tart." He winked at me, enjoying it more than I was, since I had caught the drift of both their comments. "She really is my assistant, hired for me by the music producer in Austin. And I'd wager the gate from my next concert she's read every single one of these cherished books of yours."

Standing up straight, Simon scowled at me, as if it were my fault he had judged me unfairly. "Then what were you doing in the same... room?" His face turned a bit pink, and I surmised he didn't really want an answer.

I waited for Oliver to reply, but he had grown quiet. I glanced sideways at him. Morose was more like it.

I squared my shoulders and spoke in the deepest Texas twang I could manage, giving his last name three syllables. "Mr. Goooodknight—"

"Knightley."

"What?"

"Our true last name is Knightley."

Somehow, that had a peculiar, but familiar, ring to it. "Well, then, Mr. Knightley, Oliver and I are only here to attend to some of his personal business, which has interrupted the pursuit of his usual career in music..." Hoping Simon would take a cue from the authoritative and professional tone of my voice, twang notwithstanding, I glanced at Oliver and he nodded. "We'll try not to be a nuisance to you as we make arrangements for the care of his son, George. It should only take a few days." My stomach rumbled again, louder this time. "Your kind hospitality is much appreciated."

I turned to Oliver and wondered how big a hint to drop. "Have you eaten yet this morning?"

He shook his head. "Of course not. When would I have had an opportunity, since the last time you saw me was in your room, tucked in your bed?" He gave me a smirk bordering on wicked. "I could murder some breakfast now."

Simon scooped up his cash and shoved it in his pocket. "Cook will have something for you in the private breakfast room."

I raised my eyebrows at him and fixed a meaningful gaze straight up into his dark brown eyes. *You aren't quite off the hook yet, are ya, bubba?*

"And, Miss, ... er—"

With a wry pucker of my mouth, I jerked my chin upward and stuck out my hand. "Morehead. Alice Morehead."

Stepping forward, he took my hand and gave it a light shake. "Please accept an apology for my misunderstanding."

"Thank you, Mr. Knightley."

I tried to turn sideways to follow Oliver out of the library, so I wouldn't get lost again, but Simon didn't let go of my hand. Instead he tilted his head and gave me a curious look.

"Alice Morehead?" he said, edging closer. "Where have I heard that name before?"

His hand felt firm and muscular, as if he could perform serious physical tasks if he ever had to, yet soft, because Lords-To-Be of the Manor didn't have to. My hand tingled, so I snatched it away.

"I'm sure I have no idea," I said, with a shake of my head. From this angle and proximity, I noticed his luxuriant eyelashes, ones all women would kill for. I jerked my thumb toward one of the bookshelves. "Perhaps she's a character in one of your countless novels."

"ALICE!" From the hall, Oliver stuck his head through the doorway. "I'm quite famished. Are you coming?"

With a shrug, I bounded out of the room. Half-way down the other hallway, with Oliver ten paces ahead, my hand still tingled.

CHAPTER TWENTY-TWO

The Poet's House

"Thank God for real tea in Merry Olde England."

At least, that's what Oliver said to me as we sat down at the breakfast table in what I surmised must be the private section of the manor house.

For my part, I was grateful we had dodged a tour group as their guide led them down the main staircase. I didn't want anyone to check for familiar faces. Before I skittered around the corner, however, Simon's deep baritone greeted them in the sumptuous front hall and thanked them for coming. Flashes of light bounced off the walls, as many of them stood by his side for photos.

My quick guess was, he was rather photogenic, with classic features, a strong jawline, and those exceptional dark eyes framed by wavy burnt umber-colored hair, thick as—Wait, how did I remember all that detail?

After Cook brought our plates of over-easy eggs and crisp bacon, along with a little silver caddy laced with dry toast, I studied Oliver's face to detect his mood. He appeared too focused on the food to give me any hint. Maybe I could sneak in by another route.

"So, Oliver," I said in a voice heavy with nonchalance, "what does Simon do? You know, how does he spend his time? Does he manage the estate?"

"God forbid," Oliver snickered. "Father, who spends money like a gilded wastrel, would never entrust something that important to him."

"Why not?" Seldom a good move, to be in business with your family. Years ago, my ex-brother-in-law had joined his father's accounting firm, and then, before making partner, left to start his own. Last I heard, they were barely on speaking terms.

Teaching in the same school district where your father was superintendent would also count as a legitimate family enterprise. But if I failed at this job, it wasn't likely I could launch my own school district or open my own high school.

"He's got no head for numbers, Simon has. Total rubbish at it."

I slathered orange marmalade on my toast. "Does he live here all the time?"

"Except when he's writing or teaching at Oxford." Oliver sipped his coffee. "Or is it Cambridge?" He shrugged. "I forget."

Oh, great. Another academic. "What subject does he teach?"

"Literature... um, or poetry. Something like that. And he breeds prize-winning terriers."

My ears perked up. "Does he write poetry?"

Oliver guffawed. "I should think so. He was

England's Poet Laureate last year and the one before that."

My mouth dropped open. Oliver would have called me gobsmacked.

"Can't say he's produced much lately. Been in a bit of a slump, poor bugger." Oliver shoveled the last of the eggs into his mouth and pushed his plate away. "He might forfeit the title if he doesn't come up with something soon. Perhaps he's lost the plot."

I couldn't catch my breath. Poet Laureate of an entire country? Nationally, no, internationally recognized for writing verse like no other soul, living or dead, along the lines of Shakespeare. I had been selected Poet Laureate of my high school, but all during college, my writing had been in secret until I finally gathered the nerve to submit one of my poems after Dwight and I got married. *The Journal of American Poetry* published it the following spring, and that marked the beginning and the end of my career as a poet.

Oliver stood up. "We should head out for a bimble, unless you want to just sit there and catch flies. I'll show you our lake... or perhaps you're over knackered?"

Either I was too far gone from jet lag to question his vocabulary or he was starting to make sense. That was the signal he was feeling antsy, needed to get outdoors, and wanted either to talk or to brood in silence.

"I'll go get my jacket."

"No need. We have extras in the cloakroom."

The one he selected for me came almost to my knees. I felt like a child wearing her older brother's clothes as Oliver rolled up my sleeves until my hands appeared. But the woolen jacket, a rich blue-and-green plaid, was warm against England's country air, cool and damp even with the faint sun peeking from behind the gathering storm clouds.

I glanced at the brooding sky. "Shall we take an umbrella?"

Standing in front of me, Oliver reached behind my neck. He unzipped something inside the collar and pulled a hood over my head. "There, now you won't melt if it rains." He planted his hands on my shoulders, squeezed them, and smiled down at me.

For a moment I thought he would kiss me. After all, we were in a daily habit of it, and more than twenty-four hours had passed since we last... oh, Alice, give it up! You were the stalking horse, remember? Stop thinking like a fool!

Oliver's expression turned serious. "I'm glad you've come with me. I don't know what to do... this situation has gone completely balls up."

Poking his sternum, I said, "Did I ever tell you what my family calls me?"

He shook his head.

"The Go-To Girl, because I'm the one everyone goes to for solutions to whatever problem they have. Doug learned about my nickname from Sally, and that's one reason he hired me." I wrapped my arms around him and hugged him, harmless this time since we were both fully dressed, plus I was buried alive in wool plaid. "I'll do everything I can to help you, I promise."

In silence we stood locked together, and I couldn't guess what might have been going through his mind. Worry about George and the smugglers had bumped his fear of performing in front of live audiences way down the list. My job was extra complicated now, and probably a wee bit more dangerous.

The next thing I knew, Oliver pulled my hood off and slid his hand toward the nape of my neck, against my bare skin. "Alice, Alice," he whispered to the top of my head. "I need you desperately."

From the doorway to the cloakroom came the sound of someone clearing his throat. Damn, Simon had caught us again. Although still innocent, we both stepped back like we were radioactive.

The person who interrupted us wasn't Simon, however, but Miss Entwhistle. Both her face and her voice were devoid of all expression. "Telephone call for you, Mr. Goodknight."

Oliver nodded, then clutched my arm as he gasped, "Who knows I'm here?"

Who indeed? We had all but sneaked into the country and traveled to Ramsden Grove under cover of utter darkness.

"Maybe it's Doug, just calling to check on us." I tried to sound optimistic.

"No, it's not an American, although he does have a foreign accent." Miss Entwhistle stood back to let us pass.

Oliver's eyes bugged out in fear and he didn't move.

I took his hand and led him toward the doorway. "Come on. Let's hear what he has to say, whoever he is. Then we can come up with a plan."

Sheesh, I had just jumped over the cliff and now would have to knit my parachute on the way down. Why on earth did I do it?

Truth was, I needed Oliver, too. I had grown to like the person he saw when he looked at me.

CHAPTER TWENTY-THREE

The Other House

In the library, Oliver held the receiver to his ear, but said nothing. I stood next to him and waited. Like being on stage all over again, except we had no audience. Not even Miss Entwhistle.

I peered up into his face and gave him the circular hand signal, which should have been familiar by now. Nothing. What did I expect? No live musicians stood behind us. No stage lights blinded us.

"Say hello," I whispered, my hand still in motion.

When Oliver swallowed, his Adam's apple bounced like a pogo stick. Beads of sweat peppered his forehead. I took his hand and squeezed it, and then he croaked out a "hello" just above a murmur.

After a moment, he relaxed with a long exhale of words, "Oh, Raj, it's you. Thank God!" He covered the mouthpiece with his palm and nodded at me. "My banker's assistant."

To Raj, he said, "How did you find out I'm back in England? We didn't inform anyone."

Oliver winked at me and waggled his head with vigor. "Of course. I see. Yes, every day. A capital idea, right-o."

Since Oliver seemed relieved, I breathed easier,

too. But it was obvious Raj had something important to tell him, as I could read from the expression on Oliver's face. Maybe it was the situation, or perhaps the wool jacket, but I felt too warm and took it off. He slid his arms out of his and I laid them both across the back of an overstuffed chair next to a large carved secretary crammed with books and magazines, along with several porcelain figurines of dogs. Everything an antique going back many generations. Nothing like the house where I grew up.

Oliver frowned. "Really? How long?"

More information, or useful instructions perhaps.

"What would be the penalty?"

Oliver sucked in his breath and winced. "Too much, too much." After a pause, he said, "What if I buy a house? What impact will that have? ... No, it would be the only one I've ever purchased, in my own name."

More pause for Raj's questions and explanations.

"Yes, ask your man Mickey to get in touch. I have someone here to help me, and they can sort it out together." Oliver studied my face as he listened, but I could not read his mind, other than he expected me to help him with something and someone named Mickey. The usual job description.

"No, I wouldn't live there full-time, but a member of my family would. Actually, two members." He lifted my hand to his lips, but I jerked it away before he could deliver a smooch. I needed to keep my head on straight.

Raj had a great deal more to impart regarding

this sketchy plan of action, but after a few minutes of trying to follow his comments, Oliver said, "I'll let you know when it all develops."

He hung up and turned full face toward me. A slow grin spread across his lips as he planted his hands on my shoulders. "Alice, my dear girl, with your... cooperation, this will all work out. You'll see."

I squinted at him. "Would you care to explain? Doug is expecting—"

"Oh, Doug can bugger off." He dropped his hands to his side.

"No, he can't. You're still under contract, and I have certain—uh, who was that anyway? And how did he find out you're in England?"

"Raj? That sweet boffin monitors my credit card every day at the bank, part of the fraud protection plan. The other day he saw the British Air tickets and knew I'd be traveling soon. Then charges for the coffee at Heathrow popped up, so he figured I'd arrived here."

"Smart man. Good to know someone like that has your back."

"That's not all." His tone turned ominous. "We can't stay here very long."

"I know. We have to take care of George and get back to Austin to finish your gig."

"Not that simple. If I stay longer than a week, the tax man will have my nethers in his bin bag."

I rolled my eyes at the highest volume I could manage. A week, however, would suit Doug just fine.

"Who is Mickey?"

"Oh, yes. He's an estate agent, what you Yanks would call a real estate agent."

That comment rated a severe scowl. "Not all Americans are Yanks, I'll have you know. Fact is, I'm a native Texan and I hardly know any Yanks. I didn't even meet one until I went to college."

Oliver's eyes twinkled, and I burst out laughing. He hugged me, saying, "That's my girl. You don't take any crap from anyone, do you?"

Not anymore.

The telephone rang and Oliver answered it. "Yes, Mickey, bring your portfolio round right away and we'll have a look. I don't care if it costs a bomb."

They set a time for later that day, and when Oliver hung up, he said, "Let's go for our walk and plot some strategy. Have any ideas?"

We bundled up again for our stroll around the lake. Oliver wanted to have a clear plan in place for his meeting with George and May. We thought it best if he met with them alone, and not involve me or his solicitor yet.

"Maybe you can sweet-talk her into a more reasonable arrangement, like joint custody."

"Thing is, I don't know if that will put George in the queue for the title. It's rather a sticky wicket."

At last, slang I could interpret. "But let me be sure I understand this whole primogeniture thing."

"You're an American... sorry, a native Texan, and you used the term, primogeniture? You are rather smashing, you know?"

In my best Southern belle voice, I said, "Who you sweet-talkin' now?" and gave "now" at least two dragged out syllables.

By the time we returned to the manor, we had agreed I would meet with Mickey and go through photos of the available estates. Oliver said I should select the des res where I would be comfortable, when I came round for a tour. He wiggled his eyebrows up and down until I smacked his arm.

The rest of the plan seemed simple at first. While Mickey showed me the portfolio, Oliver would meet with May and hope to spend time with George.

"Find out everything May has in mind," I said over lunch in the same dining room where we had eaten breakfast. "Remember, she's going to demand the moon and the stars. But perhaps you can offer her much less and meet somewhere in the middle."

"No moon, one star. Hardly likely, as she holds all the cards." Oliver's voice sounded glum, and I couldn't blame him. "She won't even believe me when I insist we have to protect Georgie and maybe the rest of her family, not that they deserve it."

"Tell me about May's background. Other than she's a famous young actress, I really don't know anything about her."

"She's quite beautiful, and so talented."

I nodded, but couldn't offer any personal opinion. "What about her family background?"

"Comes from poor working stiffs. Her father was

a Brummy who worked the warehouses by day and was a barman at night. No wonder, with the wife he was chained to. Her mother, a real dim wit who never shuts her clanging cake hole, was employed as a dispatcher for the fire brigade in Birmingham. They are what you'd call unrelenting social climbers."

"Birmingham?" I raised my eyebrows and gave him a knowing smile, pleased I had caught on to his slang. "Where the Brummies live?"

At UT, I had known girls from families like May's, not as Tri Delts, but in several of my classes. Smart and ambitious, they were the first of all their ancestors to attend a university, usually on scholarship. They'd rather die than go back home to a dead-end, menial job among the less educated. If presented with any rung up the ladder, they grabbed it and never looked back. They took the Mouseburger mantra seriously and made the most of themselves, many times by scoring a rung or more based on their own achievements.

What they would never in a million years have been offered, at UT or elsewhere in the States, was the chance to have a child with direct connections to the landed gentry or the nobility. Which came with a title and an estate to inherit.

"Have May and her parents ever visited here?"

"No, Father wouldn't allow it."

"Where is your father now?"

"On a European tour with his latest girlfriend, I

assume."

"Would Simon object if you invited them to tea?"

"I doubt it. He hardly ever leaves the library except to visit his best chums in the greenhouse or the kennels."

"Well, then, give some thought to showing them some gracious upper class hospitality, overlook their not-so-genteel manners, and provide them with a mouth-watering glimpse of what's in store for George one day. Should May choose to cooperate, of course, and act like a reasonable mother. And assure them they'd be invited to partake in the festivities at Christmas and St. Swithin's Day."

Oliver jumped to his feet. "Alice, you're a genius! I never thought of that angle at all." He danced around his chair, arms in the air and shaking his butt, then came to my chair and pulled me up out of it. He spun me around and laughed until he came to a dead halt. "Wait a minute."

"What's wrong?" I stood up straight and pulled the lower edge of my sweater down where it belonged.

"How do you know about St. Swithin's Day?"

I grinned. "Actually—"

"Oliver!" said a deep voice from the doorway.

Stiff as a martinet, Simon stood there, frowning at us, as he tapped a piece of paper against his palm.

Ugh, not again. At least we were fully clothed this time.

"Hey, Simon, we were just—"

"It's Father." He held out the paper, which I then recognized as a telegram.

Oliver turned as sober and serious as I'd ever seen him. "Is he... dead?"

Simon shook his head. "Married."

Like a balloon that had exchanged helium for gravel, Oliver sank into the nearest chair and stared out the window across the room. After a moment, he closed his eyes as if in prayer, and shook his head in grinding heavy movements. "Could she be any worse steaming hell than number three or number four?"

Simon pursed his lips. "I believe so. This one is expecting Father's child." He turned to stare at me. "She's about your age."

"I thought his cardiologist warned him about..." Oliver groaned. "Jeez, she must be trying to kill him."

Both brothers looked as if they wanted to throw up. I said nothing and retreated to a corner at the end of the sideboard.

Oliver stood up and squared his shoulders. "Right. We have our work cut out for us, don't we?" He stalked out of the room, brushing past Simon at a fast pace.

I peered at Simon until he shot a glance toward me, and I gave him a weak smile. "Is there anything I can do?"

He flinched, then recovered. "Come with me, please, Miss Morehead. There is something I'd like to show you. I mean, ask you." Without waiting for me, he turned and disappeared down the hallway toward the library.

Okay, let me be sure I've got this right. Oliver wants to buy a house, plus gain custody of his child so George can inherit the estate and the title, because his older half-brother has no children. Meanwhile, George's lower class mother is yanking our lad's chains about his concert tours, and the tax man will soon be banging on Oliver's door, not to mention the threats from the smugglers, which is why we crossed The Pond in the first place. But Oliver hasn't addressed that problem yet, because he's now distracted by a possible rival if his new step-mother should produce a male heir, while his father could expire during the next act-in-the-sack.

Was that everything?

Probably not, because I had no idea what Simon wanted to ask me.

CHAPTER TWENTY-FOUR
The Des Res

As I followed Simon down the hallway toward the library, Oliver was nowhere in sight. Whatever "work" he had just mentioned was not apparent right away, and I couldn't imagine what work he was cut out for anyway. Even if he could crunch any numbers by himself, he'd much rather ask me to take care of it.

When I entered the library, Simon stood next to his desk with his back to me. I crept forward alongside him, not too close, and found him pouring over a page in a book. He appeared lost in the text, and I waited, not wishing to disturb his concentration. Plus I wasn't sure he realized I was standing there.

After a few moments, he sighed and closed the book. When he turned toward me, he didn't look startled, instead rather mystified or even disbelieving. His eyes searched my face as if I spoke a foreign language and he couldn't figure out why lip-reading didn't work.

He tapped the book's cover. "Reverie," he said. "Yours? Are you that Alice Morehead?"

Giving him a shy smile, I nodded. "You know my poem?" I leaned toward him to glance at the book's title. Sure enough, an old copy of *The Journal of American Poetry* nestled in his hand.

"My students know it backwards and forwards. It's included in the syllabus for the classes I teach at Oxford."

I thought I must have been dreaming. The reigning Poet Laureate of England not only knew my one poem, published over ten years ago, but also told his students to read it and memorize it.

Gulping, I stammered, "I'm... I'm honored." Gobsmacked once more.

Simon opened the book again and read aloud, "'Like a ship returned once more to the wharf of my soul.' That image has stuck with me since I first stumbled across your work. I keep hoping... well..." He set the book on the desk. "In which volumes are your subsequent poems published? I cannot locate them, nor can Miss Entwhistle."

I winced. "Well, ah... there aren't any others. That's the only one."

"Did the publisher reject them?" Simon frowned. "That doesn't seem very likely, given the quality of your expression."

"I mean, I never submitted the rest for publication."

"Why not?"

Why indeed? A parade of reasons flitted through my mind, but they would all sound stupid to Simon. How could someone let housework and volunteer jobs take priority over the creation of something dear and tender and at times heart-wrenching? Shouldn't all normal adults overcome the lack of encouragement from parents and spouses? On the other hand, didn't the best writing arise from the ashes of pain and suffering?

"I guess I thought I would always get back to it, my poetry, that is. But I allowed other people and circumstances to take control of my life, and... and—" a wave of sorrow threatened to engulf me. "Maybe I just don't see myself as a poet anymore."

As I gazed up into Simon's face, his eyes turned misty and I knew I had touched a nerve. Hadn't Oliver told me his brother had hit a dry patch and hadn't written anything for a while?

Simon straightened his back. "I hope you can recover that earlier image of yourself."

"If yearning will serve for inspiration, then perhaps I'll manage it."

Before I could stop him, Simon took my hand and enclosed it in both of his. "Yearning? What is it you yearn for, Miss Morehead?" He leaned his head down toward me once again.

Something inside me, the tight little box where I had locked up my truths, splintered open just a smidgen. "I need to pay attention to that yearning because it will help me find out who I really am."

"Sounds like it could be one of your poems?"

The expression in his dark brown eyes held some kind of irresistible treasure, as if I could search and then find a fortune of answers. All it would take was...

"Time, if I have time to think and write anything while I'm here. You know, in between assignments, uh, for Oliver." What was I, some kind of goofy schoolgirl with a foolish crush on the student teacher? "What about you?"

"I have all the time in the world, and not a moment to lose. You see, Miss Morehead, I am stuck. My page is blank because my imagination slumbers, and I have no Muse of poetry to awaken me."

"You only have nine from which to choose!" came a booming voice from the doorway. "Find another one."

I snatched my hand away. Simon and I both whirled toward Oliver, who stood frowning at us.

"Of course." Simon edged his way around the corner of the desk and picked up a newspaper.

"Alice, come with me." Oliver grinned and waved me toward him. "Mickey is here and he brought his portfolio for you to pour over, in your usual meticulous manner."

I glanced sideways at Simon, but he had sequestered his head behind the front page.

Shifting in Oliver's direction, I said, "Of course." Only after the words escaped my lips did I realize they echoed Simon's.

Oliver linked his arm through mine and hustled me to an even grander room. The living room, I supposed, because it held massive sofas arranged in several seating areas, and the walls were covered with more paintings of ancestors and landscapes. Against the windows stood a spacious long desk or table flanked by carved, straight-back chairs.

The well-dressed man waiting next to the table greeted us in a cordial fashion. Michael Chandler, but his friends, of whom Raj was one, called him Mickey. He had already spread out a large leather portfolio with stacks of photos and maps.

"Well, you two, I'll leave you to it," said Oliver. "I have to call on the Siren of the Cotswolds and hope she doesn't lure me to my death."

"Remember what we discussed," I said with an edge to my voice. If anything terrible happened, Doug would blame me—and then fire me—for letting Oliver out of my sight. "And come back as soon as you can."

"Right-o. Happy hunting." And within seconds Oliver was out the door.

Mickey smiled at me in a fatherly way. "True love. How sweet."

"Excuse me?"

His smile faded just a tad.

No, wait, Oliver said 'excuse me' when he belched. And 'pardon me" applied to something far grosser, he had once explained, but I stopped him before he could give me an example.

"You and Mr. Goodknight, I dare say, make a very handsome couple."

I wrinkled my eyebrows. "Whatever gave you that idea?"

"Isn't he buying the des res, as he calls it, for you? He told me you'd be living there with his son."

"WHAT?"

"After you're married, naturally."

Gobsmacked had turned into a daily, if not hourly, occurrence for me. After I recovered, it dawned on me that Oliver might have taken up drinking, again, despite what he swore to me on the flight over here. Doug was going to hit the roof.

My boss, however, was the least of my worries.

CHAPTER TWENTY-FIVE
The Green House

I gave up the idea that I could straighten out Mickey by denying my engagement to Oliver. He was estate agent to British and other international stars, and keeping secrets was his lifeline to profits. One slip of the lip and he'd be shunned, with his only future referrals coming from a ghost town.

We sat in the living room, or 'lounge' as he termed it, and poured through the photos and maps. For the life of me, I couldn't figure out why 128 rooms might be better than 76 or worse than 192, on more or fewer acres, with or without a pond, a lake, or a stream. The only thing Oliver ever fished for was sex and compliments, but not necessarily in that order.

With the exception of a reliable security force on the premises, a large staff made no sense to me, unless he planned to entertain the entire county or operate a weekend B&B. Or let tour groups wander through it.

Ugh! Not on my watch.

One thing kept me concentrated on the goal of purchasing a home: influencing May. Enticing her to be agreeable to granting Oliver custody of George. As long as I remembered we had left Austin to come rescue George—and in the process deliver Oliver from the emotional devils pursuing him—I could pretend the estate would have to meet certain standards and have an unimpeachable historical pedigree. Maybe my world would turn upside down and I would become the lady of the manor after all. I slipped out of my shoes and wiggled my toes.

After about an hour and a half, we narrowed the search to three estates within short driving distance from Ramsden Grove, ranging from 207 to 352 years old. Youthful for their age, Mickey assured me.

Stacking the few photos and maps, I promised Mickey I'd go over the possible choices with Oliver and get back to him. He gave me his card and wished me good evening before he left the room. Perhaps the butler showed him out, although up to then I had not laid eyes on that person.

Oliver hadn't yet returned from visiting George and May, so I wasn't sure what to do next. I couldn't remember the last time I wasn't chasing an assignment for Doug on Oliver's behalf. In my previous life, I would be cleaning something or preparing dinner after I finished my volunteer chores.

Whatever I did from now on, I pledged to make it more fun, if not also advance the transformation of the Mouseburger-at-hand. The new Alice grew stronger and more aware every day. Finally I could relax a bit and enjoy the sense of being more in charge of myself.

Feeling smug, I grinned and, with fingers laced

together, reached my arms behind my head. At the same time I stretched my legs out straight, ready to plop my bare feet in the chair Mickey had just vacated.

"Mrs. Morehead?" said a stern female voice from corner of the room.

With my legs mid-air, I twisted in my seat to find Miss Entwhistle holding a clipboard as she all but barricaded the doorway. Startled, I rolled sideways and tucked my legs just in time to catch myself before falling off the edge of the chair. When I shot to my feet, I jostled the chair and it tipped away from me on two legs and crashed to the floor.

Before I could reach over, Miss Entwhistle appeared at my side, grasped the back of the carved chair, and set it upright. Her expression revealed nothing, but I wondered if she had ever observed such clumsiness before. Surely, the Knightley clan could supply evidence of an ancestor who went on an occasional bender, the kind with alcohol, and bumped into the furniture or broke some valuable trinket. But she herself was so cold and straitlaced, I'm sure she never took a misstep.

What was my excuse? I sighed. A place like this would never be home to someone like me, a middle class import with no pedigree. Might as well elect a koala bear to be Prom Queen. The "des res" was merely a misguided distraction, and I was a fool to entertain such a pipe dream.

We both stood up straight and faced each other. I

waited for her to speak.

"Mrs. Morehead," she said in a monotone, "your presence is requested in the greenhouse."

"Oh, is that where Oliver is now?" I smiled at her, hoping she would thaw, even a tiny bit. "I didn't know he had returned."

"He hasn't." She swept her arm out, hand gesturing toward the door opposite the one she had entered. "Would you please be so kind as to follow me?"

Who wanted to see me in the greenhouse? If not Oliver, then... oh, the other Mr. Knightley.

I had no breadcrumbs to mark my circuitous path from the lounge to the greenhouse. After a few minutes of hiking, I could have sworn Miss Entwhistle was pulling a Billie Sol Estes on me, since each drawing room we passed through seemed vaguely familiar. But perhaps all the priceless antiques and late Renassaince artwork had become repetitive.

At last we reached the exit which led outside to the greenhouse. Miss Entwhistle retreated before I could ask for a jacket, as the damp night air had turned cold. I hurried toward the lit glass pavilion and hoped Simon had turned on the heaters.

The atmosphere inside was just as humid as outside, but much warmer. I found Simon bent over an orchid among a row of blooming potted plants stacked three-deep on a long table against the back wall. I had never seen such a frilly, richly hued display.

"Cattleya," he said, without looking up. "Not as rare as some of my cymbidiums, but it carries a slight fragrance." He held it up and turned toward me. "Very pleasing, don't you think?"

I studied the blooming "face" he presented and smiled. "It's winking at me," I giggled as I leaned forward and inhaled.

Simon set the pot down and stared at me. After a moment, he said, "Miss Morehead—"

"Oh, please, call me Alice. Oliver and everyone else does."

"All right... Alice, would you be interested in discussing poetry sometime? Maybe as a way to get back into the discipline of writing it. We could use my library as our meeting place."

"Oh, please don't throw me in the briar patch!"

He lowered his head and ran his hand through his dark chestnut-colored wavy hair. "Of course not. I just thought you and I might—"

Grinning, I put my hand on his arm. "You misunderstood me. The briar patch—in this case, your library—is an American way to describe where you feel most at home. A library is my favorite place on earth."

As his dark eyes focused on mine, his long thick lashes all but swept me backward. His turn to grin. "Then you'll agree to spend time with me there? Maybe you'll let me read your other poems."

In the figurative sense, I scratched my head. "Well, I'd have to recreate them, but that's okay. I have many of them almost memorized. Then you could show me yours as well." Inside, I laughed. Too bad Oliver wasn't here so I could lay my ambiguous American slang on him and see if he could figure out the lustful undertones.

"Miss Entwhistle will take your dictation, if that would help. She can even submit them for publication, when it comes to that. And she can write a notice to the press for you…later, of course, with your approval." He paused. "I apologize for gushing forth with so many suggestions, but I haven't felt even a smattering of encouragement until now. I look forward to our—"

"That will have to wait," came a disapproving voice from the door.

We both spun around to find Oliver frowning at us. Why did people always sneak up on everyone else in this house? Because it was so huge? Or because they didn't really communicate with each other.

"Alice's full-time job is to take care of me," Oliver said as he stalked toward us, then snatched my hand, "and no one else."

Simon backed up, and I glanced at him over my shoulder as Oliver yanked my arm and dragged me out of the greenhouse and across the lawn, muttering under his breath all the way. His declaration echoed in my head, dimly familiar for a moment. Once inside, in the hallway, I pulled my hand free and stood my ground so he would stop.

He whirled to face me. "Come on, Alice," he pleaded. "I need you."

What had he said? He was my "full-time job" and therefore I was not allowed to make any choices for myself. Where had I heard that before? When did Oliver turn into a miserable, self-centered, possessive son of a bitch? How could I not have seen that he was just like Dwight? My price just went up, and if Oliver couldn't be made to understand, Doug would have to.

"Oliver, let's get something straight...."—Wow, who was this brazen creature standing up for herself?—"When you need help, that's what you get from me, in every way possible. But you don't get... me."

"I don't follow."

"Of course, I'm here to help you." I kept my voice cool and emotion free. "And we will work together to solve whatever problems we can, because, yes, that is my job. But if I have extra time for myself, you don't get to dictate how I spend it."

"Is it just the poetry or is it something else?"

"What do you mean?"

"Well, Simon needs help, too, and all, especially since he's hit a dark patch, and I just thought... maybe you like him." Oliver looked down and refused to meet my stare. "He's always trying to take something away from me. Ever since we were tots, and all through school. He repeatedly—"

"For half-brothers, while being wildly successful in your own worlds, you are polar opposites." I put my knuckle under his chin to raise his head. "Not hard to understand, but are you also competitors?"

Oliver shrugged. "A wee bit, perhaps."

A gross understatement, I suspected. Plus it helped to explain the suspicion I felt brewing under the surface whenever all three of us were together.

"That's between the two of you. I refuse to be a cat's paw caught up in your sibling rivalry. Don't make that about me."

Frowning in a pitiful and contrite way, Oliver took my sleeve and jiggled it. "Alice, I do care about you."

Liar. When had he ever cared about anyone except himself? Did he think I was a fool?

I sighed, ready to change the subject. "How did it go with May?"

Oliver sucked in his breath and, in the next second, burst into tears.

Oh, lordy, now what?

CHAPTER TWENTY-SIX
The Wee Tot

At first, Oliver had trouble explaining what went wrong at May's. She wasn't especially glad to see him, but lucky for him, he had expected her cool reception. He put his head on my shoulder while he sniveled, and for once didn't try to sneak his hand anywhere it shouldn't wander.

His distress came from George's reaction. The little boy had screamed and cried and refused to let his father hold him. The nanny came to the rescue and carted him off to the nursery.

"I guess I've been absent too long," Oliver whimpered. "He didn't even know me."

"Well, he's not old enough to understand schedules or read the fan magazines, is he?" I tried to make my voice sound soothing. "Just give him some time."

Oliver plopped into a chair in the sitting room where we had stopped our retreat from the greenhouse. "May's got an ultimatum. She starts a new movie in a few weeks, and wants to have all this settled before then."

Doug's deadline just blew up.

I sat in a chair opposite him. "But don't you have

to be out of the country by then anyway? According to the tax man?"

"Good point." He frowned, lost in thought for a moment. "Why can't George be as accepting of a stranger as Nathan? Sally's boy got used to me right away. Even cried when I left the house each morning."

"Each child is different. You can't expect George to be like Nathan, anymore than you're like Simon."

He gave me a withering stare. Stuck a nerve again, had I?

"Well, Miss Go-To Girl, what am I to do?"

"Why don't you invite George over to play? Surely, there's a nursery crammed full of toys around here somewhere. On the third or fourth floor perhaps? Did you say Simon has dogs? Are there any puppies? What child can resist a puppy?"

"We'll have to ask him, as I steer clear of the kennel." He scratched his head, deep in thought. "May will want to be here, and the nanny should come, too, shouldn't she? To guarantee he won't cry."

"Children..."—of any age, I wanted to say—"are unpredictable. You have no guarantee he won't cry. But if you're the one who can comfort him and distract him, then that's a step toward his getting more comfortable around you. Remember, you have to be patient. He's only—"

"Three-and-a-half years old."

"Oh?" I frowned. "I thought he was closer to Nathan's age. Twenty months or so."

So Oliver's relationship had been consummated sooner than he first led me to believe. No point in arguing with him. Why would it matter to me anyway? What did I care?

We agreed to get started as soon as he could convince May to agree to visit Ramsden Grove, and he would propose it to happen by mid-morning tomorrow. He left in search of a telephone, and I stayed seated to contemplate the ticking clock and organize my thoughts.

What to handle first? Oliver's situation with George kept him from addressing any other concern. Right, get the kid in line for the throne. But reaching that solution had all sorts of booby-traps, such as May, the purchase of a house, the smugglers. Not to mention Simon and their father, with his pregnant wife.

Simon. He wasn't exactly a problem, not to me anyway. More of an opportunity. A distraction. A temptation.

The whole picture came into focus a little better. Could I help Oliver unearth his fatherly side, while, at the same time, discover the real Alice Morehead? What would it take for me to grasp my personal Brass Ring?

By instinct, I knew the answer. I would have to track down the Alice who was most alive. To let that goal sink in, I sat still with my eyes closed, until Oliver burst back into the room.

"It's all set!" he sang. "They'll be here tomorrow

morning at 10:30 for playtime and stay for lunch. I'll get Cook to prepare a menu." He took off again.

I sighed. I had forgotten to show him the photos and map of the stately homes Mickey deposited with me. How would I find my way back to the lounge? How long before my path crossed with Oliver again? Or Simon?

After a moment of indecision, I returned to the hall door we had entered earlier, pushed it open, and gazed in the direction of the greenhouse, now darkened. I envied the orchids, tended so meticulously, every need answered, always valued even when they weren't in bloom. I bet Simon talked to them, sharing his hopes and worries.

But I am not a hothouse flower. I am flesh and blood. I'd have hopes and worries, too, if I allowed myself to stop living through others and unlock that tight little box where I had stashed my truths.

I turned around and, as I trudged down the hallway toward the library, I hoped I was at least headed in the right direction.

CHAPTER TWENTY-SEVEN
The Librarian

After three wrong turns and directions from one of the maids who seemed to know all about me, I ended up at the door to the library, peeked in, and found Simon at his desk, reading. I couldn't see the book's title, but I assumed it was a volume of poetry. Tall stacks of books sat balanced on either side of his desk, while several others littered the credenza behind him.

Just like Doug's office. By now I recognized the signs of creative genius.

When I cleared my throat, he looked up and gave me half a smile, tinged with wistfulness. Returning his smile, I stepped inside the room, which I had come to regard as his inner sanctum, and he jumped to his feet. Oliver should have taken lessons on good manners from him. Then I remembered their rivalry and cut Oliver some slack for his rebellion against the accepted norm among the upper class.

"I hope I'm not interrupting or disturbing—"

"I've just ordered some tea be brought in," he said, sounding shy. "Would you... care to join me?"

Not like he asked me out on a date. Why not?

I nodded and he picked up the receiver and

pressed a button, then spoke additional instructions as he gestured to one of a pair of matched chairs by the far window. The view offered a panorama of yet another garden I hadn't realized was part of the estate. I watched a gardener rake an area that already appeared free of leaves. I couldn't imagine what he scratched up.

After he hung up the house phone, Simon came to stand beside me. I turned to him and tried not to stare into his deep, expressive eyes with the long dark lashes.

I spoke first. "Hedged, trimmed, bordered, manicured, organized, well-planned, color-coordinated, neat, tidy, and so very English. Just the way I like them. Nothing wild, overgrown, disobedient, or out of place."

Maybe I hadn't thrown out everything about the old Alice.

He laughed, somewhat less than aloud, but seemed amused. "Not entirely the unexpected, is it?"

"Well, I can excuse my unimaginative attitude and preference for orderly arrangement by acknowledging that the unexpected lies in the sumptuous beauty of each individual flower. Despite our best efforts, Mother Nature is in charge."

Simon pointed to the chair, and sat down only after I did. "Is that how you view the world?"

My eyebrows shot up. "No one has ever asked me that before."

"Here's your chance." He raised one eyebrow.

A tad bit dumbfounded, I sank back against the cushions and waited for my thoughts to reveal themselves. "I think each of us has something inside us that needs to come out. Not just by communicating our emotions, although that's important. It's something we're born with, and it can be nurtured or suppressed."

"Like what?"

"It could be some aspect of our personality, something that drives us toward our goals. Or it could be a particular talent, a natural gift we can't help sharing with others, even if they don't appreciate it."

"We know what can happen when any spark of brilliance is suppressed," said Simon in a deep, melodic voice. "Or at minimum when one receives no nurturing."

I sighed. "Sometimes the spark fades."

"Then Mother Nature is still in charge, even when she works against you." He stood up and walked over to his desk, his back to me. "And is there no remedy to revive what has withered away?"

"You sound hopeless."

Simon rifled through some papers lying in the center of his desk and turned around. "Isn't that what you meant to say?"

"Not exactly. I think it's our... responsibility, our duty, to look for ways to rekindle that spark. It's not dead, only faded."

The maid brought in a tray and set it on the tea table in front of our chairs, then left the room. After

Simon sat down again, he poured my cup first, inquired if I wanted milk or lemon, and handed me the cup and saucer. I remembered reading several years ago, before I planned our trip to Scotland (the one Dwight and I never took), about not sticking out your pinkie when you drank tea, so I balanced the handle between my thumb and index finger, with my other fingers tucked below for support.

"You drink tea just like an Englishwoman," Simon said as he loaded a small plate with sandwiches and scones.

"I'm glad my sketchy education has finally paid off." My tone was smirky, then softer, maybe a trifle sadder. "Thank you for noticing."

He sat mute for a moment. "Didn't anyone appreciate your talent?"

"What talent? It's not like I drink hot tea every day." I shrugged, then munched on a cucumber sandwich.

"For poetry. You do seem to have a proficient flair for it."

"Half a spark, a long time ago. But eventually there was no point in pursuing it." I brushed a few crumbs from my lap. "What about you? If you don't mind my asking, what's keeping you from writing?"

Silence.

I squirmed, worried I had offended him. "And please don't think I'm prying. I simply meant—"

"Alas, the embers have gone cold." He shook his head. "I can't come up with a single idea that's worth a farthing."

"Then write about that."

"About...what?"

"If the fire is dwindled, but you're still searching, then you must believe something is out there, or else you're thirsty. Thirst is also a craving or a yearning. What we're missing, what we can't quite grasp, grows and grows until it's what we absolutely burn for, doesn't it?"

Simon twisted in his chair to stare out the window, but didn't seem to observe the worker in the garden. "You mean write about what I don't have or don't even know yet?"

"Kind of like an artist's negative space. You perceive and comprehend the image by what isn't there."

His gaze shifted to me and drilled into my eyes. "Yearning for the unknown."

Somehow I couldn't look away. But after a moment I tilted my head to one side. "Use your loss of words, Simon. You already recognize the burning passion. That's half the battle." I pointed to his desk. "You have paper and pen ready, don't you? Just go jot something down, as an exercise. It's not a performance, so loosen your bowstrings and see how it feels."

Simon leaned forward and squirmed, but didn't rise.

I took another chance to confront him, and maybe help him find his way back to writing. "No one has any expectations. You're free to seek for the spark to your heart's content."

He stood up and crossed to his desk, then sat down once more where I first had found him. He hesitated, and I wondered whether to prod him yet again. In less than a minute he picked up his pen and set to scribbling on the page.

Placing my tea cup on the tray, I rose from the overstuffed chair with as little noise as possible, with the intention to sneak out and leave him to his muse. I didn't get halfway across the room before he spoke, without looking up.

"Don't go, not yet," he said in a monotone.

"Oh, well... but if you're back to work, I'll just—"

"If I'm to continue writing," he said, "I need you to stay."

Our eyes met and I retreated to my chair by the window. The room grew quiet except for the scratching of his pen on the paper. I tried to relax and not be a distraction, but I couldn't get comfortable. Something bothered me and I couldn't quite put my finger on it... until it dawned on me.

With all this consuming chitchat about fire and sparks and yearning and burning, and now watching Simon write with enthusiasm, I had just lit a fuse. And the gunpowder would be joining us very soon.

CHAPTER TWENTY-EIGHT
The Big Baby

Before long, I envied Simon his fluidity in writing. Why couldn't I become my own muse? At the rate I was going, what was one more customer, even if it would be myself?

The problem was, how could I interrupt Simon to ask him for pen and paper? When he sat with his eyes closed, he was sorting verbal images. I knew how that worked. The words came dancing down the road and you picked the ones that fit together, letting the others drift by. Some phrases might whirl around again later for a second chance, if the music still played.

When Simon wrote, the ink flowed from his pen like wild horses through the split open gate of a corral. I hadn't felt a stirring like that in almost a decade, but my horses now pawed the ground inside me. Well, maybe not horses yet, but a horse. Definitely one horse getting restless.

I sat up straight and waited for an opening. After what seemed like enough time to chisel a limerick into granite, Simon stacked his papers. I stood up and cleared my throat.

"Oh, there you are," he said. "I forgot you were

here."

"No, I've been—"

"Of course. You've stayed the entire time. I would have noticed if you had left." He tilted his head and smiled at me. "Thanks to you, I can't remember the last occasion when I so completely immersed myself in writing. Lost track of the hour and the place."

"How did it feel?"

His expression turned quizzical. "Like moving my muscles after sitting for a long while. A bit creaky and achy at first, but then enjoying the stretch, working out the soreness."

"That can lay the groundwork for your next poem."

He laughed out loud—the first time I'd heard him at such a volume—and lighthearted, too. Our eyes connected again, and in that moment the tenderness was all but written on both our faces. I inhaled, ready to congratulate him, when Oliver burst into the room.

"It's all set! Cook has a scrumptious menu planned, and May is coming tomorrow with Georgie, and her parents will arrive in time for lunch, too."

His words spilled out like lit firecrackers. "Perhaps we should invite the neighbors, only the ones with titles, the aristocracy, you know, to sweeten the pot. Isn't that what you said yesterday? I'll tell Cook to increase the number." He blinked. "Has anyone learned when Father will return?"

Was he on something? If he were, I never saw

a trigger, so maybe Doug would understand and I could keep my job.

Oliver charged toward me, grabbed both my hands, and danced around me like ten lords a-leaping. "We'll have a grand time together, then I can show her the estate I've bought—"

"What?" Gobsmacked yet again. My body stiffened and I shook my hands free. "You bought a house already? You haven't even looked at anything. Mr. Chandler only—"

"I rang up Mickey to find out which one you liked best, then instructed him to offer a contract."

"What does it matter which one I like?" I raised my voice. "I'm not living in it."

"We'll find out soon if they accept my offer. Then you can choose the furniture." He linked his arm through mine and gave me a broad smile. "Just wait 'til you meet Georgie. You'll fall in love with him straight off. He takes after his father, you know."

I didn't smell liquor on his breath. Maybe he was just excited. Or deaf. Or crazy.

Over my shoulder, he winked at Simon. I could only imagine the scowl on Simon's face.

"Is that sandwiches you have there? Great. I'm famished." Oliver whirled me around as he scampered across the room. "Would you ring for more tea?"

When I faced Simon, he wouldn't even glance at me. Discomfort had displaced tenderness, as if he expected something unpleasant. He picked up the receiver and pressed the button.

"Toys!" Oliver sputtered through a mouthful of scone with lemon curd and clotted cream. "We have to purchase new toys for Georgie. What time is it?"

My watch was still set on Texas time. I glanced at the clock on the mantel. "Half past five." Might as well try to sound like a native, even temporarily.

"Alice, find us a toy store and we'll get on with it." Oliver finished off his scone and picked up a cucumber sandwich. "We shall return in time for dinner."

I sighed, hoping it wouldn't be like our excursion to the western wear shop. How wrong could you go with toys? I was about to find out.

After jumping up, refreshed but not waiting for fresh tea, Oliver announced he would get the chauffeur to meet us out in front in fifteen minutes. "Simon, by chance do you have any puppies? Or maybe we can hire a Shetland pony." He scooted out of the library.

Silence ensued.

Long enough, I decided. I turned around. "Simon?"

"The Entertainer," he said.

"Yes, Oliver's always on the job, isn't he?" One second later, I blushed, deep scarlet, I knew even without a mirror.

Simon waved a hand in front of his face. "No, what I meant was, The Entertainer is a toy shop. It's next to my favorite bookstore." His turn to sigh. "The chauffeur will know how to get there."

I crossed the room and stopped in front of his desk. He still wouldn't look me in the face, keeping his gaze lowered, fixed on his stack of books.

"Simon, I expect…"—sheesh, what right did I have to expect anything?—"we'll find time for another session soon, and when we do, I'd like a pen and paper, too."

His head shot up. Although his expression struggled against discouragement, his mouth twitched into half a smile. "I was hoping you'd say that."

"Hope is a good thing to have."

Our eyes locked and I got the feeling we both left other words unspoken, until he said. "Alice, I—"

"ALICE!" roared Oliver's voice from the hallway.

"Gotta run," I said. "But my horse is finally talkin'."

Simon frowned. "Sorry, I don't understand."

"I'll explain later." I dashed from the room.

If I was a fool, I didn't care.

What did I mean "if"—wasn't it obvious by now?

CHAPTER TWENTY-NINE

The Dictator

The trip to the toy shop lasted twenty minutes, and during that time, Oliver couldn't sit still in the back of the limo. He fidgeted, asked me questions about what toys I had bought for Nathan, and fretted about meeting his son again in the morning.

"What if he doesn't like me?" he whined.

"What's not to like?" I tried to sound comforting, but his constant patter had worn me out. "Be yourself." Questionable advice, perhaps.

I continued with what I hoped was wisdom he would find useful and then heed it. "You can't just suffocate him with fancy gifts and expect him suddenly to be in a relationship with you. You have to take your time." I mustered as much patience as I could and hoped it came through my voice. "Let him come to you. Sit on the grass and play with something to attract his attention. Eventually, he'll wander over and join in."

"Would that work with you?" Oliver smirked, as he clutched my hand and raised it to his lips.

I snatched it away. "Not without the expensive gifts first."

Unlike Simon, he roared and then acted more relaxed.

The toy store boasted few customers at first, until the word got around that Oliver Goodnight was shopping there. In less than ten minutes, the place was packed with howling fans, which he seemed to enjoy. Jet lag had taken its toll on me, however, and I searched for an escape. Ah, the bookstore next door.

The Raven's Nest looked like Charles Dickens had built it. Or perhaps Chaucer. The dimly-lit space was crammed with sloping bookshelves which were crammed with books. So far, I was the only shopper. After some searching, I located the poetry section but recognized nothing and no one. I stifled a yawn.

A bespectacled clerk appeared at my elbow. "May I be of assistance, madam?" he said.

"I hope so. I'm looking for any book of poetry by Simon Knightley. Whatever you have will do."

At the sound of my voice, another customer came around the end of the row of shelves. With no small degree of surprise, I found Miss Entwhistle staring at me. Glaring would be a more accurate description.

"Oh, good evening," I said.

She nodded, but didn't speak for a moment. Then she said in a frosty monotone, "Mrs. Morehead, I've been instructed to offer my services to you, should you require them."

What had I done? She made it sound like I had volunteered her as a target for the bomb squad. Truly, she would give that old warped Mrs. Danvers a run for her money.

"That was Simon's idea, I'm sure," I said with haste, "and you're very kind to make yourself available, but right now I can't envision what I might—"

As quickly as she had come into view, she disappeared. I shook my head in disbelief, resolved to catch that haughty English fly with genuine Texas honey.

The clerk at my elbow cleared his throat. "This way, madam."

I ended up selecting two slim volumes, but then discovered I had no pounds to pay for them. When I offered to come back in the morning, the clerk inquired if I knew the Poet Laureate personally, since he had overheard me mention Simon's name.

"As a matter of fact, I'm a guest at Ramsden Grove."

"In that case, allow me to wrap them up for you. The family keeps an account here, and I'll simply add these to their bill."

Before I could object, he tottered off and returned moments later with them encased in brown paper and tied with a string. Exactly the way Julie Andrews would have sung about them.

I turned to leave, but just as I reached the door, a young man burst through it. "Are you Alice?"

Tucking the package in my purse, I nodded.

He waved his arm as if directing traffic. "Come quick. Oliver needs you straight away."

Oh, no, I let him out of my sight, he'd gotten hurt

or into some kind of trouble. The smugglers! Doug will never forgive me. Had anyone called the police or an ambulance? Maybe the fire department? I didn't hear sirens, but perhaps the English were too civilized to let them blare through their neighborhoods.

We raced back to the toy store and I found Oliver at the cashier counter, fussing over a mound of purchases as tall as he was. An army of clerks held the crowd of admirers at bay, while Oliver sorted the packages into two piles and then stood back to assess his choices.

"Alice!" he hollered. "You've got to help me. I can't decide which of these Georgie will want. Maybe I should just purchase all of them."

The crowd cheered, and the cashier shook open a large shopping bag.

"Please wait a minute," I told her. Then I stood next to Oliver and shuffled the items like dealing cards. "Too big, too many small parts, too old, too babyish, too scary."

"But wait!" he shrieked. "That's not enough stuff. How will he know—"

I put my hand on his arm. "That you love him?"

With as solemn an expression as I'd ever seen on his face, Oliver nodded. His deep blue eyes teared up.

"Not because of any of this... stuff. He'll know when you spend time with him. You'll show him you want to be with him."

"All right, but he'll need a cape to go with the sword. And maybe some boots. You know, hero apparel. Little boys like to dress the part."

Big boys, too.

He didn't give in easily, but when we finished arguing he ended up with a stuffed animal sheepdog who was a popular cartoon character, a small soccer ball, and a plastic sword which needed batteries to light it up.

In the back of the limo riding home, still he worried. "It's not nearly e—"

"Oliver! It's enough." I waited. "Now let's enjoy a nice dinner with Simon and get a good night's sleep."

He winked at me.

I smacked his arm and scooted over, then placed the packages from the toy store between us. I needed all the protection I could get, and not just from Oliver.

CHAPTER THIRTY
The Talking Pony

Although my night wasn't entirely restful, I needn't have worried Oliver would sneak into bed with me again. When I awoke before dawn the next morning in the birdcage, I was the only one under the covers and found no indication anyone else had been there. No guides or tour groups observed my stretching and yawning.

After I showered and dressed for breakfast, I headed downstairs just in time to find Oliver tiptoeing upstairs, shoes in his hands, still wearing the same outfit from last night. I stopped midway down and waited for him to look up and realize he was caught red-handed.

"Feeling better?" I said, with an arch of my eyebrow.

"Alice!" He dropped one shoe. "You startled me."

I crossed my arms and waited, giving him what I hoped was a sardonic smile. After a moment, I moved sideways and tried to pass him.

He reached for my arm. "Let me explain."

"No explanation needed. You're over twenty-one and I'm not your mother." I continued my descent. Or your girlfriend, I reminded myself.

"But wait, Alice... I only went back to May's after dinner to see Georgie. I thought I might read him a story before he went to bed."

"And you were surprised to discover his bedtime was actually hours before you arrived."

He grinned. "How did you know?"

As I whirled around, a blank stare was my answer.

His cheerfulness faded to something this side of melancholy, although I recognized it as fake. "And besides, you won't let me in the birdcage with you, and I can't sleep very well here all alone, so when May—she's quite young, just over twenty, and beautiful, you know, red hair, green eyes—May and I got to talking by ourselves, well, we began laughing and joking about old times, and the next thing I knew, we were—"

"Enough!" Like a traffic cop, I held up my hand, palm out. "Say no more."

"Where are you off to now?"

"Until breakfast is ready, you may find me in the library." I arched my eyebrows at him and spoke in a slow distinct voice as I held my brown paper package aloft. "I bought some books last night at The Raven's Nest and I'd like to read them." No point in discussing the purchase arrangement with him, because I had already decided to bring it up with Simon later.

"Well, you should know your onions, if anyone does." He picked up the shoe he had dropped, then yawned, mouth wide as a hippo's. "God, I'm knackered. I'd give a tenner for a whole night's sleep. What time is it?"

"Six forty-five."

"Guess I'll have to settle for a brief kip. Then we'll prepare for our visitors. Can't afford a bloody shambles now, can we?"

Shrugging, I descended to the lower floor and stopped. Turn right to the library, left to the lounge. Or is it the opposite? After one wrong hook and a U-turn, I found the library. My sense of direction was improving, but jet lag was still my enemy.

The room was darkened, so I fumbled for the light switch and then settled into the big soft chair by the window. After unwrapping the paper, I selected the book on the top and began at the beginning. Simon's use of language enchanted me and I found myself re-reading certain passages while holding my breath.

The room felt cold, so I borrowed a blanket from a basket near the unlit fireplace, wrapped up like a wandering gypsy, and plunged back into the comfortable depth of the chair. I shuffled until I could hold the book with only my hands exposed, relishing the warmth. How could a thin volume of poems feel so heavy?

The next thing I knew, Simon was staring into my bleary eyes, a sheepish smile creeping across his face. "Frightfully boring, is it?"

I bolted upright and the books fell to the floor. As I leaned forward, so did Simon, and the tops of our foreheads collided. I backed up and he retrieved both volumes.

As if he'd never seen them before, he studied them for a moment. "Where did you get these?"

"At The Raven's Nest. I need to pay you for them. The clerk said—"

"I would have given you a full set." Simon grimaced. "I have a box in the closet, the remainders I rescued before their covers were torn off."

"Uh, how long have you been in here?" I hoped I hadn't drooled during my nap.

"I just came in to announce breakfast." He arose from his seat on the ottoman. "Oliver is waiting for you."

"Oh, well..." I struggled to extricate myself from the wool blanket, while Simon took my hand to help me stand erect. "I was hoping we would... have some time to ourselves again this morning. I need to get my feet wet, too."

His expression turned serious as his dark brown eyes gazed into mine. "Perhaps after breakfast."

I nodded, then stood up and padded out of the room.

* * *

It wasn't meant to be, my time with Simon in his library, going over his magical phrases, not that morning. Oliver insisted we prepare the toys on the lawn and await Georgie's arrival. Earlier, he had telephoned someone in the village to hire a pony, and we watched as the groom unloaded a tame-looking Shetland with a long flaxen tail and bushy mane.

" 'E bites a bit, 'e does," said the groom. "But only if you stand right in front o' him."

Great. That should send Georgie, along with May, screaming back to their house.

I took the toy animal, the soccer ball, and the sword from their cartons and laid them on the quilt Miss Entwhistle had spread on the lawn. While I inserted batteries into the sword's hilt, Oliver tossed the soccer ball into the air and fretted. "What if he doesn't want to stay? How are we going to get on? Oh, Alice, what if I fail? You have to help me, tell me what I'm doing wrong."

I smirked at him. "Don't get your knickers in a twist, now will ya? Remember what I said. Just be yourself—your *best* self—and take it slow."

"You're the only one I can count on to tell me the absolute truth." Oliver tossed the ball to me and I batted it back to him. He laughed and I thought he might be all right.

He was, until their car pulled round the corner. As May and Georgie descended from the limo, Oliver sucked in his breath and turned to stare at me, stark terror in his blue eyes.

I handed him the toy sheepdog and said, "Sit down and play with it."

"How?" He sank onto the quilt, like a robot following commands.

"Make it walk, then hop. Play hide-and-seek with

it." I was running out of ideas. "Imitate its voice on TV."

"The Beeb."

"Whatever. Just try to sound like the character and call Georgie's name."

That last bit worked, got the child's attention, and drew him almost to the edge of the quilt, close enough for me to see his features and determine how much he resembled Oliver. His father's same wide grin and strawberry blond hair ruffled by the breeze, his mother's perfect ivory skin. He appeared to be a darling mixture of both parents, and I could see in an instant why Oliver desired more time with him.

Under a tree, I stood behind Oliver and off to the right. I didn't move or make any noise, so Georgie didn't notice me at first. As he inched forward to the edge of the quilt, ready to join Oliver's game of tickle the doggie, Georgie stopped in his tracks and looked up at me.

"Alice, come sit with us," said Oliver in the sheepdog's voice. "Look, Georgie, it's Alice, come to play with us."

Georgie's sweet little face peered up into mine. "Ha-whoa, Ahwiss," he cooed.

It warmed my heart and reminded me of what I had missed out on, all these years. Not to be, no matter how much I longed for one of my own.

I sat down on the edge of the quilt. With a sigh, I fantasized I cuddled him in my arms, gazing into his deep brown eyes—

His WHAT?

I had passed biology and physiology with flying colors and knew my basics in genetics. If Oliver had blue eyes, and May's were green...

Oh, how would I ever tell Oliver the truth?

CHAPTER THIRTY-ONE

The Stalking Horse

I couldn't very well break the wretched news to Oliver while he waited to play with Georgie. Maybe I wouldn't say anything at all. We should just finish our business and head back across The Pond.

Let someone else be the Naysayer or the Voice of Doom. My task did not include investigating the legitimacy or assigning the batting order for heir to the title and the estate. Let the unfortunate onus fall on... whom?

Oliver and his brother didn't need any further grounds for sibling head-butting. May wasn't likely to come forward and reverse her son's fortune.

Perhaps old man Knightley and his pregnant bride would take the bull by the horns; after all, she had the most to lose. I put my money on the swelling abdomen of the latest Mrs. Knightley.

Georgie crossed over toward Oliver and patted the stuffed sheepdog. After a few moments he sat down and Oliver "walked" the dog into the boy's lap. He "talked" to Georgie in the dog character voice, and soon all three were rolling around on the quilt, two of them laughing and chattering. I couldn't help smiling and wishing I could join them.

As I watched them, I felt someone's eyes on me. When I looked up, May had fastened her gaze on my face. Rather than let her intimidate me, I decided to approach her and find out what I could about... well, what would be most helpful to Oliver, to get his messy toothpaste back in the tube, so we could return to Austin and finish out his contract.

She beat me to it, staked out her claim on the quilt, and spoke first. "You must be the so-called Go-To Girl?"

I smiled and stuck out my hand. At a snail's pace, she reached for mine and, with a limp grip, shook it once.

"Oh, that's just what my family nicknamed me years ago. My real name is Alice."

From under the dog's rump, flat on his back, Oliver called out, "Alice is a wonder. You won't believe how positively smashing she is at getting things done properly."

Georgie plopped on Oliver's torso and twisted as he repeated, "Ha-whoa, Ahwiss."

May glared at Oliver, still half-hidden under the sheepdog and now Georgie. "He certainly needs all the help he can get."

Her edgy voice raised my hackles. "It's a challenge to become a father, but I'm sure he's—"

Oliver bolted upright and both the sheepdog and Georgie spilled from his chest with a squeal. After picking up the small red ball, the little boy toddled over to me with his arms outstretched. I took the ball and he collapsed in my lap. At last, my chance came to cuddle a giggling child.

Oliver swept his arm through the air. "Just imagine, May, all this could be Georgie's some day. The estate, the title, the—"

"You have to show me you're serious. Being a parent is time-consuming."

He frowned. "But you're off to make another movie in, what is it? Two weeks? Aren't you the pot calling the kettle black?"

"My parents tend to George when I'm gone. They bring him round the set to visit, when shooting is slow."

"You're not being fair. Besides, Alice has that all solved. Just you wait until you hear our plans. "

"That's all it ever is with you, plans! When have you ever followed through?"

"This time will be different."

"And it will cost you plenty."

The testiness in the air escalated, as they mauled each other with verbal criticisms. I rolled to my knees, took the child by the hand, and stood up. "Let's go see the pony over there. He looks like he wants a friend. Could you be his friend?"

He followed along as if he'd known and trusted me all his short life. I had to protect him from getting nipped if he stood in front of the pony, which he wasn't inclined to do anyway. I picked him up to ask if he wanted to ride the pony, and as I glanced across the saddle horn, another familiar figure appeared on the far side of the lawn, walking toward us.

It was a safe bet Simon would add to Oliver's tension, but maybe the little dogs following him would help diffuse it. Puppies were magic, weren't they?

Georgie wanted to sit but not ride, and he demanded "Ahwiss" stand next to him and hold his hand. Like father, like son. Except he wasn't. By the time Simon appeared opposite me, Oliver had come from behind and took the reins from the pony's owner.

I tore my eyes away from Simon's and turned around. "Just stay here," I said to Oliver. "Georgie only wants to sit, but not ride. Okay?"

Oliver seemed distracted as he twisted the reins and shifted his weight from foot to foot. "Talk to her, won't you, Alice? You can reason with her. She's so bloody demanding, the flaming witch."

I clapped my hand over his mouth and jerked my head toward Georgie.

"Oh. Right. Sorry," he said through my fingers.

The pony stomped one hoof and tried to nip the yapping dogs circling through his legs. Georgie squealed in delight.

"Hold on, Georgie," I said over my shoulder. "I'll be right back."

I approached May with an air of being in charge, careful not to appear threatening. She regarded me with an intense but cool expression, then crossed her arms as I drew near.

"May, I'm here to help you and Oliver through

208 ◆ Cynthia J Stone

whatever misunderstanding has caused this quarrel. Surely you can both agree to do what's best for Georgie."

"And how many children do you have, if I might be so bold as to inquire?" Her voice shot poison darts straight into my heart. "Your husband left you, didn't he?"

Did Oliver tell the flaming witch everything about me? Staggered for a moment, I gave myself time to recover.

"That's not the point right now, is it?" I stared at her with as much kindness as I could muster, imagining she was an angry child on the playground. "What's got you so furious with Oliver? We all know he's a high-flying spoiled brat who has to have responsibility explained to him more than once, but I get the feeling you haven't said what's really on your mind."

"I... I just don't want to be taken for granted, not by the bleedin' aristocracy, not by anyone. My son will have a better place in the world with the title he has coming to him. But his father is going to pay through his arse for him. Oliver will have to cough it up big if he wants his boy."

Now she was a lonely angry child on the playground, behaving that way because no one wanted to play with her. A circular conundrum.

"So you want to control Oliver by placing demands on his schedule, which affects his career and—"

"That's right, Miss Hoity-Toity assistant. You

trot on back and tell your boss what I said."

Without blinking, I gave her a grim smile. "Let me be sure I understand you correctly. You said the boy's father would have 'to pay through his arse' in order to be granted custody. By father, did you mean Oliver?"

Her eyes widened as if I had turned zombie, ready to stab her. She wasn't far from wrong.

"Or perhaps you meant someone else?"

"You wouldn't dare—"

"We've just met." If my voice grew any sweeter, I'd need a shot of insulin. "You have no way of knowing what I'd dare, now do you?"

"What is it you want?" Her tone was resigned.

"I want you to be reasonable. Share custody with Oliver, if that arrangement comes to pass. Then work out a mutually convenient schedule that benefits Georgie, which means one of you isn't working when the other one is."

"Is Oliver buying that mansion for you to live there with Georgie? Because I had thought we... we might—"

May was still in love with him and jealous of me. A first, if I ever recognized one. "Perhaps Oliver will acquire the other property for purposes of Georgie's safety and security, but I live in Texas. That's my home and always will be."

Feeling a twinge of pity for May, I glanced toward the pony. Oliver stared at us, and when I waved him over, he tossed the reins to Simon. He was by our side in less than two seconds, eagerness on his face.

While May explained her side of things, and sounded reasonable, if not lovesick, I turned my back to the couple and watched as Simon lifted Georgie from the saddle. The puppies clamored over him the moment Simon set him down on the grass. Their airy chuckles carried joy to my ears and I grinned.

The child stood up and sloshed his way through the puppy puddle, little furry balls leaping up like waves. My grin faded when May and Oliver raised their voices. I thought they had been ready to declare undying love and here they were arguing about baby furniture and boarding school. My name floated in and out of their bellowing match. I took about five steps toward Georgie and waited for him to come to me.

The argument escalated to shouting. I wanted to scoop up Georgie, get on the pony, and ride away. Simon seemed at leisure, above the fracas, as he strolled behind the child, keeping tabs on the puppies.

The next thing I knew, Oliver grabbed me by the arm, swung me around until our bodies all but slammed together, and kissed me like there was no tomorrow. I couldn't breath and tried to push him away.

"C'mon, Alice," he whispered. "She's watching. Do it like you did for the cameras."

So that was it. He was using me to get to May. I

felt like slapping him.

But I didn't get the chance. Simon yanked us apart and shoved Oliver backwards until he tripped and landed on his backside. When he struggled to his feet, Simon swung his fist at him, catching him on the edge of his eye socket and knocking him down again.

May burst into tears, then Georgie screamed and came running toward "Ahwiss." I gathered him up and pressed his crying face into my neck. "There, there," I said. "It's all right. No one will hurt you. I'm right here."

I didn't know which brother to look at first. They were both red-faced and panting.

After wiping her eyes, May came forward to claim her son. "This is all your fault," she said to me in hateful tones, as I transferred Georgie to her arms. "They're both in love with you."

Gobsmacked. And. Then. Some.

CHAPTER THIRTY-TWO
The In-Laws

Before anyone could say another word, a light blue limo pulled around the corner and a frumpy older couple I took to be May's parents climbed out of the back seat. Each of us froze where we stood.

"Are we in time for luncheon?" the woman called in a loud tinny voice. "I do hope we haven't missed anything."

She took her husband's arm and waddled toward us like an overburdened parade mistress whose dress was too long. As they drew closer, I determined they weren't as old as I first thought, and it had nothing to do with their bright colors or taste in clothing.

Mrs. Farnsworth looked to be about six months pregnant. If I read the expression on Simon's face accurately, he believed the extra girth came from overdosing on scones or Bombay Sapphire gin and not because May would be getting a sibling in a few months.

I turned to Oliver, who had stayed put where he fell on the grass, hand held over the left side of his face. He winced as I caught his good eye and motioned him to stand up and greet them. His expression begged for sympathy. At that moment, I had none. In fact, I wished I had been the one to give him the blooming shiner.

"Halloo, everyone," Mrs. Farnsworth grinned and stuck out her hand to Simon, who stood nearest. Mr. Farnsworth waited behind her, expressionless except for what I deciphered as a sincere wish to be swallowed whole in a sudden earthquake.

Simon might as well have been paralyzed, because I had to nudge him in the arm before he took her hand. He mumbled his name, and then Mrs. Farnsworth turned to me.

"You must be Miss Entwhistle," she beamed as her gaze swept the view behind me. "My goodness, but you've done such exceptional work of taking care of these charming young men. What a humongous mansion. You must be exhausted, tending to every little detail for the estate. We should hire someone with your talents for our place."

Oliver scrambled to his feet and inserted himself between us. "This is Miss Morehead, my personal assistant. Miss Entwhistle works for *him*." He pointed to Simon, and then nodded to Mr. Farnsworth. "Can't get along without the ladies, now can we, sir?"

Mr. Farnsworth grunted and glanced back toward the car he had arrived in moments ago.

Oliver chattered on. "I'm dreadfully sorry Father isn't here to greet you. His Lordship"—extra emphasis on the title—"sends his apologies from the south of France, where he is still on holiday. He and his

wife were so looking forward to making your ac-
quaintance and spending time with his grandson."

While Oliver blathered on with his not-even-half-
truths, Simon made moves to corral the puppies and
return them to their pen. I bent down to help him
and scooped up one, arching my neck as the little
dickens tried to lick my face.

"Ahwiss!" called Georgie. "I want to pway again."
He squirmed until May slid him down her leg, and
then he toddled over to me. Together we petted the
puppy I held. Georgie squealed when his face got
licked.

As I looked up, Simon was heading away from
the group, leading the rest of the puppies toward the
kennel. I set the dog on the lawn and took Georgie's
hand. "Let's help Simon put the puppies in their bed.
It's time for their nap."

"I don't want to wet them go," he whined.

"You can play with them again after their nap.
Puppies get tired, and they need to rest so they grow
up big and strong. Just like little boys." I took a few
short steps to see if he and the dog would follow
along. They did.

"Simon," I called as the child and I ambled across
the lawn, skirting the playful pup.

He stopped but didn't turn around.

When I caught up to him, I put my hand on
Simon's arm. "Do you mind if I make a suggestion?"

Without looking at me, he nodded once with a
stiff jerking motion.

"Please don't take this as criticism. I realize you must consider this an invasion of the howling peasants from outer space, but things will go easier for all concerned if you play the gracious host. The sooner Oliver gets what he wants, the sooner they will leave and we can go back to our poetry."

I thought perhaps that bribe would help convince him to visualize the desired end game.

He stared at me, fire in his rich dark eyes. "Why does Oliver always get what he wants?" With that he turned and stalked away. He whistled once, and the puppy wiggled away from Georgie, yipping as he scampered to catch up.

Georgie pulled on my hand and said, "Pony again."

As I watched Simon retreat, I knew May was wrong, dead wrong. No one was in love with me, not now, not ever. And I'd be a fool to believe anyone was.

But did Simon feel that way, too?

CHAPTER THIRTY-THREE

The Rule of Thumb

For the life of me, I couldn't figure out how May came to be so beautiful. She looked nothing like either parent, who were plain as day-old dishwater. I had plenty of opportunity to study their faces as we sat through a fancy luncheon in the formal dining room.

At least that's what I would have called the space. Likely, there was another room even fancier where we would eat dinner later.

Half of our group of six adults chattered non-stop, while Simon and I pushed food around our plates and feigned interest in whatever topic made Mrs. Farnsworth howl with laughter. Oliver seemed to enjoy eliciting a high-pitched shriek from her, if only because he knew it would get Simon's goat. Payback for the black eye, for which the butler had set an ice-pack next to Oliver's plate.

After a while, I visualized her hollering directions on the firehouse radio, pushing her argument for equipment and resources at the Birmingham town council meeting, and corralling all the neighbors for a fundraising picnic. At one point, I thought the footman might drop his tray of veal chops as he stood next to her, waiting for her to stop cackling and take the serving fork.

Mrs. Farnsworth made no effort to tone herself down, something her huband must have wished for daily, if not hourly, durng the last twenty-five years. He sat in abject silence, eating everything on his plate as if it were his last meal. Perhaps she blathered so much because he provided no balance to their conversation.

She didn't ignore him altogether; rather she would add a phrase to the end of her sentence— "Isn't that right, Mr. Eff?"—then go right on talking because she knew from experience he wouldn't bother to answer.

At one time, the local magistrate would have allowed Mr. Eff to beat his wife into silence with a small cane no bigger in diameter than his thumb. Oh, horrid thought. But, alas, the husband and wife were born a century too late.

I wondered if Mr. Eff had discovered other ways to amuse himself, or simply decided to endure marriage to the person his wife had become. Lest I was unfair, maybe her outgoing manner was her method of survival in the face of disinterest and perhaps disdain. I concluded their behavior couldn't compare to Dwight's and mine, because, well... how can anyone see inside another couple's marriage with any degree of accuracy, no matter how well you know them?

And if she wanted to thumb her nose at the aristocracy... then who was I to object? No law said she had to tone herself down. Maybe what we saw was a woman with guts enough to be the authentic Mrs. Farnsworth, a woman who was comfortable in her own skin, even when she got under other people's. She probably would have been all the more annoying if she sported false genteel manners.

Georgie had insisted on sitting in his high chair only if it were placed next to me, so when the adult conversation turned unintelligible, I had a dinner companion to keep me occupied. He still ate with his fingers, something I found unusual in a three-year-old, but I encouraged him to quit sucking his thumb and finish his green beans along with his strawberries. He held one up for me to eat.

"Gobble, gobble," I said to his peals of giggles. I waited until he slipped it into his mouth, like a game of cat-and-mouse.

When I glanced across the table, I found Simon gazing at us, an absent-minded half-smile on his face. After a moment, our eyes met, and I could swear he blushed.

From the other end of the table, Oliver called, "Georgie, what's my name?"

Georgie wrinkled his nose at him, but kept silent, as did all the adults. For the first time, the entire room went utterly quiet.

"Come on, my little chap, say it," Oliver pleaded.

"Ah-wiss!" Georgie looked pleased with himself.

"No, say my name, like Nathan does. Say Oh-Oh."

Everyone at the table turned to stare at Georgie as if he would recite the Gettysburg Address at any second. Instead he chose that moment to toot, and not just a minor pop, but a drawn-out honker of a toot, like a channel tugboat.

I'm sure my face went pale, and I refused to look at anyone else's.

"Ah, well," Oliver said with a chortle, "I've been called worse."

Mrs. Farnsworth screeched, "He comes by that talent naturally, don't he, Mr. Eff?" She jerked her thumb at her husband, but spoke to Oliver. "He should know perfectly well, all right."

I was certain at least two of us would testify in Mr. Eff's defense, should he take a thumb-sized cane to his wife's back. We might even help him by holding her down.

Dessert was served, a crisp, lightly browned creme brûlée, but I was too tense to enjoy it. I couldn't tell if May were warming up to the idea of letting Oliver have joint custody. By hook or by crook, I'd have to address the question of the house Oliver wanted to buy, since I wouldn't be living there. Then the larger problem of the smugglers loomed in my mind's eye, and I knew from just this brief exposure to Georgie that I'd never let them get their ugly paws on him without a fight to the death. And I couldn't forget my boss Doug and his expectations for our immediate return.

These were external concerns, however, and I had others on the inside, such as my truths, clamoring to get out. Craving a turn at writing poetry, I wondered if my horse would talk to me in the quiet of Simon's library.

And Simon. He had become a bit of a mystery to me. And I had to admit I felt drawn to him, but why? We weren't in an equal league on any level, but somehow we spoke the same language. Language we both loved: poetry. But our depth of feeling for it shouldn't be confused with feelings for each other. Unless we were both fools.

Before we finished our desserts, Oliver stood up and held out his hand to Mrs. Farnsworth. "How about a tour of the place?"

"Oh, my, I think that'd be quite lovely, but our dear little Georgie's too tired." She flashed a toothy smile in our direction. "Maybe another time, say, when your father is here to meet his grandson?"

Oliver waved his hand as if shooing a fly. "Don't worry. Miss Morehead has things well in hand." He shot me a meaningful glance. "Haven't you, Ah-wiss?"

"Of course." I rose from my seat and used my napkin to wipe Georgie's hands and face. Before I could lift him from the high chair, Simon scooted around the table and slid the tray out. Once aloft, the fatigued little boy snuggled against me and laid his head on my shoulder, with his thumb returned to its comfort zone in his mouth.

"There's a rocking chair in my library," Simon whispered.

"Perfect," I mouthed.

Mrs. Farnsworth looked disappointed, since I had deprived her of a return visit when she could meet His Lordship, but Mr. Eff was relieved. I could tell he wanted to get this business over with and return to his... whatever he did. During our entire conversation, no one had taken the trouble to ask him anything.

Oh dear, had we taken a cue from his wife?

"This way, my lovelies," Oliver said with a grand sweep of his arm.

May and her parents followed him in one direction, while Simon and I headed the opposite way. Once in the library, he fluffed the pillow on the rocking chair and dragged a footrest in front of it before I sat down. Then he took the same blanket I had used earlier and tucked it around the drowsy child. You'd have thought I had just delivered the baby.

"Thank you," I said, softer than a whisper.

Once Simon was satisfied I was comfortable and Georgie was asleep, he sat down at his desk and took up pen and paper once more.

Perfect, I thought. But...

CHAPTER THIRTY-FOUR
The Awakening

As I rocked at a gentle pace, I wondered how long Georgie would stay asleep. I didn't mind holding him for as much time as he needed, but after about fifteen minutes, my left arm tingled while it edged toward numbness.

"Hmmmmm," I murmured as I stirred in the chair.

Simon jumped up from his seat at his desk. "May I get you anything?" he whispered.

I crinkled my face and shook my head. He came around from behind the desk and tiptoed over to me, then bent down. With his palm on the crown of Georgie's head, he said in a low voice, "Are you at all uncomfortable?"

"Getting there," I mouthed, frowning. I raised my shoulders in a circular motion and tried not to disturb the slumbering child in my arms.

"Here, let me take him."

What did a bachelor in his late thirties know about cuddling unconscious toddlers? Enough, it seemed. Or at least he wasn't afraid to try.

Switching places without waking Georgie played out like a game of Twister in slow motion. First,

Simon put both hands on the back of my elbows to pull me out of the chair. Then he scooted the footrest out of the way and, standing across from me, placed one forearm against mine. Together we attempted to roll Georgie into the cradle of Simon's chest, but the conked-out child held fast to my neck. Worse, Georgie seemed to gain weight as I stood there.

Next Simon tried standing to the left of me and wrapping his left arm on the outside of the blanket. While I tipped forward, hoping gravity would separate Georgie from my chest, Simon inserted his right arm into the two inches between the child and me, ready for the transfer.

I swung the tangled bundle sideways, like a quarterback's underhand shuffle to a running back. Georgie moaned but didn't awaken.

Simon smiled, then jerked his head toward his desk. "My turn for this means your turn for that," he whispered as he sat in the rocking chair.

My turn. He intended for me to sit at the desk and write a poem. A new one, not a recycled one from years ago. But what did I have to write about? If I waited for my truths to surface, first I'd have another birthday. Then another.

What had I used to coach Simon? Negative space; write about what isn't there.

I sat down and stared at a blank sheet in the center of his desk until I was snow blind. After a moment I picked up Simon's pen, then put it down as if it were radio-active, and instead prayed for a rush of angel's wings to transport me elsewhere.

With my eyes closed, I imagined myself as a younger women, even a girl, again. What had I yearned for then? For "love" to be the answer sounded trite, but it was true. Love is a big room, however, with lots of hallways leading to it, and I was trapped in one of the outer ones.

Write about that, Alice, said the voice in my head.

I grope the walls beyond not being there and
search for the bright cleft, waiting for
the distant light to beam its welcoming grin at me
and lead me to the center of

the room where Love is.
I've visited there once before but
it was so long ago, I barely remember it. And
time was cold and scarce then, since

I couldn't put my feet up and get
comfortable enough to feel
at home. Home must be another place, farther away,
and a different encounter with

someone who will show me
how it feels to be chosen for Love.
Then I will no longer ache or spend hours groping
and searching with skinned knuckles

for I will be at the very center,
the heart of the room where Love is.
And I can stay home as long as I want, even until time
warms up and loses all its meaning.

Not bad, for a beginner. Or re-beginner. A little tweaking, moving words around a bit, and I'd be finished. The next several minutes I spent reworking a few phrases, shifting or deleting commas, and rereading in silence. When I had changed everything that struck me as awkward or incomplete, I recopied it on a clean sheet, folded it, and planned to put it under my pillow. I set the new sheet in front of me and propped my chin on the back of my hands.

Nothing else, no other yearning, came to me. Those words were enough. For now.

After a few moments, I felt eyes on me, and I glanced at Simon to find him staring at me. I gave him a shy smile and nodded. He seemed pleased, even relieved, that is, until voices in the hallway disrupted the peace and comfort of our silence.

I stood up and was about to move closer to the rocking chair when Georgie stirred, moaned, and opened his eyes. Startled, he stared up at Simon, gasped, and then let out an ear-piercing wail.

Simon bolted to his feet and thrust the blanket-wrapped child toward me. "What did I do wrong? Here, quickly, you take it!"

Before we could achieve another transfer, the library door sprang open and Mrs. Farnsworth bounded through it. "Hold on now," she called. "What are you doing to my boy?" She flounced up to Simon and snatched Georgie out of his grasp, leaving the blanket dangling over his arms. "There, there," she cooed while Georgie's bawling subsided. "Granny's right here. No need to worry. I won't let these strangers hurt you." She had to shift the boy sideways over her hip, so his leg stretched halfway across her protruding stomach. It struck me as odd to consider that bulge would soon be his aunt or uncle.

Oliver and May had followed her into the room and came to stand behind her, forming a semi-circle. Oliver wore a serious frown, and May looked bored. Mr. Eff waited in the hall, eyed closed, leaning against the wainscoting, asleep for all I could tell.

"Simon, what in bleeding hell did you do to him?" said Oliver in an accusing tone.

Simon turned pale, but before he could answer, I spoke up. "He did everything right. Georgie had a good, comfortable nap. He just woke up and found himself in a strange place, with someone he scarcely knows."

At the sound of my voice, Georgie perked up, twisted in his granny's arms, and reached for me. "Ah-wiss!" he called.

"We have to be going now." Mrs. Farnsworth whirled around and swept past Oliver and May. "We'll finish the tour another time," she said in a frosty voice as she flounced out of the room. May fell into step behind her.

Oliver glared at Simon. "Look what you did! You always ruin everything. How could you have made my son cry like this?" he snarled, then huffed out the door after them.

Simon frowned and then turned to drop the

blanket on the rocking chair. His expression said 'volcano, ready to blow.'

"You really looked like you knew what you were doing," I said. "Like you've had experience with sleeping children."

He hesitated. "Not really... but one of my friends, someone I used to see on occasion... well, she had young children and I spent a bit of time..."

Dangerously close to cracking, his voice faded into... how would he like me to phrase it? Reverie? His ship returning to the wharf?

But I knew that some memories are better left at sea. Seemed as if he had learned that lesson as well.

"ALICE!" came Oliver's voice from the hallway.

I sighed and tried not to roll my eyes before heading out the door. I passed an expressionless Miss Entwhistle on the way and gave her the slightest nod I could manage. The Texas fly-catching honey would have to wait.

CHAPTER THIRTY-FIVE
The Hot House

By the time I caught up to Oliver at the front door, he had lost his pique. We stood together and waved good-bye to the Farnsworth clan, one of us—if not both of us—hoping never to see that rowdy gang again, except for Georgie.

"Looking forward to tomorrow," Oliver called as their limos pulled away.

I struggled to suppress a loud groan. "Did you have any luck with May?" We turned to stroll toward the entrance.

"She's warming up to the idea that I should share custody with her."

"What about the issue of Georgie's security? Remember, your family has been threatened."

"I mentioned it to her, and that's one reason she's so angry. She blames me for all the mess. But she agrees there is reason for concern. It's her clot of a mum who's the problem. That cack-handed Chavette will drive me to—"

"Clean up your language around Georgie?"

He put his arm around my waist. "If you insist," he said in a teasing mood.

With my fingertips, I removed his arm like I

believed it could spread leprosy and stepped inside the front door. "It's what good fathers do," I said over my shoulder.

"When would I have learnt?" His tone turned defensive as he followed me inside. "Mine was never around much and when he was, he didn't spend his precious time chatting with me."

I whirled to face him. "Here's another lesson you might not have learned."

"I'm all ears," he grinned at me, and then winced and covered his left eye with his palm.

"You owe Simon an apology."

Lowering his hand, Oliver frowned, wrinkled his nose like he smelled something foul, and wouldn't look at me.

"Come on now, Oliver," I said in a gentle tone. "Surely you can see your outburst in the library was uncalled for. When Georgie cried and ran away from you, would you have liked it if someone spoke to you that way?"

"That's just it. May's mum, that ignorant gummy, she was too quick to criticize me when things turned pear-shaped. How would I know what to do with a kid throwing a wobbly?"

"So she came to a hasty conclusion without knowing all the facts. If you didn't care for the way she treated you, then you should be able to imagine how Simon felt, shouldn't you?"

Oliver shifted his weight from one foot to the other as he wailed, "Well... what about him? He knocked me down"—he pointed to his blackened eye—"and gave me this horrific injury. Does it require sutures? I'll be lucky if I don't go blind."

"Do you have any idea why Simon hit you?"

"I thought perhaps you could inform me." His tone changed to irritable.

I took a few moments of silence to gather my thoughts. "I cannot justify his reaction, but it had to do with your improper behavior."

"Oh, that. Why should he—"

"You can't pretend it's the same as when we were... working. Anyway, on extremely short notice, Simon went out of his way to make May and Georgie feel welcome. He brought the puppies and helped your son have a great experience, one that will entice him to return. You should be grateful."

"Maybe if he gave Georgie one of his prize-winning mutts..."

As if our roles had switched, I took him by the hand and dragged him to the library. We expected to find Simon at his work, but the person standing there was Miss Entwhistle. She perked up erect and tapped the stack of papers against the top of the desk, as if she had something to hide.

"Good afternoon," I said with a grim smile. "Would you be so kind as to inform us where Simon can be found?"

She gave me a blank stare and said nothing while her pale eyes darted to Oliver, then back to my face.

Oliver brightened up. "Well, I suppose Simon is nowhere around." He backed toward the doorway.

I clasped his hand tighter and anchored him in place. "Where is he?" I said in a firmer voice.

Oliver sighed. "You may as well answer her. She won't let go of me until you do."

Miss Entwhistle blinked. "In the greenhouse."

"Thank you." I turned to exit, tugging Oliver behind me, him bawling protests like a calf to slaughter.

Once outside on the lawn, Oliver grew more resistant. "Alice, what's the big fuss? Why is this so important to you? Simon and I have rows every other day when we occupy the same lodgings and no one seems to mind."

I turned to face him. "Apologies are important. Simon offered me a sincere one, once he discovered his mistake."

Oliver guffawed at the memory. "You mean, when he first met you and thought you were a common tart? He offered to pay you, didn't he, for services rendered?"

"His apology changed how I saw him as a person and subsequently I learned to regard him as trustworthy." With my lips pursed, I glared at him, then softened. "When I was a student at the university, one of my dearest longtime friends—or so I thought—asked me for a personal favor at some expense of time and effort to me. Gladly, I did my part right away, and she raved about it privately to me, but she lost track of my... contribution, shall we say? She let herself get distracted, and when her project didn't turn out quite perfectly, and she couldn't meet expectations, she blamed me. She lied to everyone about the whole thing, and took credit for what I had done. It ruined our friendship."

"Sounds like you didn't lose much."

"Maybe not, but the point is, I would have blown it off if she had acted like an adult by assuming responsibility for her mistreatment of me and apologized. And if she had not misled others about it. We might not have regained our close friendship, but we would have parted with a buried hatchet."

"A hatchet? How drastic." Oliver peered at me with one raised eyebrow, the one over his uninjured eye. "Are you certain you've forgiven her?"

"Both parents are tempestuous alcoholics, so she comes from a crazy family, and—"

"Who doesn't?" he scoffed.

"And that's no excuse for your behavior toward Simon. For goodness sake, he's your brother."

"Half-brother."

"Well?" I waited and tapped my foot on the grass, hoping to appear stern. "I'm pretty sure he would be mature enough to apologize to you, if he needed to." Since the memory of Oliver's inappropriate kiss still lingered, but not in a good way, I was inclined to view Simon as my defender, my handsome, wavy-haired knight in armor, shiny or otherwise.

"All right, but only because I want to get back into your good graces. I don't wish to wake up tomorrow morning and find your hatchet embedded in the middle of my skull."

The unfriendly sun had sunk behind the outlying oak trees and the evening lights came on in the greenhouse. I could discern Simon's tall silhouette as he puttered among the orchids. Was he concentrating on the blooms to get his thoughts off what had occurred?

But then, other than Oliver's outburst, what else had happened? Were those moments in his library—just the three of us—of any lasting significance? What did they represent to Simon?

If I let my mind's eye hover over that scene, what would I have beheld? The image of a happy family, celebrating togetherness and joy and peace. Had I departed from, even for a while, the cold remote hallway of my poems where I had been wandering and found the warm center of the room where Love is? Or was it an illusion?

"ALICE!" Oliver called from several paces ahead. "Come on, let's get this hatchet burial ceremony over with."

CHAPTER THIRTY-SIX

The Hot Seat

Components of Simon's greenhouse could have served as a metaphor for all of us, if I'd been inclined to write another poem.

With good reason, he was steamed at Oliver enough to vaporize him for his unkind outburst, no matter how much of it might be factual. Given Oliver's penchant for exaggeration, I couldn't imagine how much of it might be, and in truth, didn't want to.

Oliver played the part of a delicate orchid, needing special attention, with just the right setting and amount of light. In the far reaches of my mind, I expected a cameraman and sound engineer to emerge from behind the exotic palm tree in the corner.

And what was my role here? I had vowed not to become entangled in their sibling rivalry, but somehow I was involved, unwitting guest that I was. They needed an opportunity for brotherly growth, and all of a sudden my duty became clear to me.

Fertilizer.

I was to be the organic compound. And I couldn't take sides.

We entered the greenhouse, and Oliver slinked

behind me as we approached Simon. The younger brother hadn't become an an adult yet. I wouldn't do his work for him, but I could prepare Oliver's 'soil.'

I took several steps ahead and waited for Oliver to catch up. When I was certain he stood to my immediate rear, I said, "Simon, Oliver has something to extend to you, following his reaction in the library earlier."

Simon looked up, clippers mid-air, his expression a complete blank. Oliver cleared his throat. I marked time as I retreated.

"Uh...," Oliver began in a soft voice. "Well, Alice pointed out to me that I... overreacted back there in the library, and, you see..."

He picked up a potted orchid and in silence I took it from him before he tipped it again and more bark spilled out.

"...and I quite concur," he continued. "In fact, I always agree with her since she never fails to be spot on the mark."

Not true, but I wasn't about to interrupt his performance.

Simon glanced at me, bewilderment on his face, as if Oliver had sprouted pink hooves and a sparkly tail to match. At this point, Oliver must have believed he had consummated the apology, since he plastered a fake smile on his face.

I nudged him in the ribs hard enough to make him say, "Ooofff!"

Simon resumed clipping dead leaves, but I could sense he was still fuming, too angry to recognize

Oliver's first venture into maturity. He was in no mood to be encouraging or even receptive.

Again I poked Oliver, and he turned to me with a 'What?' expression. I gave him the evil eye and nodded toward Simon. Say you're sorry, I mouthed.

His expression changed to that of deflated tire, as he muttered soft as a distant echo, "And for that I apologize."

Simon whirled to face us, icy daggers shooting from his eyes straight at Oliver. "Apology accepted," he said through clenched teeth.

Probably thinking he had been let off the hook easier than he anticipated, Oliver turned to leave. As for me, I had had no expectations for a joyful reunion and considered this to be a satisfactory outcome for now. My fertilizer job was complete.

Not so Simon. "You're not finished yet," he said with more force. "You must apologize to Alice, too."

Oliver's expression became jaunty, almost a challenge, daring Simon to make him do something else. "Why should I?"

"For assaulting her dignity with that... that outrageous—"

"You mean that kiss?" Oliver crowed. "We've had at each other better than that, and for the camera, too. Haven't we, Alice?"

My face turned scarlet hot. And I felt like slinking under the potting table. Diving headfirst into the compost pile. Slipping an empty pot over my head.

"That is no manner in which to behave toward

a lady. Don't you dare touch her like that again," Simon shouted. "Or—"

"Or what?" Oliver poked him in the collarbone, even though Simon loomed a good four inches taller.

Simon shoved his hand away and took a menacing step toward Oliver. "Ever!"

"What May said is true then," said Oliver, the decibels increasing with each word. "You are in love with Alice. Well, you can't have her. She's mine!"

Next thing I knew, the brothers were rolling on the floor, struggling for supremacy. They knocked over a bench and spilled several pots. The potting table rattled as they slammed each other into it. I stood paralyzed for several seconds as they cursed and fought, letting out years of resentment on both sides.

How to stop them? Whether to stop them? They weren't vicious enough to kill each other. Maybe I should just turn on the sprinklers and let them come up for air in separate corners.

Before I could make a move to the control box, Miss Entwhistle appeared at the door to the greenhouse.

"Mrs. Morehouse," she called, loud enough to capture the embattled siblings' attention.

All the noise and commotion came to a standstill, both men with arms drawn back in mid-punch. Simon's white button-down shirt was torn at the collar, underneath which was a large wet spot, and Oliver's swollen cheek sported a dirty smudge. Or maybe it was fresh blood.

"It's Morehead," I said with matching frosty words.

"You're wanted on the telephone."

"Who could be calling at this hour?"

"It's an American."

"Man or woman?" Had to be either Doug or my mother.

"Man."

Doug had probably called for a status report. Or to fire me, after I explained how little progress we had made since our arrival.

Before she departed, Miss Entwhistle glanced over my shoulder at the two brothers, who had scampered to their feet and stood there, dusting leaves, spilled bark, and garden soil from their hair and clothes. If I comprehended her attitude, Miss Entwhistle blamed me for their fisticuffs. Was she wrong?

I spun around to give them the full bore of my disapproval. "Once I leave the greenhouse, you may tear each other to bits or not. But in my presence, you will behave yourselves like proper gentlemen, both of you! Is that clear?"

Somber as undertakers, they nodded without looking at each other.

Alice, the great and powerful, the former Miss Mouseburger USA, had spoken. Best to take heed, lest I became displeased again.

CHAPTER THIRTY-SEVEN

The Out-Laws

The person who had called me was neither my mother nor my boss.

"Hey, Leo, what's up?" Friendly voice, since I was honestly glad to hear from him. "Is Doug looking for me?"

"Doug is on a different planet right now. He's got more deals going than a Las Vegas blackjack addict on a hot streak."

"So he doesn't miss me?" I laughed through my sarcasm.

"Oh, he probably would if he weren't distracted by the next big show. He and Willie have cooked something up for New Year's Eve. You'll be in Austin by then, won't you?"

"Leo, it's not even Halloween yet."

"When will you be coming back? Do you have a target date?" He sounded anxious.

"We're working on it. The child's mother is a piece of work, and the overbearing grandmother is even worse. After every encounter, Oliver lets loose an endless stream of invectives to describe her. Fortunately, I can't understand all of them, but I get the drift."

"Well, I'd step it up, if you can."

"Why? Is there something else going on?"

Leo was low-key to the point of hesitancy to get involved, but our brief friendship had struck me as genuine. He had been more forthright with me than anyone else associated with my job. Both Doug and Oliver could take lessons in candidness from him.

"Some guys came around the set today, asking about Oliver. Said they were reporters, but wouldn't show me any credentials. They weren't Americans."

"Describe them, if you would, please. Maybe Oliver will know who they are."

He reported on their appearance. "Typical Mafia hit men, except they were French."

"I'm impressed. How do you know they weren't impresarios, for example?"

"I learned to speak French in 'Nam, back in the early 60s, but I played dumb and listened to their exchange with each other. They weren't interested in Oliver's singing voice. One sported a prison tattoo, and the other had a large knife scar on the back of his left hand."

"Okay, I'll keep my eyes peeled. Some day you'll have to tell me more about yourself as a young man."

"I could but..."

"I know. Then you'd have to kill me." I laughed. "Given your outstanding skills in audio and video, to the point where nobody knows you're listening in, were you a spy?"

Leo kept quiet. Had I guessed it?

After a moment, he said, "Listen, Alice, these guys looked serious. Watch your back. And Oliver's."

"We're talking about how best to secure the safety of his young son. That's the most important thing to him right now."

"Only until the most important thing becomes keeping himself alive."

After a little more idle chitchat, I thanked him and we hung up. Next I had to get Oliver's undivided attention and explain how the situation could turn deadly if the two French hit men figured out where he was.

Perhaps his buying the des res was a good idea in the long run, if he could keep the acquisition quiet. Mickey, the agent, wasn't likely to spill the beans, and May, the flaming witch, would come to see the logic of it. Maybe her mother, the vulgar Mrs. Eff, would finally be forced to tone herself down. After all, in a few months she'd have another squawking mouth to feed. Poor Mr. Eff.

As these thoughts raced, I lingered in Simon's library and scanned the room. Lately it was the only place I had felt completely... me.

Was that due to the tranquil space or the stirring activity of writing again? Or to the realization of acceptance and encouragement Simon gave me?

Somehow turmoil—no, more like sadness—balled up in my chest and rose in my throat, threatening to overwhelm me. How could a man who had only just met me—exactly the Alice I was—offer me the very things I'd been aching for? He didn't try to make me over into a person of his vision, something my family or my ex-husband had never hesitated to attempt.

Inside, another plank shook loose from my box of truths, letting one of them escape.

My gaze landed on the top of Simon's desk, where Miss Entwhistle had been tidying up. Surely she stashed the papers with my hard-won new poem in a drawer. Next chance Simon and I had, we'd reconvene there for another round of discovery.

Meanwhile, the French smugglers were hot on our trail and I had to devise a plan of action before something dreadful happened.

It wasn't hard to figure out how the smugglers found out Simon was in Austin. While the press hadn't gone total bonkers over his arrival, it was well known he had come to town for *Austin City Limits* and for his music video for the new TV station dedicated to that format.

Was it only a matter of time before they discovered he was back in England? I should have gone to the toy store without him yesterday. No more taking chances in public.

Oliver had once involved Scotland Yard, or they had recruited him. Maybe it was time for another phone call. The first hurdle would be to get Oliver to agree without delay.

When we talked about it later, I assured him we could meet with the detectives away from Ramsden Grove. Simon would have nothing to fret over, May would be on the alert, and Mr. and Mrs. Eff would be kept in the dark about everything.

"What if May took Georgie and her parents on vacation somewhere? Australia?" I said as we faced each other over tea. Just the two of us, as Simon had gone with the local veterinarian to attend to one of his pregnant dogs with another litter of blue-ribbon puppies due any minute.

"Then how would I get to spend time with my son?" Oliver whined. "I've just arrived. I can't let anyone send him to the other side of the world now."

"You would if it protected him from kidnapping or other danger."

Oliver sighed with such depth, I thought he would cry.

"Just until the smugglers are caught. Then you can persuade May to agree to let you bring him to Texas. We can go to Sally's father's ranch and Georgie can learn to be a real cowboy."

"Why can't we go there now?"

"What? And have a shoot-out at the OK Corral? You aren't Wyatt Earp."

"Who?" He shook his head. "I suppose it is best to let Scotland Yard handle it."

"What happened last time around with the sting operation?"

"Well, I didn't actually go through with it. At the last minute, I decided I didn't want to be live bait."

"Can't say as I blame you, but let's at least talk to them and see if they can hatch another plan."

"Bury the hatchet. Hatch another plan!" Oliver laughed. "Alice, I'll never understand your amusing lingo."

Said the totty old duff with the squiffy bollocks.

Before we helped ourselves to hot tea with scones and cucumber sandwiches, Oliver made the phone call to Scotland Yard. A Senior Detective Forsythe would be over first thing in the morning.

All we had to do was survive until then.

CHAPTER THIRTY-EIGHT

The Detective

The next morning, we sat in a huddle in the small drawing room, which was decorated in Wedgewood blue walls bursting with still life oils, mostly dead trout and pheasants, with a few apricots thrown in for flavor.

Seated on the dark green velvet sofa, Oliver scooted close to me, in snuggling range, while the police officer chose the straight-backed chair across from us.

Detective Forsythe was nothing like characters in the movies or on PBS Mystery. Neither handsome nor plain, well-dressed but not stylish, assertive but never overbearing. His demeanor belied the bumbling English stereotype who never caught on to the most transparent clue. His job was to listen while Oliver got the ball rolling, then question me.

He spoke first. "How did you first learn of the threats to your son?"

"May told me, when she telephoned me in Texas." Oliver's tone sounded weepy, but I couldn't tell if May and Georgie were the cause. "Last week."

Had the weekend already passed? No wonder Leo was worried about how long we'd been gone. So far

Doug was too busy to notice, thank goodness.

"We'll need to interview Miss Farnsworth, if you can assist us to contact her and make arrangements for it."

"I've spoken to her already this morning, but she's now headed to Brighton." Oliver squeezed my hand.

Frowning, I said, "I thought she was bringing Georgie over here again today."

He gave me a gloomy half-smile. "Don't you hate it when people are so terribly unreliable, not to mention unpredictable?"

I tried not to snort my recently devoured English breakfast sausages out of my nose.

The detective cleared his throat. "Will she be gone long?"

"Something about an audition for a horror show," he whispered toward me from the side of his mouth. "She's taking her fright wig, not that she'll need it."

My eyebrows shot up. "Did Georgie accompany her?"

Oliver scowled at me. "Of course, and that blathering mum of hers as well."

Which meant poor Mr. Eff could kick up his heels if he wanted to. Or revel in the mysteries of peace and quiet for a rare change.

"When will she return?" the detective said.

"Who knows?" Oliver shrugged and his distracted gaze couldn't settle on any object, as if he searched for something. "What do we do now?"

Ignoring him, Detective Forsythe flipped a page in his notebook. "Miss Morehead, I understand you have an update for us."

It was Oliver's turn to be surprised. He leaned sideways and backed away a few inches as he glared at me.

"Yes, I received a phone call from Austin yesterday evening. It seems some French Mafia-types were poking around the music scene asking about Oliver."

Oliver clasped my arm. "Why didn't you tell me this before now?"

"Because I didn't want you to panic and bolt from the country. We have to help Scotland Yard catch these guys once and for all."

"Did you get any description?" The detective's voice was calm, almost matter-of-fact, which I hoped would be a soothing influence on Oliver.

I shared what Leo had observed, including the knife scar and the prison tattoo. "They didn't use their real names, of course."

Oliver winced and buried his face in his hands, as if he could hide.

The detective scribbled on his pad. "How did this Mr. Leo become aware of their deception?"

How much would Leo want me to reveal about him? Very little, I decided.

"Leo understands French."

"Oh, that's astonishingly clever." Oliver raised his voice. "Why didn't he telephone the police?"

"You can't arrest someone for asking questions.

And Leo couldn't determine on the spot if they were wanted for something in France or anywhere else."

A helpless air clouding his expression, Oliver turned to Detective Forsythe.

"She's right," he said. After he closed his notebook, he studied Oliver's face until Oliver met his gaze. "What became of your bodyguards?"

"They were active participants in the betrayal the first time around. Right away, after the sting operation... uh, failed to materialize, they disappeared. Maybe they've returned to England by now." Oliver pursed his lips until his eyes crinkled. "I've been hesitant to hire any replacements, that is, except for Alice."

Eyes widened, Detective Forsythe turned to me. "I'll need to register your weapons license. Do you carry a pistol or other firearm?"

"Absolutely not. No permit, no guns." A power drill or a pole saw was as dangerous as Alice the former Mouseburger could get. "I'm just a personal assistant, not a bodyguard." Not a fool either, not about firearms anyway.

"Then we'll station an undercover officer at the entrance by lunch time. He'll report any suspicious activity."

Oliver jumped up and paced back and forth. "What about Georgie? He's in Brighton for now, but someone could easily have followed May. She's quite popular, you know."

He came to a stop in front of us and his voice

turned falsely sheepish. "Well, not as well known as I am, but her photo gets splashed throughout all the gossip rags."

The detective rose to his feet. "We'll notify the local department to keep a sharp watch on them. We have to proceed carefully so the smugglers don't go into hiding again. No sense in tipping our hand, so to speak."

"Your hand," said Oliver, "but my neck. And also Georgie's."

"Meanwhile, continue your routine, but with a greater degree of caution." Detective Forsythe gave us his card with his private telephone number. "Please do not hesitate to contact me at any time, should you see or hear anything irregular."

Irregular? Didn't he realize that was Oliver's specialty?

CHAPTER THIRTY-NINE
The Suspects

After the detective left, Oliver grew even more antsy.

"I need to think," he said, sniffling and rubbing his forehead. "And walk." He staggered toward the door.

"Do you want me to come with you?"

"Not this time. I need to be alone."

I didn't believe my ears. Oliver had insisted he couldn't stand to be by himself, crawled into my bed when we first arrived, and never gave me a moment's peace while he was awake, except for that interlude when I had settled in Simon's library to read and revive the Muse for both of us. Maybe here was another chance to rekindle... what had Simon called it? That ember.

"Come back soon," I called after him, not meaning a word of it. Yes, I felt sorry for him, since none of this mess was his doing, but I couldn't help but believe he should have contacted law enforcement before we left Texas.

Whenever Oliver returned, we'd review our new strategy and take steps to bring Georgie here for safety's sake, if nothing else. Meanwhile, feeling the

Muse get itchy inside, I had poetry to write.

I found Simon alone in his library, chatting on the phone about the new puppies. He grinned when he saw me at the doorway and gestured to come in and sit down. I chose my favorite chair by the window. After a few moments of proud declarations as to quality of breeding, he hung up.

"Congratulations," I said. "How many little critters are there?"

"Quite a sizable litter. Eight tiny mewling newborns." He eyed me nose-to-tail like a Westminster judge. "Do you appreciate dogs?"

"Yes, as a child, but we never could have any, I mean, as adults." Heartache swept through me. Dogs, not children, silly. "You see, my husband, uh, ex-husband was allergic."

"She had a fine delivery. Should be a blue ribbon or two in that batch somewhere."

"How soon will you know?"

"Not for some months. We'll have to see how they develop, what their markings are, which ones display the appropriate show temperament, that sort of thing."

"Stubborn won't do, then, will it?"

"If they take after the mother, it will all turn out fine. The sire is another story altogether." He paused. "I suppose that's true of many families."

"Which do you take after? I'd have to guess it's not your father, based on what I've learned."

Simon was silent for a moment, and I thought maybe I had spoken like a fool and embarrassed him.

"Don't answer, if I've made you uncomfortable," I said. "I'm just trying to figure out a few things... well, because Oliver and you seem...so different, and..."

What a lame excuse. But I blathered on.

"... And truly I don't know him all that well, but I need to help him through this muddled affair so we can return to Texas and I can assure my employer that—"

"You're departing?" He jumped to his feet. "When?"

"Eventually, yes. I have to get back. My boss depends on me, basically to run his life, while he chases opportunities in the music business."

Simon crossed the room and plopped in the matching chair across from me. "Which muddled affair is it this time?" His voice sounded tired. "May and Georgie?"

"They're only a small part, thus far. Before his bass guitarist died, Oliver tried to help Bennie get away from the drug dealers. But it turned out the smugglers were even more dangerous, and so Oliver backed out of a sting operation with Scotland Yard here and fled into hiding in a rehab center in Texas. But he swears he has no problem with drugs or alcohol."

Expressionless, Simon stared at me.

"He has a performance contract with Doug, my boss, and when Oliver escaped from rehab, I picked him up and got him settled at my friend's house so he could work on both new television programs without too much distraction." My words spilled out faster. "But then May called him and said someone had threatened Georgie, so immediately we flew over here to the rescue."

Folding my hands in my lap, I waited, while Simon gave an almost imperceptible shake of his head.

"I'm leaving out a lot of details."

"Quite all right," he said. "Now what will you do?"

"Oliver has gone for a walk to sort things out in his head. When he returns, we'll work on a strategy for taking care of Georgie, which depends on how far May is willing to cooperate. And what Detective Forsythe recommends."

"This is a bigger muddle than I suspected. All I had considered was the issue of the boy's paternity, which seems to be a bit of a sticky wicket—"

"So you know?"

Simon nodded.

"Please don't say anything to Oliver about it. His heart would break. And May would become even more difficult."

"Hard to imagine," he said under his breath as he shrugged. "I won't mention anything until Father returns with his new bride and we see what the ramifications turn out to be."

"You mean, if she has a girl?"

"Father believes he is capable of producing nothing but male heirs."

"So far, he's two for two."

Simon stood up and reached for my hand. "Would you like to see the newborns?"

I took his hand and let him pull me to my feet. "Yes, very much. I adore puppies."

We left the house and crossed over the back lawn to the kennel. The kennel manager assured us we wouldn't be disturbing the nursery if we wanted to take a peek.

Tiny, soft, clumsy, squeaky little bundles, cuddled in the circle of their mother's tender love and nourishment. Another wave of sadness, a different yearning from what was else missing from my life, brushed past me.

Simon unhooked a leash from the wall and attached it to the collar of a terrier he called Amber. "Look at the unique color of her eyes."

"Did she win a ribbon for that?"

"Several. And she's now very much in demand for breeding. The top of the charts."

We strolled outside along the gravel path toward the lake, indulging the dog's pauses to sniff, then turned left at the far end of the driveway. We hadn't gone more than fifty yards, when the kennel manager hustled up behind us.

"Beg pardon, sir," he said, with his plaid hat in his hand. "Someone has already rang up an inquiry about the new litter. You be wantin' on the telephone, sir."

Simon handed me the leash. "I'll be right back."

The sky let loose a light sprinkle as they hurried back to the kennel. I turned to the dog. "Well, Amber, it's just you and me now." Wishing for an umbrella, I patted her head and let her lick my wet hand. Sweet thing.

As I stood up, a sports car came racing around the corner toward me and skidded to a stop. The passenger door flew open. I recognized Oliver in the driver's seat, clutching the steering wheel of the Jaguar XKE he had whimpered about not being allowed to drive since his license was revoked.

"Get in, quick, get in!" he shouted.

"It's not raining that hard."

"It will be in a few seconds. Get in."

"What about the dog?"

"Bring the bloody dog!"

I picked up Amber and folded both of us into the passenger seat. "Thanks for rescuing me. Is something wrong?"

He switched on the windshield wipers and adjusted their speed. "It's Georgie. May called and she's seen a few suspicious people hanging about the audition." He stomped on the gas pedal and we zoomed down the driveway, away from the kennel. The rain fell thicker and thicker, blurring the road ahead.

I frowned, feeling anxious. "Where are we going?"

He slowed down around the next several curves to splash through puddles in the road and then increased speed again as we exited the estate property. "Brighton," he said.

"Wait," I sputtered. "Don't we want to refer this to Scotland Yard, or at least notify Detective Forsythe?" I petted Amber in frustration. "What about Simon's dog? I can't just leave with her."

"The dog will be fine." He pressed harder on the gas pedal "You can phone Simon when we arrive."

"How long will that take?"

"We'll be there in less than one hour." Tears, real ones, leaked from the corners of his eyes. "There's no time to waste."

I might have mentioned to Simon that I didn't know Oliver all that well, but this much I did know. Nothing I said would have stopped him.

We were on our way to Brighton. Oliver, Amber the prize-winning terrier, and I. It was just an afternoon's outing. What could possibly go wrong?

CHAPTER FORTY

The Next-to-Last Resort

Oliver ignored the speed limit on the M23, which took us due south to Brighton. It was a challenge to get used to riding, not just on the wrong side of the highway, but also on the opposite side of the car. He explained that Brits called it the 'proper' side of the road.

We passed through woods and rolling farmlands as lush and green as anything I'd ever seen, small quaint villages with not much more to offer than a ancient church and a pub, and in the distance a private golf club when we reached Pyecombe, just north of Brighton, where we stopped for gas. 'Petrol,' he called it.

Oliver said his father had taken them there once as boys, but he never enjoyed the sport at all. "Simon kept at it longer than I did, but eventually he gave it up as well. I guess Father was rather disappointed in us."

"It's really unfair of parents to expect us to live up to their ambitions for us, isn't it?"

"Evidently, you survived better than I did. You're

the strongest woman I've ever met." Oliver took his eyes off the road for a moment to glance at me. "What did your parents expect of you?"

A rare day for Oliver to care enough to ask me a personal question. Maybe adulthood wasn't too far off. "Oddly enough, it wasn't too much, but instead too little."

"How so?"

"They expected me to cater to everyone else's needs, especially my husband's, and let my own hopes and dreams slide. They thought, especially my mother, that getting a marriage certificate was the best I could accomplish." I snorted in derision. "Little did she realize..."

"But at least you have a degree from a university. Surely that counts for something, even if it's a public institution."

"Lot of good it's done me." I stroked Amber's back starting at her perky little ears. "What about you? Did you attend a private school?"

"Oh, yes, several of them. We weren't well suited to each other. They kept wanting me to get up early and attend their boring lessons, while I wanted to stay out late and play my music in the local pubs and dance halls."

"I can see," I giggled, "that must have been a bit of a mismatch."

"The thing is," Oliver said in a serious tone, "I don't believe Father even knows what I do. He has no concept of how successful I am or what my career is like. The man hardly acknowledges he has children at all. I can't imagine what he'll do with another one."

"What about your mother, his second wife, I believe? You've never mentioned her."

"After I left for boarding school at age six, she took up with a tango instructor and moved to Argentina that year, right before Christmas. I've seen her a few times a year since, but she has another family now. Father has never forgiven her, I'm certain."

"Have you?"

He shrugged. "I don't think about it much."

I patted his arm. "But Oliver, it obvious you want to be a different kind of parent to Georgie, and that's very commendable."

He gave me a shy smile. "Think so?"

Nodding, I added, "So we have to come up with a plan that gives you more control, which means more responsibility. You have to become the adult."

"Come on, Alice," he whined, "why can't you simply stay here and be the adult for both of us? Georgie and I would really appreciate it."

Time to get tough.

"He's your son, not mine." Inside, I winced at my own words. "Very soon, I'll be going back to Texas, where I live, permanently."

"But—"

"No buts allowed. Cooperate to the fullest extent and assist Scotland Yard to catch the smugglers. Mickey will help you purchase whatever des res you

choose... or not. Then you can work out an arrangement with May for custody. Hire a reliable English
nanny or governess." I stared out the side window.
"I'm not your Jane Eyre."

"Who?"

"Life is about choices, Oliver. Each one you make
has consequences."

I had learned that lesson the hard way, but when
I thought more about it, I decided there was no easy
way for any of us. Otherwise we'd keep repeating
our same mistakes. Unless we were all fools.

"Here we are," said Oliver as he pulled into a
parking spot near the ocean. "This is the Waterfront
section of town, and the marina's farther beyond
there."

"Where is May's audition being held?"

"The Theatre Royal on New Road. Do you mind
walking a few blocks?"

"Not at all. You can be my tour guide."

After he put on his UT knitted cap and dark sunglasses, we climbed out of the car. Still tethered to
the leash, Amber immediately relieved herself on
the sidewalk. We passed the Brighton Town Hall at
Bartholomew Square on our way to 'The Lanes,' the
fashionable historic district of narrow cobblestone alleys lined with antique and jewelry shops, designer
boutiques, and restaurants offering works of edible
art. I could have strolled all day, and Amber seemed
to enjoy herself, too, but Oliver was in a bit of a rush.

Meeting House Road took us to North Street,

where we zig-zagged to find ourselves in front of the theater at last. I paused on the sidewalk to admire a charming multi-story building with arched windows—were they called Palladian?—surrounded by warm red bricks above a balconied colonnade.

Once we slowed our pace, I noticed Oliver kept looking over his shoulder. Taking the cue, I struck a watchful pose and wished Amber were larger and scarier.

"I have to go in alone," he said in a secretive voice. "May wouldn't exactly cheer up at the sight of you." He lifted my hand toward his lips. "She's insanely jealous, you see, but—"

I yanked it away before he could make contact. "For no reason."

He lowered his sunglasses down the bridge of his nose and winked his one good eye at me. "If you insist."

"Amber and I will keep watch out here. How long will you be?"

Oliver shrugged. "As long as it requires."

"Remember we have to phone Simon and let him know his prize dog is all right and we'll be back very soon. He must be frantic by now."

"Oh, let the silly old boffin pace around the lake if he's that cheesed off." Oliver pulled the UT cap off his head, handed it to me, and fluffed his blond locks before he pushed open the front door and disappeared inside the theater.

I felt awkward just standing there on the wide

sidewalk with Amber at the end of her leash. What was I going to do? Watch the dog pee every five minutes? When had she last eaten? My stomach growled and I asked myself the same question.

A quick glance at the establishments on either side of the theater revealed them to be restaurants, but I suddenly realized I didn't have my purse. Not that it would have done me any good, with the few dollars it held. In frustration brought on by this ridiculous situation and by hunger, I squeezed Oliver's knit cap and mentally kicked myself.

Until I felt something flat and stiff inside his cap. I turned it over and dug out his credit card. Hooray! Luncheon to go, with a little something on the side for the pooch. My order was ready in less than ten minutes.

Oliver's absence gave me an opportunity to consider his reaction to May's news while I sat on the curb and chewed my boiled beef sandwich, feeding tidbits of it to Amber. He hadn't shared with me any details of what May said, but his panic was real. What if she had concocted the whole story? Because...

Maybe the threats were her way of yanking him around, to see if he would jump through the burning hoops she held up to prove something. Maybe she was truly in love with him and had a peculiar way of showing it.

But I also had new information from Leo, who was genuinely worried about our safety. I trusted him to stick to the facts as kindly as possible, not exaggerate or fabricate, but also to shoot straight with me.

Two French gangsters had figured out Oliver was in Austin recently. Could they also figure out where he was now?

I peeked over my shoulder in both directions. The sidewalk was devoid of tourists.

Surely Oliver could convince May to let us take Georgie back to Ramsden Grove with us, so we could arrive before Simon sent out a search party. If everyone would just stay calm and behave in a reasonable manner. Yeah, right.

Oh, what I fool I was!

CHAPTER FORTY-ONE
The Diddling Trickster

I waited for over an hour for Oliver to come back outside the theater, and when he did, he was alone.

"Where's Georgie?" I said as I handed him his UT cap, along with credit card. He put it on right away, as well as his sunglasses. It amazed me no one recognized him as we sat on the curb and watched Amber try to chase to passers-by.

"The loud-mouthed minger is bringing my son here in a little while, after he awakens from his nap."

"I take it you mean May's mother?

Oliver nodded.

"So what were you doing in there all this time?"

"Oh!" He grinned. "Watching May perform, in a lengthy audition. She's quite wonderful, you know. A feast for the eyes and ears. And then we ate lunch with the cast."

What a thoughtless toad he was! I was a fool to believe otherwise, but now was not the time to let my anger surface. "Is the project a play or a movie?"

"Undetermined. Maybe the telly."

Not really caring which, I handed him the leash. "Here, look after Amber for a while. I need to find a—"

"Don't call it a bathroom. Ask where the loo is. Or the toilet."

As I arose, I wrinkled my nose.

"Here it's not at all the disgusting term like in America. We don't put baths in the same closet as our toilets. No one rests in there either."

When I was certain he couldn't see my face, I rolled my eyes and headed inside. The lobby was well marked and I located the facility without having to search for an usher.

When I came outside again, a large blue limo had just pulled up to the curb. The doors swung open. Before we even laid eyes on her, the sound of Mrs. Farnsworth's voice rang like a bell. Clanged like a fire alarm is a better description.

I stood about two feet behind Oliver, now on his feet, and waited. He twisted around, eyes closed as if in prayer, and whispered, "Lord help us! Here she is again. I never saw such a hovering grandparent."

"Concentrate on Georgie, and just endure the few minutes until she's gone." Good advice, as I had started to count the days until I could leave for home.

Handing me the leash, he took a deep breath and then faced them as the pair edged toward him. Georgie sucked his thumb and appeared uninterested in Oliver's offer of his hand.

Amber wagged her tail and yipped, which served like a magnet to the child. He tottered over and patted her head. "Wet's take the doggie on a walk, Ah-wiss," he said.

With his huge brown eyes, he looked so adorable in his blue sweater, matching knit cap, and corduroy overalls, my heart leapt. I didn't want to let him out of my sight ever again. It occurred to me that perhaps this was what falling in love felt like.

I squatted on my haunches to reach his level, but also to keep out of the line of sight and the inevitable crossfire. "Maybe in a short while," I said. "Can you scratch behind Amber's ears while we wait? She'd like that."

He set to work and the dog rewarded him by licking his palm. He giggled and repeated the action.

"What would you two be doing 'ere?" Mrs. Eff demanded, as she eyed me up and down with bare-faced suspicion.

"May telephoned me. She's worried about... strangers getting too close to Georgie. I thought we could—"

"Hah!" she snorted. "What a load of cobblers. May's just diddling with you, don't you know?"

"What?" Oliver stole a glance at me. "You mean, no one has threatened my son?"

"Shut up, Mum!" came an angry voice from behind us.

Oliver and I whirled around to find May shooting visual daggers, first at her mother, then at Oliver. I was the final target of her expressive ammo.

I stood up and peered straight into Oliver's face,

using my firmest tone. "I think I'll take Amber for a walk and let you two resolve this."

"Ah-wiss, wet's go!" Georgie tugged on my hand.

"May, with your permission?"

She nodded, and with Georgie clinging to one hand and Amber's leash wrapped around the other, I led the three of us down the sidewalk at a slow pace without a backward glance. The first sound that reached my ears was a shriek—as only Mrs. Eff could—followed by the slam of the limo door.

Score one for May.

Next, the engine started up and the limo pulled away from the curb.

Score another one, for Oliver this time. And maybe for May as well, since I knew how liberating it felt to be out from under your parents' thumbs at last.

By the time we had strolled half a block, their voices had crescendoed into shouting again. I thought British temperaments were supposed to be restrained to the point of being laid-back and calm even when bombs were dropping, but they proved me wrong.

Well, Oliver was on his own now. I couldn't fix this, whatever it amounted to. Was May in love with him? She'd have to be a a fool, but that never stopped anyone before, not even me.

But that would explain her yanking his chain, to see how he responded. So far, he didn't disappoint, since each time she held up the hoop of fire, he plunged right through it. Would Oliver awaken one day and figure out he was in love with her?

Wasn't that the reason they shouted at each other? If they didn't care, they would shrug and walk away. That was how I had treated Dwight at the end of our marriage. Over time, his neglect and indifference had eroded the caring right out of me. But May and Oliver were light years away from acting detached and impassive.

Oh, well, their true feelings for each other were for them to decipher. Coupled or otherwise, they posed little obstacle to me. I just needed to help get Georgie's custody issue resolved and return to Austin with Oliver so he could fulfill his contract with Doug and I could keep my job. Perhaps Georgie would come along.

Erase that last thought, I scolded myself. *Do not get attached to that child. He isn't yours and never will be. He's not even Oliver's, but that is of no consequence now.*

My speeding thoughts got so tangled up, I missed Georgie's chattering.

"Wook, Ah-wiss." He pointed ahead. "A weally big dog."

Sure enough, another dog on a leash, a large Doberman, stood at attention, as if waiting for us to provide his afternoon snack.

"Let's turn around, Georgie, and take Amber back to…" What did he call Oliver?

"Oh-Oh," he sputtered.

"Yes, that's who we're going to see, right back there."

When we turned around, the only person left standing on the sidewalk was Oliver. He wore a fat and sassy grin, and his body language indicated he heard dance music. Or possibly he had just taken a victory lap around the block.

He picked up a small child's suitcase, probably deposited there by Mrs. Eff. "Let's saddle up—isn't that what you Texans say?—and head back to the ranch."

Oh, sweet relief. After confessing her deception, May had agreed to allow Oliver to keep Georgie, at least overnight, to ascertain their compatibility, as long as I kept in the background and only helped him through any rough spots. Such as eating, pooping, bathing, and sleeping, I thought.

"Go inside and call Simon first to let him know what's going on."

"He can wait until we return."

I glared at him until he agreed. He disappeared through the theater door for less than three minutes, and returned with a grim frown.

"How did he take the news?"

"Not well."

We'd be home in just over than eighty minutes, and I felt certain I could explain everything to Simon by blaming the entire escapade on Oliver. Except I would first extract a solemn promise from Simon not to clobber his brother. Reserve that punishment for me to inflict.

Oliver took off down the sidewalk, leaving me with the child, the dog, and the suitcase. I stood my ground until he glanced over his shoulder.

"Eh, what now?" he said.

"Pick one." My tone was firm. Don't mess with the ex-Mouseburger.

He retreated and picked up Georgie's bag. When I passed him, I called Oliver a 'cheeky monkey' under my breath, hoping I got the insult correct and Georgie didn't hear me.

We wound our way through 'The Lanes' again, stopping for tea in one of the pubs. Cookies for Georgie, who called them "biskitties." He ate five of them with his juice.

"We'll take a drive through the marina so Georgie can see the lovely boats before we leave," Oliver promised, once we were back on the sidewalk. "Would you like that, Georgie?"

Skipping faster was the child's answer.

When we reached the parked XKE, a man in a dark blue suit was leaning against the driver's side door, smoking a cigarette. Before Oliver could demand his removal, a second man came up close behind Oliver, took him by the elbow, and poked a pistol in his ribs.

I gasped and snatched Georgie up into my arms, as I clutched the leash tighter. When I spotted the tattoo and the scar on their hands, it dawned on me. These men were the French mafia types Leo had deflected in Austin. How on earth did they find Oliver here?

Someone had to tip them off. But who?

CHAPTER FORTY-TWO
The Marina

"You will come wiz us to ze marina," said the man against the car, as he tossed his cigarette butt to the pavement and pointed to a gray van parked behind the XKE

"Leave the child out of it," pleaded Oliver. "I'm the one you want."

Incredible. You can't abandon a child of three on the street. And what about me?

"All of you, get in!" said the man with the gun.

One problem solved. Oh, dear.

"Georgie, we're going to the marina now," I whispered in his ear. "Sit very still and don't make a sound, all right? Very soon, we'll see some super big boats. Would you like that?"

"Oh, yes, Ah-wiss."

We climbed into the back of the van, all four of us, five if you included the suitcase. Of course, I couldn't leave Simon's prize-winning terrier or Georgie's essentials on the sidewalk either.

The man with the gun kept it pointed at Oliver as he scuttled into the front passenger seat. The other man slid behind the steering wheel and started the engine. At first he drove in the right hand lane, until his partner screamed curses at him in French. At least, that's what they sounded like.

Had May played a treacherous trick on us? Surely, she wouldn't endanger the life of her own son, no matter how angry she had become with Oliver.

Somehow, afraid to look over my shoulder, I kept hoping Detective Forsythe would appear, as if by magic, to rescue us. Or Simon. Or even the Doberman.

I cuddled Georgie tighter as we raced along a bumpy road toward the marina.The ride took less time than I had hoped. Not that I relished being seated in the back of a van and held at gunpoint by drug dealers.

Somehow every single thing that had gone wrong was Oliver's fault. And I hadn't yet caught on to all he had done, but his pulling something stupid had gotten to be a daily occurrence.When my patience reached the end of its rope, which I anticipated the moment we were rescued from this dangerous can of worms, I wanted to hang him with it.

The marina wasn't too crowded, just a few locals cleaning or loading supplies, so no one noticed how we were escorted at concealed gunpoint to a yacht-sized cabin cruiser. Georgie gushed and wiggled, as he tried to wrest free and escape from my grip on his hand. Amber barked and refused to board until I scooped her up and carried her over the gangplank.

Oliver and his thug came last. Oliver had

already removed his hat and sunglasses, and sure enough, a teenaged girl on the boat two stalls over squealed and came running toward him, shrieking his name.

The thug pulled Oliver tighter to him and, through lips that barely moved, whispered in his ear.

Nodding, Oliver waved to her and edged toward the gangplank at the pace of a snail.

She ran straight toward him. "Is it really you? Oliver Goodknight! Oh, please, please, may I have your autograph?"

Oliver glanced at the thug, who then jerked his head toward the gangplank.

The girl turned and hollered to someone on the boat she came from. "Katie, bring a pen and paper! It's Oliver Goodknight!"

"I'd hate to disappoint such an enthusiastic fan, now that you've recognized me and can alert everyone where I am, here on the *Taj Mahal*." He said the last phrase directly into the face of the thug.

The thug frowned and glanced toward the upper deck of the yacht. I followed his gaze but couldn't see anyone.

Katie dashed below from her station on the other boat, I assumed to get autograph materials, and reemerged in less than ten seconds. She raced to joined the first girl and handed Oliver pen and paper.

"What are your names?" he said to the eager

girls. "I mean, other than Katie."

I couldn't see his expression, as Oliver had turned his back to the thug, but experience had taught me he was winking at them. His good eye, not the blackened one.

The girls' gazes never left his face as they muttered their names. Oliver scribbled on their paper and handed it back to them. He let his grasp linger on theirs as he shook hands with both of them. Was he sending a signal? Doubtful a hormone-infested, rock-star-addicted, sugary-drink swilling pre-adult would, could, notice anything except his deep blue eyes.

The thug jerked Oliver's arm and all but dragged him up the gangplank.

"Ta ta, my lovelies!" he called, blowing them a kiss as a crew member—another thug?—pulled the ramp onboard.

Who did he think he was? Errol Flynn? Well, then, Captain Blood would be most welcome on this voyage. Haul out the cutlasses now, please.

The thug with the gun—heck, they all probably carried them— escorted us downstairs to the deck below and into a crowded storage room, filled with oars, life preservers, and other equipment, with a tiny view of the entire port and English channel beyond.

"I want to drive the boat," Georgie begged.

"Seet over zhere." The thug gestured with his pistol, now in plain view.

Just as we had gotten seated on the long blue

canvas banquette, the roar of the motor's ignition filled the airwaves, then settled into a low hum, like an undercurrent. In another moment, the floor under me felt like it glided backward. I glanced out the long narrow windows and spied the tall masts of neighboring boats sliding forward.

We were headed out to sea.

CHAPTER FORTY-THREE

The Gormless Pillock

We hadn't sat for more than three minutes when another person, a dark-skinned man of Asian ethnicity, who wore a turban, entered the equipment room. Yet another thug followed him at a tight proximity. I assumed he also poked the Asian man's ribs with a gun.

Oliver jumped to his feet. "Raj!" From the side of his mouth he whispered, "The young guy from my bank."

I recalled Oliver mentioning a sweet boffin who kept track of his credit card usage. Must be this Raj, but he hardly looked old enough to have a college degree, much less a full-time job as a banker.

"Seet down!" ordered the thug at our side.

Raj burst into tears, then spoke in a voice some would identify as approaching soprano. "Oh, Mr. Knightly, sir, I apologize most profoundly. They forced me to reveal your location. I had no option to resist and couldn't inform my supervisor of their brutal misconduct toward my family and myself.

You must forgive my contemptible weakness of the lowest rank. I pray—"

"Shut up!" yelled the thug nearer to Raj, and he whimpered again.

Oliver sat down and the other thug escorted Raj to the banquette opposite ours. Raj wiped his eyes on his sleeve and sniffled like a soap opera queen without a date on Saturday night.

"Bleeding hell, Raj. Don't go all barmy on me. You sound gutted, all right?"

As we passed the harbor's edge heading due east, the *Taj Mahal* picked up speed. Amber settled at my feet and rested her chin on top of my right shoe. Georgie slid off the seat and toddled toward his suitcase, which Oliver had placed on the floor between us.

Alert as an eagle on the hunt for prey, I watched him and the group as Georgie tipped it over and tried to unzip the lid. All eyes except mine stayed glued to him, as if he could produce some magical solution to our quandary. The thug next to us stood up and took a step toward the child.

In a flash, I inserted myself in his path, balancing as the boat pitched toward the open sea, and leveled my harshest steely glare at him. Rather audacious of me, wasn't it?

"Don't interfere!" squealed Raj. "They'll not hesitate to harm you an any possible way, and therefore I implore—"

The thug near him swatted his shoulder. Thank goodness, Georgie hadn't reacted to the retaliation and was preoccupied enough to ignore Raj's shriek.

"Georgie," I said from over my shoulder, "what do you need from your bag?"

"My book, Ah-wiss." He hiccoughed, then burped. "Weed me a sto-wee."

"All right, let me help you find it." I knelt down, and the thug hovered above us while I unzipped the bag and fumbled for a book among the clothes, toys, overnight diapers, and baby shampoo. The boat rocked, smoothed out, lurched, then rocked again.

"In dere." Georgie pointed a stubby finger to an elasticized pocket inside the lid.

I pulled out several children's book and he chose one about Babar, also a childhood favorite of mine. We snuggled on the banquette, primed to read, but then Georgie crawled into my lap and leaned back against my chest.

"Now, Ah-wiss." His stomach gurgled and he burped again.

The thug sat next to us as if he wanted to hear the story of the elephant king.

"Georgie, you don't have a case of the collywobbles, do you?" said Oliver. "Then say 'Excuse me' when you belch."

Hah! As if he could teach anyone to be considerate of others.

"Cuse me," said Georgie. "Ooohhhh—"

Without further warning, he leaned over and puked all his juice and biskitties into the lap of the thug. The thug screamed obscenities in French and jumped up as if his pants had caught fire, dropping his pistol on the floor. Then he bent over double and heaved his own lunch, unable to control his innards or his posture.

Swift as a racer, I shoved Georgie toward Oliver.

"You wee bugger, no more honking, please," Oliver said to his son in a cheerful tone.

I grabbed the pistol, and pointed it at the thug. "Don't move," I said through clenched teeth.

Oliver's tone changed in a second to frightened. "Crikey, Alice, what are you doing?

Meanwhile, across the room the other thug leapt to his feet and pointed his gun at me. "Drop eet," he said as he adjusted his aim to include both Oliver and Georgie, "or zhey will sooffer."

For a split second I wondered if I could wing him, but lowered the pistol instead. What a fool I was, taking this ex-Mouseburger persona too far. I had no business even holding a weapon, must less threatening to shoot someone. I could have gotten us all killed.

Before I could drop my arm all the way down, Raj sneaked up and whacked the other thug across the back of his head with an oar, and he collapsed unconscious on the floor. After he retrieved that one's pistol, Raj stalked across the room, looking like he would do the same to the other one. I couldn't stop him until after he landed one strike.

"Way to go, Alice and Raj!" beamed Oliver, as he dangled Georgie out in front of him like a stinky sack of potatoes. "You make a smashing crime-fighting duo. Get a rope and let's tie the sorry bastards up."

Amber licked the heaving thug's sodden face while we laced large ropes around their wrists and ankles. I showed Raj how to make it secure.

Raj picked up the second pistol, pocketed it, and then tied ace bandages around their mouths from a first aid kit he had found in a storage locker. "How are you acquainted with the techniques of fastening unassailable bondage? Most captivating."

"My uncle took us to the rodeo in San Angelo when we were kids. Showed us how they rope calves and tie their ankles so they can't move. We practiced on his goats."

Oliver hadn't shifted from his spot, still holding Georgie away from him. Not that I blamed him, but he would need to step it up and participate as we planned our next maneuver.

After arising and leaving our inverted victims to wiggle helplessly on the floor, I studied the contents of the room and noted a few items. "Who is piloting this boat? How many others are there?"

Still bent over, Oliver shrugged and made a face.

"Raj, what did you see as you boarded?" I said.

"There is only a solitary person at the helm, a most vicious perpetrator of criminal behavior, who terrifies everyone by subjecting them to—"

"Anybody else?"

"He acted in concert with these two, but I fear there are others involved who have made arrangements to intercept them in the middle of the channel. Unbeknownst to them, I overheard them discussing plans and conjecturing ransom figures."

Oliver jerked his torso erect. "Ransom? What are you on about?"

"They have knowledge of your conspiracy with Scotland Yard, and they intend to exact revenge. Also they would like the three million English pounds' sterling worth of cocaine returned, the drugs which your drummer, a Mr. Benjamin Lockeheart, absconded from them last year in Paris. All that stash, as I believe they term it, has never been recovered."

While Raj yammered in his excessive florid vocabulary, I sorted through the contents of Georgie's suitcase and selected fresh clothes. Poor little guy, every time he puked, he said, "What happen to me?" Together Oliver and I exchanged Georgie's soiled overalls for clean ones.

Our discussion centered on who would risk their life by approaching the captain and trying to knock him unconscious. Then we could return to Brighton, contact the police and Scotland Yard, and get this unholy mess cleared up for good.

The argument that ensued turned into something like the riddle about how to get a fox, a duck, and a sack of cornmeal across the river when your boat only held one extra passenger. If you left the duck with the fox or with the cornmeal while you rowed across with the other, one of them would get a tasty meal. You had to figure out how to leave the fox with the cornmeal.

At last Raj insisted he should be the one, since Oliver was the target and I was only a woman, who should remain responsible for the child and the dog. Besides Raj convinced us he could pretend to ask for help, acting as a messenger for the two thugs, and the captain would believe him and be caught off guard.

Oliver agreed, with too much enthusiasm, I thought, but I shouldn't have expected him to volunteer. And I decided to let Raj's men-first comment pass, secure in the knowledge I could rope and hog-tie him if I had to.

We wished him luck, with Oliver adding encouragement to 'be a real man,' and Raj slinked out of the doorway, a pistols in either pocket, and headed toward the ladder to the upper deck. When he had disappeared, Oliver dashed to the storage locker and pulled three life preservers out.

"Here, put this on!" he said.

"What for?"

"We're going over the side fast as we can. Raj, that gormless pillock, won't make it back here alive. We'll have to swim to the dock in Brighton."

"Have you lost your mind? The water is cold, we are stuck in the middle of the English Channel, and it'll be dark out there in a few hours. And even if we were champion Olympic swimmers, how could we take a child and a dog with us?"

He stared at me, then retrieved another life

preserver. "Can the dog wear this?"

"Oliver, you can't possibly think we'd survive out there."

"Alice, it's not like you to be so negative." He pulled an orange life preserver over his head and set about untangling the straps. "What has happened to my lionhearted Go-To Girl?"

I stormed over to the wall and pulled down another oar. "See, there are more of these. Let's find an inflatable raft or a skiff. Surely this yacht has another method of escape. No way will—"

Three gunshots pierced the air. We stared at each other, gobsmacked, not daring to say another word, even a whisper.

After a few moments, the engine went dead.

As the *Taj Mahal* rocked in the waves, I wondered how long it would take us to swim back to Brighton.

CHAPTER FORTY-FOUR
The Sweet Boffin

When Raj reappeared in the storeroom, his shirt sleeve was torn and bloody, and he carried a large duffel bag.

I ran to his side and linked my arm through his uninjured one. "You're hurt. What happened?"

"The captain attempted to intimidate me with his revolver, a quite impressive piece of metallic machinery with a large bore, and—"

"We heard three shots."

Raj sat down and sighed. "Fortunately, the captain was most surprised to see me but became immediately suspicious that I had committed an act of aggression against his collaborators. When he withdrew his weapon, I had no possible alternative except to discharge my pistol. He capitulated without hesitation."

Heaven forbid Raj should ever try to tell a joke.

"This whole thing has gone totally balls up," said Oliver, "but I hope you killed the sorry bastard!"

I pulled an alcohol swab and a bandage from the first aid kit. "Who turned off the engine?"

"He did, as he had received a signal from the other party that they were within twenty minutes of arrival."

"The kidnappers!" Oliver shrieked. "We have to get out of here." He snatched up two life preservers and shook them at me. To Raj, he said, "Go up again and start the engine. We can race them back to Brighton. Can't we radio the harbor patrol or something?"

"Alas, no," said Raj. "Their boat is a prodigious craft, and they would overtake us forthwith. And the radio is now defunct." He pulled up his torn sleeve and jutted his wounded arm toward me.

Trying to conjure the possibilities, I squinted at him as I applied the alcohol swab. "How did that happen?"

"It was quite unnerving," Raj winced and whimpered. "The captain was in communication with the co-conspirators to provide them our location, so without a moment's reflection, I fired a bullet into the radio. Then he shot at me but with no degree of precision, perhaps fortunately for me, only shaving a little skin from my arm. I returned fire, but can conjure no estimate of the injury I may have caused him. I was able to ascertain, however, that I left him in such a state as to render him immobile and unable to resume his duties."

He twisted his shoulder forward to gaze at his upper right arm, still oozing a trickle of blood. Gulping at first, he collapsed into sobs.

Feeling sorry for him, I wrapped a clean bandage around his arm and put pressure on the wound. "You've been quite brave," I said in a tender voice.

"Hold very still." I tied another length of bandage to fashion a sling and threaded his arm and neck through it.

Oliver stood at attention, holding an oar like a sentry's rifle. "Let's get moving. We have to escape before the kidnappers arrive."

Raj nodded as he arose and picked up the duffel bag. "There is a medium-sized motor boat attached to the rear of this vessel and available for use by any person familiar with its attributes. Without expecting much in the way of comfort, we can lower it into the water and embark from that position."

After donning the life vests, we gathered our things, which included Georgie and Amber along with improvised flotation devices for them, and trudged toward the aft part of the yacht. Like a pro, Raj worked the winch with his one good arm and lowered the boat, holding it steady as we climbed aboard and found our seats in the middle.

Exhausted, Georgie curled up in my lap, and Amber zigzagged through my legs, trailing the leash like a snake. She shivered, then settled between my feet for mutual warmth.

I scanned the horizon in all directions, torn between yearning for rescue and hoping the kidnappers had gotten lost at sea. Only two small fishing boats did I spy between the yacht and the port we left behind.

The sea was as welcoming as a hot-tempered bronco, bouncing us up and down, side to side, and front to back. My stomach turned queasy and at first I prayed not to vomit, then prayed I would.

"Ah, just like the boat on our lake, only a wee bit smaller. I'll take my usual spot at the helm." Oliver stepped over the seats behind us until he reached the motor, which started following two pulls on the cord. After tossing something small and metallic from the duffel bag onto the deck behind him, Raj shoved the skiff away from the yacht and sat down in the front to face us.

"Merry Olde Brighton, here we come at last," said Oliver. He steered the skiff around the yacht, bound for northwest.

Raj pulled his arm from the sling, extracted a pistol out of the duffel bag, and aimed it at Georgie and me. "Not so fast, Mr. Knightley."

I gasped. "What are—"

"Shut up," said Raj in a deep baritone. He removed his turban, revealing a closely-cropped head of black hair. After he extracted from the inner folds what looked like a passport, he tossed the ball of white fabric into the sea.

To Oliver he said, "If you want them to live, turn the boat around."

"Where are we going?" said Oliver, with a mixture of wonder and anger in his voice, as he pulled the handle on the outboard motor to one side. The boat made a wide circle as it reversed direction.

"I've always wanted to see what Paris has to offer," said Raj with a smarmy smile.

No further drawn out, high-pitched, flamboyant explanation needed. Raj, the shape-shifter, didn't want to see Paris. He wanted the three million English pounds' worth of cocaine.

After we skirted the yacht and headed southeast, Raj checked his watch, then lugged several emergency hand flares from a pocket of the duffel bag. Once we were about 100 yards away from the yacht, Raj fired a flare in a low arch at it. The fireball traveled far enough but landed in the water to one side.

The second one made contact, and within ten seconds, the yacht exploded, sending fragments, smoke, and sparks blazing upwards into the sky, as if the sun had crashed into the dark blue waves.

CHAPTER FORTY-FIVE

The Row Boat

The only effect we felt from the explosion came through the airwaves, as Raj had instructed Oliver to speed up, right after he launched the flare.

I couldn't make myself watch the remains of the boat as it swirled amid the vapor and detritus of its former grandeur. The wind had become merciful and insignificant, so whatever ripples it created on the surface of the ocean caused little delay in our progress toward the west coast of France.

Oliver's expression had turned stoic, which didn't mean he was planning an escape. He had already established his discretion, or perhaps lack of bravery, by sending Raj, his 'sweet boffin,' or rather the 'gormless pillock,' to overpower the captain.

Even if I knew a pillock with a gorm, I never would have believed the wimpy banker's assistant was capable of murder, not even if his victims were hired assassins.

So far, Raj had demonstrated extraordinary skills at preparation—although he couldn't have anticipated a toddler and a dog—and legerdemain masking his true personality. The high voice and the cowering attitude were ideal distractions, red herrings to hide his evil intentions. He had tracked our location by the use of Oliver's credit card, with which we purchased gas and my lunch. How did Raj outsmart—and out-gun—the kidnappers?

After about fifteen minutes, Georgie sat up and looked me in the face. "Ah-wiss, I tursty now."

"Let's ask Raj how much longer 'til we arrive," I said, hoping if our captor engaged with us on a humanitarian basis, he'd be less likely to shoot us later. "Then we can get you some juice—"

"And more biskitties!"

I gave Raj a fixed look, but he refused to return my glare from his seat in the forward section of the boat. "How soon before we land?" I said in a stern voice.

He ignored me still.

I set Georgie on the bench beside me. "Let's look in your suitcase and see if Mommy packed anything else for you."

When I leaned forward and unzipped the lid, the boat hit a sudden monster wave. Screaming, Georgie and I both crashed backward and bounced to the floor. In an abrupt reaction, Oliver cut the speed to almost nothing.

Raj slid forward, then landed on his butt, clanging the gun in his hand against the side, while the suitcase slithered under the nearest bench between us. Amber barked, then jumped up on the seat and ran under and around it twice, until her leash forfeited all its slack.

Oliver scrambled forward from the stern and offered his left hand to me, while tugging on Georgie to regain his seat with his other. I couldn't get my balance yet and didn't accept his assistance.

When I planted my hands behind me for stability, my right one bumped something that rolled an inch sideways.

Without looking, I let my fingertips identify the object: another flare? Perhaps one extra Raj had removed from his duffel bag, in case the second one he fired missed as well.

Up front, Raj was still preoccupied with regaining control of his position and command of the vessel. He didn't see me slip the flare into Georgie's suitcase and tuck it beneath his overnight diapers.

Once Raj returned to his seat, he waved the gun at all of us like he was shooing flies. "Sit down, back where you were," he barked. "You! Knightly, turn on the navigation running lights. Then start the engine and get going."

After a few minutes, I had untangled Amber and returned the suitcase to its proper spot. Georgie and I searched the top layer of its contents until we found a paper bag with kiddie snacks and candy.

"I want strawbear-wee," he said with a smack of his lips. "I wike wed."

A red lollypop proved useful to soothe his rumbling stomach and give him a little energy boost. We could worry about cavities some other time.

Once we settled in again, Georgie in my lap and Amber at my feet, I stared hard at the darkening eastern horizon directly over Raj's shoulder, veiled from any tell-tale lights except on the far outer edges. Oliver must be headed to one of those inlets south of Boulogne. I hoped he kept a tight watch and knew when to slow down again without causing havoc.

Or maybe havoc was a method of survival. How could we throw Raj off balance another time? I eyed the suitcase, envisioning the flare, and wondered what benefit it could provide.

No one was aware I had scooped it up, and if I were to ignite and fire it, a diversion was necessary, one that didn't involved the child or the dog. No taking a chance with them.

That left Oliver or me. He was the logical choice, since he had his hand on the tiller and could twist the forward thrust sideways and rock the boat enough to toss all of us overboard. He had probably used that maneuver on Simon more than once at Ramsden Grove. Oh, when would we ever see that lovely place again?

But how do I get a meaningful signal to Oliver, but also hang onto the boat, Georgie, and Amber, plus the flare, long enough to fire it?

I glanced over Raj's shoulder and stiffened. About 200 yards to the northeast, a large cabin cruiser matched our course head on. It hadn't passed us, so it must have originated its journey in France.

The kidnappers had failed to deliver us to the

drug smugglers, because Raj killed them when he blew up their yacht. My guess was, the drug kings hadn't taken kindly to his thwarting their scheme and they had come to overtake us and finish the job.

I considered my options. The first one was to unhook my life vest, slip my arms out, and lean overboard until I fell in the ocean. While the boat sped ahead, I could dive under water and swim to... Okay, next option.

No way could I leave Georgie or Amber, now both dozing. Simon would never forgive me if anything happened to her.

And Georgie... well, my dormant motherly instincts were in full bloom. Alice, the great and powerful, the ex-Mouseburger, was a lioness, fixing to transform into attack mode.

Or maybe I was a fool, fixing to die.

CHAPTER FORTY-SIX

The Escort Service

Toward the northeastern horizon, the larger boat was narrowing the distance between us and, if it maintained its course, could pull alongside in less than ten minutes. Could it be the French Coast Guard? No official markings were visible in the dim light.

The window of opportunity was fast closing, and I had to make a decision about whether to contact it, while nursing the hope we might be rescued instead of hastening our capture at the hands of the ones who had hired the recently liquidated assassins. Ha, no sympathy here!

With his duffel bag tucked securely between his feet, Raj seemed to be unaware of the other vessel. I expected him to have a scheme in place, but since my mind didn't tend toward criminal theory and enterprise, I came to no conclusion.

Which meant I had to anticipate possibilities while concocting a plan of my own and somehow enlist Oliver's assistance. And I had to be sure neither Georgie or Amber got hurt.

Besides flares, what was in his duffel bag? Was it a grenade he had tossed on board the *Taj Mahal*?

What else could have caused such a large explosion? How many more did he have?

He wouldn't risk blowing himself up, so I had to assume he meant to use them against any other vessel that interfered with executing his strategy. Pistols would be no match against rifles, but that didn't matter if you had grenades. No wonder he appeared calm.

The question in my mind became how to get Raj to look the other way so I could reach the hidden flare and launch it. What would make him turn around?

Within seconds, the answer came to me.

"Raj," I called out above the roar of the outboard motor. "I have to pee."

He glanced at me and sneered.

"I'm not kidding," I said. "You have to let Oliver stop the boat."

"What are you saying?" Oliver yelled. "I heard my name, but nothing further."

Typical.

I twisted in my seat to catch Oliver's eye and made a slashing motion across my throat, then pointed to the motor. He tilted his head and squinted his one good eye at me. The other one had turned dark purple. Good for you, Simon.

"Cut the motor!" I hollered.

Oliver looked past me at Raj. I turned around in time to see him nod, and then Oliver slowed the boat down before killing the power. Georgie startled awake and whimpered, which goaded Amber into letting out a gruff yap.

"Turn around, both of you." Shaking while I stood, I set Georgie on the seat next to me, but he cried and reached for me. I picked him up and tried to hand him to Oliver. "Here, let Daddy hold you for a few minutes. He's feeling all alone back there by himself and he needs you to be his friend. Can you help Daddy, maybe with the engine, too?"

Georgie perked up and stretched his arms toward Oliver.

"What's going on?" Oliver said as he accepted the transfer of his son.

"I have to pee and my body, as I'm sure you realize, is not equipped the way yours are." I peered over the side of the boat. "It's going to take a little maneuvering to get the balancing act just right."

"Make it fast," said Raj, brandishing the pistol in our direction.

I unzipped my slacks. "Turn around *now!*"

He didn't face entirely the opposite direction, more like 145 degrees, but it was enough for privacy. When I was certain he wasn't looking, I reached in the suitcase for the flare, fumbling until my fingers closed around its cool metal casing.

"What are you doing?" said Raj in an accusing tone while he peeked over his shoulder at me.

"I can't very well use my bare hand when I finish." I pulled out one of Georgie's diapers and waved it at him, praying women's private anatomy was still a mystery to him. "I need this."

"Okay, but—"

"I'm hurrying." That much was true.

I kept my eyes fixed on Raj, as well as the approaching cruiser, while I extracted the flare.

"Ah-wiss, what's dat?" squealed Georgie. "Dat's mine."

I froze, expecting Raj to whirl around and shoot me. When he didn't react, I studied his body language, which seemed to say, 'I can't hear you because I'm zoomed in on that large boat coming straight toward us, which will be here any minute.'

All at once, it occurred to me that the captain of the large cruiser hadn't spotted us, despite our running lights. We floated in the path of something so large and powerful, no one aboard it would even know they ran right over us.

Now or never.

Just pretend it's the Fourth of July.

I twisted the cap off the flare. Nothing.

Where was the damn fuse? Did I need a cigarette lighter, like setting off a Roman candle? If so, we might as well have let the cruiser sink us or dived overboard right then.

I rubbed my thumb on the inside of the cap. It felt like an emery board. Aha, the strike surface!

But scratch it against what? I peered down at the top of the flare and spotted a black button. I scratched the cap across the black button, held the flare out over the water, and waited. After about one second, I pointed it toward the starlit heavens.

It fired a shimmering halo of light that put me in

the center of the known universe. Nothing existed outside its reach, and all eyes at the edge of the watery darkness focused on me.

To this day, I cannot explain how I connected the dots, or rather connected the proper surfaces to each other. Angelic mermaids, I was certain.

The cruiser came to a floating stop about twenty-five yards away.

In a daze, as if sound and sight crawled in slow motion through a long tunnel before they reached me, I watched as Oliver and Georgie cheered and clapped their hands. In the front of the boat, Raj cursed, groped his way to his feet, and raised his arm, pointing his pistol at me.

Raj fired at the same moment the waves from the cruiser arrived in time to pitch our boat upwards, then plunge it down in rapid succession. Raj lost his balance and plummeted over the side.

Sound and sight returned to normal, and Raj's thrashing and screaming spurred me to action.

"I can't swim," he gulped. "Help me, please."

"You're wearing a life jacket, you biscuit-arsed slag," Oliver jeered from the aft seat. "Alice, leave the snookered devil there as bait for the next famished octopus that slinks along just below the surface. Ooh, there's one now!" He made a loud slurping-sucking sound through his lips and Raj screamed again.

I reached into the water and pulled the back of his life jacket to the outside edge of the boat. "I've got you," I said, "but please remember I'd rather set you adrift and let you get gobbled up by a hungry hammerhead shark."

Before I could haul him into the boat, a spotlight illuminated us, like we were onstage at Carnegie Hall. Then a voice came over a loudspeaker:

"ATTENTION!" The accent was French.

"This is the Gendarmerie Maritime. Do not attempt to escape, or you will be fired upon. You are in violation of..."

I paid no attention to the remainder of the announcement. We had been rescued by proper authorities, French law enforcement—we must have crossed the maritime boundary into their jurisdiction—and Raj could no longer threaten us.

Georgie was safe, along with Amber. No one else was hurt, except for Raj, a slight wound, and the men he killed.

Very soon Oliver would cooperate with the French government's officials to apprehend all the criminal conspirators, and then we could return to Merry Olde England for a brief good-bye before heading back across The Pond to Texas, problem solved.

My original intentions had come to pass, proving to Doug and everyone else—but most importantly to myself—I wasn't a fool after all.

It would have all worked out very nicely, except when I boarded the cruiser, the first words I heard were, "Madame, you are under arrest."

Then the officer slapped the handcuffs on me.

CHAPTER FORTY-SEVEN
The City of Lights

Despite my difficulties present and impending, I fell asleep in the back of the paddy wagon on the route to Paris. The entire experience—whisking the dog to Brighton, tracking Oliver and his son, trying not to get killed by Raj and the kidnappers, riding in the boats and witnessing the explosion—had worn me out.

Plus it was hard for me to believe I was under arrest, when I hadn't done anything wrong. Just because I took charge of Raj's duffel bag—to prevent him from grabbing another grenade—didn't mean it belonged to me, but the maritime police weren't listening. Regardless of the handcuffs, I wasn't the criminal in this unsavory affair.

A simple explanation would fix everything. In the peace and calm of headquarters, I could have the whole episode and all our actions accounted for and justified with my usual clarity and logic.

Oh, what I fool I was!

Four hours later, which must have been somewhere around midnight, we faced a hollering riotous army of papparazzi armed with cameras outside the Paris police headquarters. Who tipped them off? Why did they keep shoving lenses in my face, blinding me with the flashes?

Next came the fingerprinting and the list of charges read aloud, once Oliver and I were seated across the desk from the police captain.. Kidnapping, dognapping, illegal entry, weapons and drug running, plus smuggling, and more. Oh my!

* * *

And now we are back where I began this... this frenzied, crazy misadventure.

* * *

The police captain speaks broken English, but I am too tired to wrestle my way through his heavy French accent. After what sounded like a lecture from a hall monitor, he gestures to a subordinate who unlocks our handcuffs, separating Oliver and me where we had been joined at the wrists.

Oliver stands up and extends his hand, then thanks them for superior service. "And, oh yes, would someone be kind enough to escort us to the airport?"

The captain orders him to sit down. "You have no passports," he says. "You cannot leave ze country."

In a huff, Oliver plops in his chair.

Unused to anything resembling even a bracelet, I rub my wrists, and wait. And sob. And gasp. Then, for reasons I still can't explain, I let loose a drawn-out manic giggle.

Across the desk, the humorless captain glances up, then resumes filling out paperwork. Oliver steals a sideways peek at me, then shakes his head.

"If I've gone bonkers," I whisper, "it's your fault."

He gives me a sly grin.

Wait, did I say something about sex? Not again.

I don't know where they've taken Georgie or Amber. Upon arrival, other officers assumed charge of them, and I hope have given them both a meal by now.

My stomach rumbles. The energy from the sandwich I ate yesterday afternoon has expired, and, having reached the end of my rope, I'm about to faint from hunger.

And what have they done with Raj? I want to hear what he has to say, since he's an expert at falsifying first impressions.

Before I can inquire, the captain's phone rings, and he answers in French, but switches to his brie-slathered English. I cherry-pick phrases until I figure out he's talking to Interpol. Someone from the national office is on their way to the police station.

The phone rings again, and he answers in monosyllables. "Oui." He nods for emphasis. "Oui. Très bien."

The captain fingers his dark mustache, then stares at us for a moment. "We will transfer you to a holding cell until ze proper authorities arrive."

"I hope that means Detective Forsythe will soon appear," says Oliver in an imperious tone. "Look, my good man, I don't wish to linger here any longer than I—"

"Shut up!" I bark at him through clenched teeth. The rope has finally snapped. "This whole mess is all your fault."

"But, Alice..." he wheedles.

"Don't do or say anything." I shake my finger at him, in as threatening a way as I can manage. "You'll only make it worse. Just keep your mouth shut until someone who is not bonkers shows up to help us."

Oliver leans back in his chair and pouts, but I'm not buying his suffering. Not for a moment.

To the captain, I say, "Please put us in different holding cells, preferably at opposite ends of the dungeon."

The captain nods, then gestures to two of his subordinates again, who escort us to the elevator. In silence we ride to what I suspect is the basement and then march our separate ways down long corridors.

The dimly lit cell they put me in offers a cot, attached to the wall, with a thin mattress and not much else. The door clangs shut, and I have nothing to do but lie down and drift off to sleep.

After an indeterminate, time, I rouse at the sounds of footsteps and men's voices coming down the corridor. How long have I been asleep? No windows in the holding cell to give me a hint of the sun's position in the sky.

I swing my feet to the floor and shake myself fully awake. When I look up, the men have stopped at the door to my cell. One of them, the one not in uniform, is none other than Simon Knightley. His expression lacks any emotion.

Standing up, I try to smile at him but I can sense my face turning bright red and hot. "Oh, Simon, I'm so sorry about your dog. Amber is—"

"We'll discuss that later," he says in a grim tone. "For now, she's quarantined but in reasonably good hands. My task at present is to get you and Oliver, along with Georgie, out of here and back to Ramsden Grove, with as little fuss and publicity as possible."

"Are the journalists still clamoring at the front door?"

"Yes, but the captain has agreed to let us use the rear exit. He also approved the release of you into my custody, so I have posted bond. Detective Forsythe is now upstairs sorting out the details."

"What about Raj?"

"He'll likely be charged with three counts of murder in the first degree and extradited back to England. It seems Scotland Yard had been tracking his involvement for quite some time. They kept him in their crosshairs at almost every moment. Oliver was not aware of it, but... I can't say as I blame them for withholding the details from him."

I sigh, too relieved to ask more questions. The jailer unlocks the door to my cell and steps back. Before I exit, hesitation overcomes me, or maybe it's embarrassment. How could I have let such a simple thing get so out of hand? Not that a custody battle can't be complicated, especially given the two insane parties involved.

But now it will be an ordeal to discover who was telling lies and who wasn't. May had lied to Oliver, who had lied to me and to Detective Forsythe. But somehow, a kernel of truth nestled in each of their stories.

In the elevator, I wonder how I'll ever get back to Texas.

As if Simon can read my mind, he turns to me and pats the breast pocket of his tweed jacket. "I took the liberty of retrieving your passport."

The elevator doors open, and I shrink behind Simon at the hubbub and flashing of bulbs from cameras. Questions from reporters bounce off the walls, as I trudge along, following Simon across a large room toward another hallway.

"Who allowed these wangling hyenas inside?" says Simon under his breath.

A wave of excitement pulses through the room as we come to a stop. The answer sits on a counter in front of us. Perched there for all the world to see is Oliver, basking in the glow of attention, devouring the scrutiny, swilling up the compliments.

"Ah, here she is!" he calls, pointing at me. "The heroine of my story, my intrepid maiden in shining armor. Alice, my own true love, tell them how you dodged bullets, pushed the evil villain overboard, then fired the flare and saved my life." He clasped his hands together. "Oh wait 'til you hear how she adores me!"

Huh?

Simon peers at me, disbelief—or disappointment—on his face like an egg splattered against a wall. He steps aside to let me pass, as more cameras flash in my face.

Figuring I will choke Oliver to death before he utters another word, then be escorted in chains right back downstairs to my cell, I stomp toward him with my fists clenched.

"Ah-wiss, dere you is," Georgie calls from the other side of Oliver's lap.

My heart melts.

I'm so cooked.

CHAPTER FORTY-EIGHT
The Cake Hole

Before I can take more than two or three steps, a blaring, brassy voice makes everyone spin toward the entrance.

"There you are, Georgie, my darling boy. We thought you were dead, slaughtered by evil kidnappers and those other spawn of Satan," wails Mrs. Farnsworth as she bursts through the door, arms outstretched. "And here you are, right as rain. Oh, my prayers have been answered. How could you let this happen?" Without taking a breath, she glares at Oliver.

She pauses for photos, and pulls May into the shots with her, but leaves Mr. Eff in the background. He doesn't seem to mind.

Cheering, Georgie stands up on the counter and stomps his feet, balancing himself with one hand on Oliver's shoulder. The photographers eat it up, encouraging him to sing one of the Goodknight Lads' top hits.

"So talented, isn't he just the most adorable wee sprog?" Mrs. Farnsworth shoves her way into the center of the throng. "Takes after both his parents, don't he? But especially my own daughter May. Have you seen her latest film? The absolute bee's knees!"

She blathers on for several minutes about a variety of subjects, including details of her recovery from morning sickness. She fails to notice, however, that most of the reporters have reverted their attention to May and Oliver. Who, I have to admit, make a gorgeous couple.

Hoping no one detects the little aberration in eye color, I duck behind the counter and call Georgie's name. He turns and I hold out my arms. "Jump!" I say.

"Whee!" he squeals as I catch him and whirl around.

Simon leans against the wall, waiting for the media circus to fold up its tent and leave town. Every time Mrs. Farnsworth emits a shrieking laugh or criticism, he winces, imperceptible to anyone but me. Most likely because he cannot imagine her as an in-law. Or a neighbor. Or even a repeat visitor to Ramsden Grove.

I can sympathize with Simon's predicament, embarrassed as he must be by Oliver's antics and associates. Goodness knows, I'd die of humiliation if my family showed up.

Even as this thought settles, I spy a tall man with a familiar face coming through the entrance. It can't be! What is Nate Wallace doing here?

My faces heats up like an ember. How did he find out? Do my parents know?

The crowd divides in two groups like they're

lining up for a barn dance, and he moves forward with purpose in his stride. Older than I remember, but just as handsome as the last time I saw him, when Sally's boy Nathan was baptized.

His apparel is so exquisite, his demeanor so imperious, even Mrs. Farnsworth shuts her cake hole, as Oliver would term it. A low-key buzz circles through the crowd, but no one dares take his picture. Maybe they suspect he's European royalty, or divine, or somehow off-limits.

When he approaches the counter, he glances around, then settles his intimidating gaze on Oliver, almost eye-to-eye. More timid than I've ever seen him, Oliver extends his hand, but before they can shake, Detective Forsythe pops around the corner.

"Thank you for coming, sir," he says to Mr. Wallace.

They clasp hands without looking at Oliver.

"I appreciate your phone call," Mr. Wallace says. "Is it all settled?"

"Yes, I have expedited the additional paperwork through the proper channels and you have clearance to take her home."

Her? I am the only 'her' involved. Where is Mr. Wallace taking me? Back to Texas? But...

As I kiss Georgie on the forehead, my heart skips a beat. I turn to pass him to Simon, but find Simon staring at Mr. Wallace. Frowning—no, glaring—at him.

"Who is that gentleman?" Simon's tone is curt.

He accepts the child, while seeming not to realize it.

"Sally's father, Nate Wallace. She's my close friend from school, who helped me find a job with Doug, which is how I came to be assigned to Oliver, who lived in Sally and Mike's guest house until May contacted him and then we came to England and found ourselves in the middle of all this trouble..."

I can't tell if Simon is even listening to me. He hasn't taken his eyes off Sally's father and Detective Forsythe.

"Nate must have already been in Europe on business, or maybe even Paris, since he has contacts all over, so maybe Sally found out and asked him to pull some strings, which is apparently something he can do anywhere in the world, or maybe he flew here in his private jet... or... say, why do you care if—"

Simon frowns, like he can't quite catch their drift. "Has he come to retrieve you?"

"Looks that way but I won't know for sure until I manage to speak to him in private, which, in this crowd, hardly seems possible, unless someone blows a whistle or..."

I'm standing close enough to hear Simon exhale. Was that a sigh?

"What's wrong?" I cock my head to one side. "If he takes me off your hands, well, then that's one less—"

"You are my responsibility, and no one else's."

A turf war? Another first for me, but then, this trip has produced so many surprises, I can't keep track of them.

"And why would you care if Nate escorts me back to Texas. I'm sure he won't even sit in tourist class on the plane with me. Not that I'll be there either, since Simon bought me a first class ticket."

Oh, jeez, Mrs. Farnsworth is contagious. I'm the one with the clanging cake hole now.

Simon shifts Georgie to the other hip. Leaning down, he gazes into my eyes until I can see nothing except his face. "You are..." He gulps. "I want..."

"You cheeky monkey! What nerve!" squawks Mrs. Farnsworth. Unnoticed, she has waddled up behind me.

Simon bolts upright like someone struck him with a cattle prod. Giggling, Georgie clutches Simon around the neck and won't look at his grandmother. It's a game to him.

"See what you've done!" she wails. "You've turned my own grandson against me. What will May and Oliver have to say about this, I wonder? Mistreating me in such an odious manner. Some Poet Laureate you are!"

A few reporters pick up her accusation and swirl around us, posing questions, poking their lenses closer, and snapping photos. Simon looks like he wants to magically disappear. Or vomit.

"No comment," he says.

"I should report you to the proper authorities," Mrs. Farnsworth rattles on. "There ought to be a law to keep people like you from—"

"From what?" came a stern male voice a few feet

behind her.

I whirl around to find Mr. Wallace commanding everyone's attention from his breathtaking height, if not his air of dominion. Mrs. Farnsworth, a good eighteen inches shorter than he, shrinks even lower.

"Nothing," she mutters, then scuttles away.

"Hello, Alice," says Mr. Wallace. "I've come to take you home."

My relief is short-lived. I glance at Simon, but he won't look at me.

Yes, I want this sordid mess to be over. I want to go home. I want to resume my uncomplicated life.

But first, most of all, if I'm honest with myself, I want Simon to finish his sentence. What does *he* want?

CHAPTER FORTY-NINE
The Merry-Go-Round

The return to England happens in a mind-numbing blur. Sally's father has a well-earned reputation for getting what he asks for, and that's how he shepherds me out of France. He revises his plans, juggles his schedule, and pulls whatever strings need pulling, in the netherworld or the upper reaches of the stratosphere, or anywhere in between.

After a short trans-Atlantic chat with Doug on the phone in Simon's library, we decide I can't go back to Texas without Oliver. My job isn't finished yet, he informs me.

So here we are, Nate and I—he insisted I call him by his first name—sitting at dinner at Ramsden Grove, waiting to learn if Oliver's deposition satisfied the French authorities enough to release him into Simon's custody and leave the country. Before long, Miss Entwhistle appears at one end of the long dining room to let us know they are expected at any moment.

Her tone hasn't changed, still frosty, as usual. I

am too exhausted to wonder if she blames me for all the trouble. Or maybe I just don't care any more.

Sure enough, before the second course is served, voices raised in argument reach my ears from the hallway. Nate looks at me, expectation on his face.

"They're half-brothers, complete opposites. Oliver told me they are as different as chalk and cheese," I say. "Rivals, at times bitter ones, for anything in their path."

Including me, but that will be over as soon as I'm back in Texas.

I continue. "Both of them have an astonishing talent that will not be suppressed. They are each flawed, wounded, and full of life, with fierce intentions to do their 'thing.' Just at incompatible speeds in contradictory directions."

"That's a very generous assessment," Nate says. "How long have you known them?"

I am silent for a moment. "I hardly know them at all, yet they are familiar to me in every way."

"How's that?"

"They both want what I want."

"Which is?"

I am not certain why I feel comfortable sharing my innermost thoughts with Nate. Sally once said something about understanding him better, after she learned how her mother died. Nate took good care of Sally, even from the great distance she had put between them. Maybe that's the reason I trust him.

"We each want to nurture what's trying to ra-
diate from inside us, something that won't be held
down or denied. For Oliver, it's music. For a year
after his bass guitarist died, Oliver couldn't sing a
note on stage, but he figured out how to reinvent
himself and keep going."

Nate nods, but doesn't reply. I bet he understands
what I'm talking about.

Somewhere near, in the other part of the house,
a door slams twice in succession, and the bickering
voices go silent.

"When I arrived, I found out Simon couldn't write
his poetry. He was despondent, thought he had lost
his genius. My word, not his. Imagine the Poet Laureate of England hitting a dry patch, but something
had cut the switch and he was in the dark."

I grin and shake my head. "How's that for a mixed
metaphor? But he made sense of his emotional paralysis and found a way to get back into the rhythm."

"What about you?"

"Until I took this job, I spent my life doing what
other people expected. I gave up my dreams and
tamped my square self down into the round hole
they created for me. What a weakling I was..."

I cringe at the memory. "Then one day I just
couldn't do it any longer. Since then, I've grown
stronger every day, making my own choices, with
varying degrees of success, but lots of satisfaction.
There's a difference, you know."

Who am I, explaining things to one of the most

successful men on the planet? What nerve!

He laughs, but I get the feeling humor is a rare experience for him. Maybe he's been getting more practice lately, since he's a new grandfather.

"So you enjoy your job with Doug Creighton?"

"Oh, very much. It's full of the unexpected, which is a one-eighty from my previous. life. Do you know him?"

His voice grew soft. "I first met Doug when he and Angelique were married."

"Sally misses her every day. Like losing a member of her family."

"Yes."

Silence overtakes both of us, but it's not uncomfortable. Or long-lasting.

Both Oliver and Simon burst into the room, after they untangle themselves from the wedge they created by trying to go through the doorway at the same time. Still jockeying for position, I see.

In short snapping barks, they greet Nate and me and grab seats at either end of the long table. Although they might have taken time to freshen up, only Simon is dressed appropriately, having changing into a dark suit. Oliver, on the other hand, is still Oliver, wearing the same casual slacks, loafers, and pullover from yesterday. He hasn't combed his hair.

I can't wait any longer. "Where is Georgie?"

Oliver sniffles, like he's been crying. "With his mother. And with that pain-in-the-arse dip stick of a grandmother."

"Here or still in Paris? Is he all right?"

"They've returned, settled in at May's home." Oliver tapped his fork on the table like a drumstick. "Georgie feels no longer dicky, my brave little soldier, but May is furious."

"You can understand that, can't you?" I kept my tone soft and devoid of confrontation. "She must have been worried to death."

"Well, it was her fault anyway, concocting that wild story about Georgie being in danger from those smugglers. She admitted she was only trying to throw me off balance." He shrugs. "No, she's angry about something else entirely."

"What then?"

"It's Georgie, but—"

"Is he sick? He threw up in the *Taj Mahal*. Maybe he has the stomach flu. That can be harmful in little kids."

I glance at Simon, who is frowning. Uh oh, I shouldn't have mentioned illness at the dinner table, especially the queasy, retching kind.

Oliver shakes his head. "When it was finally time to leave the police station, Georgie called for you. He cried when you didn't answer or come get him, so much that no one, not even May, could comfort him. He only wanted you."

My eyes tear up, and I give Oliver a wry smile for twisting my heart so much. I had hoped to leave England without suffering the pain of separation, but I can't help loving that little guy.

Shoving his chair backward, Oliver stands up and his napkin falls over his plate. He marches around the end of the table and comes to stand next to my chair. When I shift to face him, he drops to one knee and takes one of my hands in his.

"Alice, my love, my own true love," he says, first rubbing the back of my hand with his palm, then piercing my eyes with his deep blue ones. "Will you marry me? I can no longer live without you, and neither can Georgie. You are the perfect soul mate for me and I worship you."

Oliver smooches the back of my hand, and for once, I don't snatch it away. Then he leans forward, extending his head until his face is about two inches from mine. He expects me to kiss him.

But I am too gobsmacked.

Before I can react further, Simon scrambles to his feet, knocking his chair over backward. He throws his napkin on the table like it's a referee's penalty flag. As he passes us on his way to the door, he mutters under his breath, something about a 'beastly bugger.'

I'd never heard him use slang and I'm exactly not sure what he referenced, but Oliver has no such confusion.

He clambers upright and follows Simon. "Beat you to the punch, didn't I? Well, as usual, you're ponderously slow and you missed your chance. I asked her first and she's mine! All mine! I'm going to purchase that des res she adores, and Alice and I will settle there with Georgie and be one big happy family. But we'll drop in on occasion so you can see what you've failed to win."

Simon whirls around and takes a swing at him, but Oliver ducks, laughing in a smarmy way. Simon hustles through the doorway with Oliver in hot pursuit, and the sounds of scuffling and grunting emanate from the hallway as they brawl all the way down it.

My mind goes blank. I push my plate forward and lay my head, face down, on the table. At first, my breath comes in shallow gasps, then makes a gradual transition to a deeper and more peaceful rhythm. After a moment, I raise my head and find Nate studying me.

"Alice, Doug told me what you did for Oliver. The way you enabled him to sing on stage again. Did you do the same for Simon and his poetry?"

As I nod, my eyes water at the edges. "What do I do now, Nate?"

He smiles. "The chalk and the cheese are both in love with you because you bring something into their lives they've been missing, and can't live without. They both value you for it."

"Is that enough?"

He shrugs. "Not many couples I know can say that."

"I couldn't, not the first time around with Dwight. Mike and Sally can, can't they?"

His expression turns wistful. "They are blessed."

"But is it love, this thing with Oliver and Simon?"

Nate stares past my shoulder, as if he can see through the wall. "Love is a decision. Make it, then follow your heart."

A decision. Of course.

All I had to do was choose the right brother. And not be a fool.

CHAPTER FIFTY

The Home on the Range

O n the way to Simon's library, I ponder my options while weighing the positives and negatives. Not exactly like a job interview, but somehow it feels like I'm the employer with two candidates for the same position.

Oliver. He is a challenge, never dull, usually unpredictable, but intends well, except when acting selfish. Life with him would be fun, maddening, and give me an opportunity to enjoy parenting whenever May granted partial custody of Georgie. We could avoid the unpleasant in-laws by traveling to Texas. The sex would be breathtaking, but I push that thought aside.

Oh, Texas. My tap root goes to China, but that doesn't mean I can't live elsewhere for part of the year. Oliver would buy me a first-class ticket whenever I wanted. One issue resolved.

Back to Oliver. How will he learn to sing without me on stage with him? With a toddler in the house, I can't always go on tour with him. Will I even want to? Learning to handle his shell-shock from the death of

Benjamin Lockeheart is an effort that could draw us closer in more significant ways. He will have to grow up and work on it.

Georgie. Not my biological child, not even Oliver's. Don't care. My heart is already invested heavily in him, and he is my dream come true, despite the zigzag route by which it arrived.

But.

Wanting to be a step-mother to Georgie doesn't translate to wanting to be married to Oliver, especially if he figures out he isn't the father. At this point, neither May nor I will spill the beans, but the risk is there. And Oliver is mercurial, with a tendency toward instability. Not attractive qualities in a husband.

Simon. He is sweet, caring, slightly dull and stuffy, but tends toward quiet surprises. Such as the puppies for Georgie. Held the sleeping child so I could get started on reawakening my poetry. He would not adjust well to the unpretentious, outgoing friendliness of Texans, where he'd be unlikely to want to visit.

I arrive in Simon's library and find no one there. I sit behind his desk and survey the room. It feels comfortable to me, a good sign.

Oliver or Simon?

One thing I've forgotten. Love.

They both indicate in their own ways they love me, but what are my feelings for them? I glance at the top of the desk and see my poem on a printed page. I am chosen, but am I in the heart of the room where love is?

The answer echoes in my heart: yes!

The answer is Simon. It must be Simon. With him, his love and encouragement, I will become the Alice I am meant to be.

I glance down at my poem, and all of a sudden wonder how it came to be printed. I snatch up the page only to discover it's a newspaper with a blaring headline across the literary section:

POET LAUREATE BACK TO WORK AGAIN.

Next to a small photo of Simon is printed my poem. My poem! Not his! Mine!

This is worse than gobsmacked. I am gutted.

Why would he steal my poem? I have been so wrong about him. He is worse than Raj. It stuns me to think of what a fool I've been.

Clutching the newspaper, I head down the hallway and yell Nate's name at every corner. Take two wrong turns before I reach the salon where Nate and Simon are sitting and chatting.

Simon leaps to his feet. "What's the matter?"

I smack him in the chest with the newspaper. "Explain this, if you can!"

Befuddled, his gaze bounces between my face and the headline. "I... I don't—"

"Nate, is your private jet standing by?" I drop the newspaper on the floor.

He stands up. "Yes."

Simon bends down to pick up the paper.

"I can be ready to depart in less than fifteen minutes. Let's go home."

Nate heads toward the doorway. "I'll contact the pilot." He passes Oliver on the way out.

"Alice, what—"

"Get out of my way!" I shove past him.

If the two half-brothers resume their argument, I'm not listening. I gather my things, meet Nate at the front door, and within two hours, we are airborne.

I cry all the way back to Texas.

After three days' worth of mourning all by myself in my little apartment and refusing to answer my parents' phone calls, I return to work at Doug's office early the next morning, unsure of what my current duties will be. Or if I still have a job.

To my surprise, Doug sits at his desk waiting for me. "Nate called me and explained what happened. Not in any detail, just the highlights. By the way, Leo was the one who tipped him off. He sent photos of those two goons to Scotland Yard."

I nod and get myself a cup of coffee, silently thanking Leo for his undercover connections. At the first sip, I screw up my face and spit it back in the cup. Doug really sucks at making coffee.

"Oliver will be here next week, to finish the shoot."

"What do you need me to do?"

"Not much. Chelsea would like your help about selecting a college. Woody wants to hear from you.

You'll have to call the realtor and cancel the sale of my house."

My eyebrows shoot up.

Doug shrugs. "DeeAnn changed her mind."

"I'm sorry." I might be, if I could feel any emotion.

"Chelsea thinks I should marry you. She says you understand me perfectly, and we make a good team."

Not certain I heard right, I stare at him and try to suppress what I know would be an hysterical laugh. Bonkers again. Not about sex.

Doug sips his coffee in silence.

We both jump at the sound of a knock on his office door. I get up to answer. The man in the hall-way is the last person on earth I expected to see.

"Dwight! What are you doing here?"

He ducks his head in a sheepish fashion. "Alice, can we talk?"

Doug excuses himself out the door, and I invite Dwight in. We sit across from each other at the conference table.

"Alice, I made a huge mistake. My life is a big mess, and I'm... I'm sorry about that. I need you and hope you'll take me back."

I'm in Texas now, so I can't be gobsmacked. Flabberghasted will have to do.

"What happened? Aren't you a father by now?"

"Well, somebody is, but not me."

I frown. "Please explain." I don't care if I sounded unsympathetic.

"Rhonda's baby isn't mine." His tone is bitter.

"How do you know?"

"Because I don't have dark skin and nappy hair!"

My mouth clamps shut as I try to suppress another hysterical laugh. Soon the effort will be for naught.

"Her boyfriend got sent to prison after she got pregnant. She seduced me and told me it was mine. That's why I married her. Boy, was I—"

"A fool?" Here comes the laughter, like a river gushing through a crack in the dam. The dam breaks apart. It's all I can do to keep from falling out of my chair. I pound the tabletop and then wipe my eyes.

"Go ahead and laugh, if you want to." Dwight makes it sound like his feelings are hurt, as if he has feelings.

"Dwight, go home." I stand up to usher him out the door. "Go fix your own mess."

"But Alice—"

I slam the door in his face.

The next several days I spend cleaning up the shambles of Doug's affairs. He can't fix his own mess, but at least he pays me well to do it for him and I don't have to take him home with me. I am happy to see Chelsea, less so poor Woody. Doug doesn't mention marriage again.

When Oliver arrives the following week, we greet each other as if nothing has happened. He seems chastened, if that's possible.

Our first moment alone once we finishing filming, we head for the trail around Town Lake. After a short pace, he says, "Alice, I have something to tell you."

"I'm listening." I maintain my stride.

He tugs on my arm until I stop and turn around to face him.

"May and I are getting married. We think it's best for Georgie."

I jerk my head to stare across the lake at the red oaks, which have begun their transition in the cooler weather. "Good for you."

He takes off his UT cap and twists it in his hands. "It won't be easy. May's a handful."

"So are you." I pat his arm. "I wish you both well. Hug Georgie for me."

After Oliver returns to England, my next visitor presents another surprise. I open the door to my apartment to find Simon standing there.

"What are—"

"It was all a misunderstanding."

"What was?" After a moment's hesitation, I step back to invite him in, refusing to be self-conscious about my humble, less-than-des res.

"It was Miss Entwhistle. She mistook your poem for mine and submitted it, all without my knowledge. The editors were so excited, they published it immediately." He hands me a newspaper. "Here's the retraction."

Somewhere, deep inside, I sigh in relief.

We sit on the second-hand couch in my combination kitchen/living/dining room, talking for hours. He excuses himself once to visit the loo, my tiny bathroom cluttered with hair products for blondes. I resolve to make an appointment with Binky and return to my natural color.

By the time we realize we've skipped eating, I suggest dinner at the Night Hawk. He agrees and we laugh and chat over Down South hamburgers until closing. Who knew he was so entertaining?

Simon encourages me to go back to writing poetry, and I confess to him I have already attempted it. Before I drop him off at his hotel, I invite him to meet Sally and Mike tomorrow. She picks up on the burgeoning undercurrent right away, and they request the pleasure of his company at Nate's ranch for Thanksgiving. My family will be there, too. Simon checks with me before nodding.

When I drive him to the airport, he hesitates on the curb next to baggage check, then gathers me in his arms. I can hardly breathe. The tingle—more like an earthquake from head to toe—from his kiss lasts for days, and I can always summon it whenever something reminds me of him.

By the time he returns at Thanksgiving, we've spoken on the phone just about every other day. We've exchanged poems and discussed them. And jokes. Amber is pregnant, he tells me.

"I can't wait to see her puppies," I say as we sit on the couch in my apartment.

"Soon enough." He inquires about my family.

After glossing over the latest, I say, "How's your father?"

"Enjoying his new daughter."

We laugh, but in a light-hearted way. Babies or puppies. All bring joy.

When it gets dark outside, he suggests dinner at a fancy restaurant.

"I have a better idea."

I stand up, take him by the hand, and pull him to his feet. He gives me a surprised grin as I lean up to kiss him. Then I loosen his tie and let it drop to the floor.

He tries to kiss me again but I turn, his hand still in mine, and lead him to my bedroom. As we wrestle off each other's clothes, he says, "Don't you need... protection?"

I stop dead in my tracks. Should I tell him now? Honesty won't just kill our mood, it will terminate our relationship. Still...

"I never could have children. We tried, but I'm—"

He puts his hand under my chin and raises my face to his. "Alice, you are more important to me than anyone ever has been or will be. I love you and want to spend the rest of my life with you. Will you marry me?"

Tears and deep passionate kisses are my answer. The unbridled sex is pretty spectacular, too.

We announce our engagement at the ranch, with an intimate wedding planned just before Christmas, and I bask in the glow of my family's astonishment and my triumph. Simon and I can't wait to get back to my apartment, just the two of us.

When Simon arrives the week before Christmas, he won't stop smiling. "I have a surprise for you."

"I have one for you, too. But you go first." I quiver with excitement. And not because his family will arrive in three days.

"I've been offered a guest professorship at the University here. A graduate program in English literature."

"And you accepted."

"Of course. Should I have asked you first?"

Roaring with laughter, we hug. Then he holds me inches away from him. "What's your surprise?"

"You *have* to marry me."

"I know. Because I adore you and can't live one more day without you."

"There's another reason."

He squints, then raises his eyebrows. "Which is?"

"Remember the first time we made love and you asked about protection, and I said I didn't need any because I never could get pregnant? Then we didn't worry about it any more all the other fantastic times... well, anyway when you left after Thanksgiving and returned to England, I wasn't feeling so hot. I thought maybe I was depressed from missing you so much, so I went to my doctor, who referred me to a specialist."

Simon tightens his grip on my arms. "Alice, what are you saying?"

"It took a week or longer, seems like a year, but after running a bunch of tests, we discovered... I still can hardly believe it, but it turns out, it wasn't my fault. Dwight was the problem all these years, and you're going to be a—"

"Alice!"

Tears streaming down my cheeks, I gaze up into his dark, fathomless eyes.

"Shut your clanging cake hole!"

I close my mouth. After all, I'm not a fool.

THE END

ACKNOWLEDGMENTS

To the many close friends who have encouraged me and believed in me over the years: Pan Adams-McCaslin, Ann Arnett, Paula Damore, John Fincher, Dr. Suzanne Novak-Nemeth, Sylvia Simpson, and Betty Trimble, among others.

To Kim Greyer, a terrific artist and designer who makes a passionate soul sister and teammate. Her talent knows no end.

My heartfelt appreciation goes to Gerald, a husband and soul mate who always knew what I could accomplish. And here's to my son Jordan, actor and writer, who shares his own creative streak with so much enthusiasm.

Also by

Cynthia J Stone

MASON'S DAUGHTER

Sally Edwards' teenage son Colton is headed for a major meltdown, and she is desperate to avert another disaster by proving her husband's recent death was an accident, not the suicide determined by the coroner. Everyone in town, even Colton, seems to know something particular about Jack's last days, but no one in Mason's Crossing wants to help her put all the pieces together.

On the morning she discovers secret notes in Jack's appointment book, she finds something else to convince her she's right. But the deeper she digs for the truth, the more destructive Colton's behavior becomes, until Sally is left with one choice: ask her father what really happened.

The problem: Sally hasn't spoken to him in fifteen years.

Includes a Reading Group Discussion Guide

Available on Amazon

TREATY OAK PUBLISHERS
www.treatyoakpublishers.com

MASON'S KEEPER

From the author of ★★★★★ *Mason's Daughter* ★★★★★
comes another fascinating tale of family, loss, and recon-
ciliation. Set against a background of historical events, *Mason's
Keeper* begins right after WWI and takes readers through the
ups-and-downs of the Jazz Age, Prohibition, and the Mafia,
Southern debutants and the Klan, pandemics and the rise of
gasoline-powered automobiles.

Young Nate Wallace is determined to keep his impover-
ished family together, but when his choice to defend his mother
results in disaster, he must flee his home and rebuild his life
alone. Every effort, every step in his search to reunite with
those he abandoned – and an unforeseen discovery – forces him
to remake himself.

As his personal losses multiply, Nate believes shutting
down his emotions while pursuing success in business will be
the answer to his survival, but another surprise awaits him,
one that will turn his world – and his heart – upside down.

Includes a Reading Group Discussion Guide

Available on Amazon

TREATY OAK PUBLISHERS
www.treatyoakpublishers.com

ABOUT THE AUTHOR

Cynthia Stone believes she and Sting were twins separated at birth, because they share the same birthday and original last name. Since she's a native Austinite, some complications in proving their kinship are sure to arise.  All of which provides creative fodder for the tangled tales she loves to write. Cynthia wrote her first story at age five and has continued to indulge that Muse ever since. Also the owner of a marketing company, her checkered career includes magazine publishing, copywriting, professional fundraising for the fine arts, and antiques importing. She still lives in Austin with her ever-patient husband.

Connect with Cynthia online:
www.TreatyOakPublishers.com

Also by Cynthia J Stone

Mason's Daughter
Mason's Keeper

Available in print and digital from Amazon.com